W9-DHG-879

Bret Harte

SHORT STORY CLASSICS

(AMERICAN)

VOLUME TWO

EDITED BY
William Patten

WITH
AN INTRODUCTION
AND NOTES

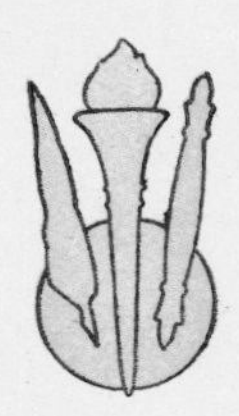

P. F. COLLIER & SON
NEW YORK

CONTENTS—VOLUME II

THE BRIGADE COMMANDER

BY J. W. DE FOREST

John William De Forest (born March 26, 1826, in Seymour, Ct.) at the outbreak of the Rebellion abandoned a promising career as a historian and writer of books of travel to enlist in the Union army. He served throughout the entire war, first as captain, then as major, and so acquired a thorough knowledge of military tactics and the psychology of our war which enabled him, on his return to civil life, to write the best war stories of his generation. Of these "The Brigade Commander" is Mr. De Forest's masterpiece. Solidly grounded on experience, and drawing its emotive power from our greatest national cataclysm, like a Niagara dynamo the story sends us a thrill undiminishing with the increasing distance of its source.

THE BRIGADE COMMANDER

BY J. W. DE FOREST

THE Colonel was the idol of his bragging old regiment and of the bragging brigade which for the last six months he had commanded.

He was the idol, not because he was good and gracious, not because he spared his soldiers or treated them as fellow-citizens, but because he had led them to victory and made them famous. If a man will win battles and give his brigade a right to brag loudly of its doings, he may have its admiration and even its enthusiastic devotion, though he be as pitiless and as wicked as Lucifer.

"It's nothin' to me what the Currnell is in prrivit, so long as he shows us how to whack the rrebs," said Major Gahogan, commandant of the "Old Tenth." "Moses saw God in the burrnin' bussh, an' bowed down to it, an' worrshipt it. It wasn't the bussh he worrshipt; it was his God that was in it. An' I worrship this villin of a Currnell (if he is a villin) because he's almighty and gives us the vict'ry. He's nothin' but a human burrnin' bussh, perhaps, but he's got the god of war in um. Adjetant Wallis, it's a —— long time between dhrinks, as I think ye was sayin', an' with rayson. See if ye can't confiscate a canteen of whiskee somewhere in the camp. Bedad, if I can't

By permission of "The New York Times."

buy it I'll stale it. We're goin' to fight tomorry, an' it may be it's the last chance we'll have for a dhrink, unless there's more lik'r now in the other worrld than Dives got."

The brigade was bivouacked in some invisible region, amid the damp, misty darkness of a September night. The men lay in their ranks, each with his feet to the front and his head rearward, each covered by his overcoat and pillowed upon his haversack, each with his loaded rifle nestled close beside him. Asleep as they were, or dropping placidly into slumber, they were ready to start in order to their feet and pour out the red light and harsh roar of combat. There were two lines of battle, each of three regiments of infantry, the first some two hundred yards in advance of the second. In the space between them lay two four-gun batteries, one of them brass twelve-pounder "Napoleons," and the other rifled Parrotts. To the rear of the infantry were the recumbent troopers and picketed horses of a regiment of cavalry. All around, in the far, black distance, invisible and inaudible, paced or watched stealthily the sentinels of the grand guards.

There was not a fire, not a torch, nor a star-beam in the whole bivouac to guide the feet of Adjutant Wallis in his pilgrimage after whiskey. The orders from brigade headquarters had been strict against illuminations, for the Confederates were near at hand in force, and a surprise was proposed as well as feared. A tired and sleepy youngster, almost dropping with the heavy somnolence of wearied adolescence, he stumbled on through the trials of an undiscernible and unfamiliar footing, lifting his heavy riding-boots sluggishly over imaginary obstacles, and fearing the while lest his toil were labor misspent. It was a dry camp, he felt dolefully certain, or there would have been more noise in it. He fell over a sleeping sergeant, and said to him hastily, "Steady, man—a friend!" as the half-roused soldier clutched his rifle. Then he found a lieutenant, and shook him in vain; further on a captain, and exchanged saddening murmurs with him; further still a camp-follower of African extraction, and blasphemed him.

"It's a God-forsaken camp, and there isn't a horn in it," said Adjutant Wallis to himself as he pursued his groping journey. "Bet you I don't find the first drop," he continued, for he was a betting boy, and frequently argued by wagers, even with himself. "Bet you two to one I don't. Bet you three to one—ten to one."

Then he saw, an indefinite distance beyond him, burning like red-hot iron through the darkness, a little scarlet or crimson gleam, as of a lighted cigar.

"That's Old Grumps, of the Bloody Fourteenth," he thought. "I've raided into his happy sleeping-grounds. I'll draw on him."

But Old Grumps, otherwise Colonel Lafayette Gildersleeve, had no rations—that is, no whiskey.

"How do you suppose an officer is to have a drink, Lieutenant?" he grumbled. "Don't you know that our would-be Brigadier sent all the commissary to the rear day before yesterday? A canteenful can't last two days. Mine went empty about five minutes ago."

"Oh, thunder!" groaned Wallis, saddened by that saddest of all thoughts, "Too late!" "Well, least said soonest mended. I must wobble back to my Major."

"He'll send you off to some other camp as dry as this one. Wait ten minutes, and he'll be asleep. Lie down on my blanket and light your pipe. I want to talk to you about official business—about our would-be Brigadier."

"Oh, *your* turn will come some day," mumbled Wallis, remembering Gildersleeve's jealousy of the brigade commander—a jealousy which only gave tongue when aroused by "commissary." "If you do as well as usual to-morrow you can have your own brigade."

"I suppose you think we are all going to do well to-morrow," scoffed old Grumps, whose utterance by this time stumbled. "I suppose you expect to whip and to have a good time. I suppose you brag on fighting and enjoy it."

"I like it well enough when it goes right; and it generally does go right with this brigade. I should like it better if the rebs would fire higher and break quicker."

"That depends on the way those are commanded whose business it is to break them," growled Old Grumps. I don't say but what we are rightly commanded," he added, remembering his duty to superiors. "I concede and acknowledge that our would-be Brigadier knows his military business. But the blessing of God, Wallis! I believe in Waldron as a soldier. But as a man and a Christian, faugh!"

Gildersleeve had clearly emptied his canteen unassisted; he never talked about Christianity when perfectly sober.

"What was your last remark?" inquired Wallis, taking his pipe from his mouth to grin. Even a superior officer might be chaffed a little in the darkness.

"I made no last remark," asserted the Colonel with dignity. "I'm not a-dying yet. If I said anything last it was a mere exclamation of disgust—the disgust of an officer and gentleman. I suppose you know something about our would-be Brigadier. I suppose you think you know something about him."

"Bet you I know *all* about him," affirmed Wallis. "He enlisted in the Old Tenth as a common soldier. Before he had been a week in camp they found that he knew his biz, and they made him a sergeant. Before we started for the field the Governor got his eye on him and shoved him into a lieutenancy. The first battle h'isted him to a captain. And the second—bang! whiz! he shot up to colonel right over the heads of everybody, line and field. Nobody in the Old Tenth grumbled. They saw that he knew his biz. I know *all* about him. What'll you bet?"

"I'm not a betting man, Lieutenant, except in a friendly game of poker," sighed Old Grumps. "You don't know anything about your Brigadier," he added in a sepulchral murmur, the echo of an empty canteen. "I have only been in this brigade a month, and I know more than you do, far, very far more, sorry to say it. He's a reformed clergyman. He's an apostatized minister." The Colonel's voice as he said this was solemn and sad enough to do credit to an undertaker. "It's a bad sort, Wallis," he continued, after another deep sigh, a very highly perfumed one, the sigh of a barkeeper. "When a clergyman falls, he falls for life and eternity, like a woman or an angel. I never knew a backslidden shepherd to come to good. Sooner or later he always goes to the devil, and takes down whomsoever hangs to him."

"He'll take down the Old Tenth, then," asserted Wallis. "It hangs to him. Bet you two to one he takes it along."

"You're right, Adjutant; spoken like a soldier," swore Gildersleeve. "And the Bloody Fourteenth, too. It will march into the burning pit as far as any regiment; and the whole brigade, yes, sir! But a backslidden shepherd, my God! Have we come to that? I often say to myself, in the solemn hours of the night, as I remember my Sabbath-school days, 'Great Scott! have we come to that?' A reformed clergyman! An apostatized minister! Think of it, Wallis, think of it! Why, sir, his very wife ran away from him. They had but just buried their first boy," pursued Old Grumps, his hoarse voice sinking to a whimper. "They drove home from the burial-place, where lay the new-made grave. Arrived at their door, *he* got out and extended his hand to help *her* out. Instead of accepting, instead of throwing herself into his arms and weeping there, she turned to the coachman and said, 'Driver, drive me to my father's house.' That was the end of their wedded life, Wallis."

The Colonel actually wept at this point, and the maudlin tears were not altogether insincere. His own wife and children he heartily loved, and remembered them now with honest tenderness. At home he was not a drinker and a rough; only amid the hardships and perils of the field.

"That was the end of it, Wallis," he repeated. "And what was it while it lasted? What does a woman leave her husband for? Why does she separate from him over the grave of her innocent first-born? There are twenty reasons, but they must all of them be good ones. I am sorry to give it as my decided opinion, Wallis, in perfect confidence, that they must all be whopping good ones. Well, that was the beginning; only the beginning. After that he held on for a while, breaking the bread of life to a skedaddling flock, and then he bolted. The next known of him, three years later, he enlisted in your regiment, a smart but seedy recruit, smelling strongly of whiskey."

"I wish I smelt half as strong of it myself," grumbled Wallis. "It might keep out the swamp fever."

"That's the true story of Col. John James Waldron," continued Old Grumps, with a groan which was very somnolent, as if it were a twin to a snore. "That's the true story."

"I don't believe the first word of it—that is to say, Colonel, I think you have been misinformed—and I'll bet you two to one on it. If he was nothing more than a minister, how did he know drill and tactics?"

"Oh, I forgot to say he went through West Point—that is, nearly through. They graduated him in his third year by the back door, Wallis."

"Oh, that was it, was it? He was a West Pointer, was he? Well, then, the backsliding was natural, and oughtn't to count against him. A member of Benny Havens's church has a right to backslide anywhere, especially as the Colonel doesn't seem to be any worse than some of the rest of us, who haven't fallen from grace the least particle, but took our stand at the start just where we are now. A fellow that begins with a handful of trumps has a right to play a risky game."

"I know what euchered him, Wallis. It was the old Little Joker; and there's another of the same on hand now."

"On hand where? What are you driving at, Colonel?"

"He looks like a boy. I mean she looks like a boy. You know what I mean, Wallis; I mean the boy that makes believe to wait on him. And her brother is in camp, got here to-night. There'll be an explanation to-morrow, and there'll be bloodshed."

"Good-night, Colonel, and sleep it off," said Wallis, rising from the side of a man whom he believed to be sillily drunk and altogether untrustworthy. "You know we get after the rebs at dawn."

"I know it—goo-night, Adjutant—gawblessyou," mumbled Old Grumps. "We'll lick those rebs, won't we?" he chuckled. Goo-night, ole fellow, an' gawblessyou."

Whereupon Old Grumps fell asleep, very absurdly overcome by liquor, we extremely regret to concede, but nobly sure to do his soldierly duty as soon as he should awake.

Stumbling wearily blanketward, Wallis found his Major and regimental commander, the genial and gallant Gahogan, slumbering in a peace like that of the just. He stretched himself anear, put out his hand to touch his sabre and revolver, drew his caped greatcoat over him, moved once to free his back of a root or pebble, glanced languidly at a single struggling star, thought for an instant of his far-away mother, turned his head with a sigh and slept. In the morning he was to fight, and perhaps to die; but the boyish veteran was too seasoned, and also too tired, to mind that; he could mind but one thing—nature's pleading for rest.

In the iron-gray dawn, while the troops were falling dimly and spectrally into line, and he was mounting his horse to be ready for orders, he remembered Gildersleeve's drunken tale concerning the commandant, and laughed aloud. But turning his face toward brigade headquarters (a sylvan region marked out by the branches of a great oak), he was surprised to see a strange officer, a fair young man in captain's uniform, riding slowly toward it.

"Is that the boy's brother?" he said to himself; and in the next instant he had forgotten the whole subject; it was time to form and present the regiment.

Quietly and without tap of drum the small, battle-worn battalions filed out of their bivouacs into the highway, ordered arms and waited for the word to march. With a dull rumble the field-pieces trundled slowly after, and halted in rear of the infantry. The cavalry trotted off circuitously through the fields, emerged upon a road in advance and likewise halted, all but a single company, which pushed on for half a mile, spreading out as it went into a thin line of skirmishers.

Meanwhile a strange interview took place near the great oak which had sheltered brigade headquarters. As the unknown officer, whom Wallis had noted, approached it, Col. Waldron was standing by his horse ready to mount. The commandant was a man of medium size, fairly handsome in person and features, and apparently about twenty-eight years of age. Perhaps it was the singular breadth of his forehead which made the lower part of his face look so unusually slight and feminine. His eyes were dark hazel, as clear, brilliant, and tender as a girl's, and brimming full of a pensiveness which seemed both loving and melancholy. Few persons, at all events few women, who looked upon him ever looked beyond his eyes. They were very fascinating, and in a man's countenance very strange. They were the kind of eyes which reveal passionate romances, and which make them.

By his side stood a boy, a singularly interesting and beautiful boy, fair-haired and blue-eyed, and delicate in color. When this boy saw the stranger approach he turned as pale as marble, slid away from the brigade commander's side, and disappeared behind a group of staff officers and orderlies. The new-comer also became deathly white as he glanced after the retreating youth. Then he dismounted, touched his cap slightly and, as if mechanically, advanced a few steps, and said hoarsely, "I believe this is Colonel Waldron. I am Captain Fitz Hugh, of the —th Delaware."

Waldron put his hand to his revolver, withdrew it instantaneously, and stood motionless.

"I am on leave of absence from my regiment, Colonel," continued Fitz Hugh, speaking now with an elaborate ceremoniousness of utterance significant of a struggle to suppress violent emotion. "I suppose you can understand why I made use of it in seeking you."

Waldron hesitated; he stood gazing at the earth with the air of one who represses deep pain; at last, after a profound sigh, he raised his eyes and answered:

"Captain, we are on the eve of a battle. I must attend to my public duties first. After the battle we will settle our private affair."

"There is but one way to settle it, Colonel."

"You shall have your way if you will. You shall do what you will. I only ask what good will it do to *her?*"

"It will do good to *me,* Colonel," whispered Fitz Hugh, suddenly turning crimson. "You forget *me.*"

Waldron's face also flushed, and an angry sparkle shot from under his lashes in reply to this utterance of hate, but it died out in an instant.

"I have done a wrong, and I will accept the consequences," he said. "I pledge you my word that I will be at your disposal if I survive the battle. Where do you propose to remain meanwhile?"

"I will take the same chance, sir. I propose to do my share in the fighting if you will use me."

"I am short of staff officers. Will you act as my aid?"

"I will, Colonel," bowed Fitz Hugh, with a glance which expressed surprise, and perhaps admiration, at this confidence.

Waldron turned, beckoned his staff officers to approach, and said, "Gentlemen, this is Captain Fitz Hugh of the —th Delaware. He has volunteered to join us for the day, and will act as my aid. And now, Captain, will you ride to the head of the column and order it forward? There will be no drum-beat and no noise. When you have given your order and seen it executed, you will wait for me."

Fitz Hugh saluted, sprang into his saddle and galloped away. A few minutes later the whole column was plodding on silently toward its bloody goal. To a civilian, unaccustomed to scenes of war, the tranquillity of these men would have seemed very wonderful. Many of the soldiers were still munching the hard bread and raw pork of their meagre breakfasts, or drinking the cold coffee with which they had filled their canteens the day previous. Many more were chatting in an undertone, grumbling over their sore feet and other discomfits, chaffing each other, and laughing. The general bearing, however, was grave, patient, quietly enduring, and one might almost say stolid. You would have said, to judge by their expressions, that these sunburned fellows were merely doing hard work, and thoroughly commonplace work, without a prospect of adventure, and much less of danger. The explanation of this calmness, so brutal perhaps to the eye of a sensitive soul, lies mainly in the fact that they were all veterans, the survivors of marches, privations, maladies, sieges, and battles. Not a regiment present numbered four hundred men, and the average was not above three hundred. The whole force, including artillery and cavalry, might have been about twenty-five hundred sabres and bayonets.

At the beginning of the march Waldron fell into the rear of his staff and mounted orderlies. Then the boy who had fled from Fitz Hugh dropped out of the tramping escort, and rode up to his side.

"Well, Charlie," said Waldron, casting a pitying glance at the yet pallid face and anxious eyes of the youth, "you have had a sad fright. I make you very miserable."

"He has found us at last," murmured Charlie in a tremulous soprano voice. "What did he say?"

"We are to talk to-morrow. He acts as my aide-de-camp to-day. I ought to tell you frankly that he is not friendly."

"Of course, I knew it," sighed Charlie, while the tears fell.

"It is only one more trouble—one more danger, and perhaps it may pass. So many *have* passed."

"Did you tell him anything to quiet him? Did you tell him that we were married?"

"But we are not married yet, Charlie. We shall be, I hope."

"But you ought to have told him that we were. It might stop him from doing something—mad. Why didn't you tell him so? Why didn't you think of it?"

"My dear little child, we are about to have a battle. I should like to carry some honor and truth into it."

"Where is he?" continued Charlie, unconvinced and unappeased. "I want to see him. Is he at the head of the column? I want to speak to him, just one word. He won't hurt me."

She suddenly spurred her horse, wheeled into the fields, and dashed onward. Fitz Hugh was lounging in his saddle, and sombrely surveying the passing column, when she galloped up to him.

"Carrol!" she said, in a choked voice, reining in by his side, and leaning forward to touch his sleeve.

He threw one glance at her—a glance of aversion, if not of downright hatred, and turned his back in silence.

"He is my husband, Carrol," she went on rapidly. "I knew you didn't understand it. I ought to have written you about it. I thought I would come and tell you before you did anything absurd. We were married as soon as he heard that his wife was dead."

"What is the use of this?" he muttered hoarsely. "She is not dead. I heard from her a week ago. She was living a week ago."

"Oh, Carrol!" stammered Charlie. "It was some mistake then. Is it possible! And he was so sure!

But he can get a divorce, you know. She abandoned him. Or *she* can get one. No, *he* can get it—of course, when she abandoned him. But, Carrol, she *must* be dead—he was *so* sure."

"She is *not* dead, I tell you. And there can be no divorce. Insanity bars all claim to a divorce. She is in an asylum. She had to leave him, and then she went mad."

"Oh, no, Carrol, it is all a mistake; it is not so. Carrol," she murmured in a voice so faint that he could not help glancing at her, half in fury and half in pity. She was slowly falling from her horse. He sprang from his saddle, caught her in his arms, and laid her on the turf, wishing the while that it covered her grave. Just then one of Waldron's orderlies rode up and exclaimed: "What is the matter with the—the boy? Hullo, Charlie."

Fitz Hugh stared at the man in silence, tempted to tear him from his horse. "The boy is ill," he answered when he recovered his self-command. "Take charge of him yourself." He remounted, rode onward out of sight beyond a thicket, and there waited for the brigade commander, now and then fingering his revolver. As Charlie was being placed in an ambulance by the orderly and a sergeant's wife, Waldron came up, reined in his horse violently, and asked in a furious voice, "Is that boy hurt?

"Ah—fainted," he added immediately. "Thank you, Mrs. Gunner. Take good care of him—the best of care, my dear woman, and don't let him leave you all day."

Further on, when Fitz Hugh silently fell into his escort, he merely glanced at him in a furtive way, and then cantered on rapidly to the head of the cavalry. There he beckoned to the tall, grave, iron-gray Chaplain of the Tenth, and rode with him for nearly an hour, apart, engaged in low and seemingly impassioned discourse. From this interview Mr. Colquhoun returned to the escort with a strangely solemnized, tender countenance, while the commandant, with a more cheerful air than he had yet worn that day, gave himself to his martial duties, inspecting the landscape incessantly with his glass, and sending frequently for news to the advance scouts. It may properly be stated here that the Chaplain never divulged to any one the nature of the conversation which he had held with his Colonel.

Nothing further of note occurred until the little army, after two hours of plodding march, wound through a sinuous, wooded ravine, entered a broad, bare, slightly undulating valley, and for the second time halted. Waldron galloped to the summit of a knoll, pointed to a long eminence which faced him some two miles distant, and said tranquilly, "There is our battle-ground."

"Is that the enemy's position?" returned Captain Ives, his adjutant-general. "We shall have a tough job if we go at it from here."

Waldron remained in deep thought for some minutes, meanwhile scanning the ridge and all its surroundings.

"What I want to know," he observed, at last, "is

whether they have occupied the wooded knolls in front of their right and around their right flank."

Shortly afterward the commander of the scouting squadron came riding back at a furious pace.

"They are on the hill, Colonel," he shouted.

"Yes, of course," nodded Waldron; "but have they occupied the woods which veil their right front and flank?"

"Not a bit of it; my fellows have cantered all through, and up to the base of the hill."

"Ah!" exclaimed the brigade commander, with a rush of elation. "Then it will be easy work. Go back, Captain, and scatter your men through the wood, and hold it, if possible. Adjutant, call up the regimental commanders at once. I want them to understand my plan fully."

In a few minutes, Gahogan, of the Tenth; Gildersleeve, of the Fourteenth; Peck, of the First; Thomas, of the Seventh; Taylor, of the Eighth, and Colburn, of the Fifth, were gathered around their commander. There, too, was Bradley, the boyish, red-cheeked chief of the artillery; and Stilton, the rough, old, bearded regular, who headed the cavalry. The staff was at hand, also, including Fitz Hugh, who sat his horse a little apart, downcast and sombre and silent, but nevertheless keenly interested. It is worthy of remark, by the way, that Waldron took no special note of him, and did not seem conscious of any disturbing presence. Evil as the man may have been, he was a thoroughly good soldier, and just now he thought but of his duties.

"Gentlemen," he said, "I want you to see your field of battle. The enemy occupy that long ridge. How shall we reach it?"

"I think, if we go at it straight from here, we shan't miss it," promptly judged Old Grumps, his red-oak countenance admirably cheerful and hopeful, and his jealousy all dissolved in the interest of approaching combat.

"Nor they won't miss us nuther," laughed Major Gahogan. "Betther slide our infantree into thim wuds, push up our skirmishers, play wid our guns for an hour, an' thin rowl in a couple o' col'ms."

There was a general murmur of approval. The limits of volunteer invention in tactics had been reached by Gahogan. The other regimental commanders looked upon him as their superior in the art of war.

"That would be well, Major, if we could do nothing better," said Waldron. "But I do not feel obliged to attack the front seriously at all. The rebels have been thoughtless enough to leave that long semicircle of wooded knolls unoccupied, even by scouts. It stretches from the front of their centre clear around their right flank. I shall use it as a veil to cover us while we get into position. I shall throw out a regiment, a battery, and five companies of cavalry, to make a feint against their centre and left. With the remainder of the brigade I shall skirt the woods, double around the right of the position, and close in upon it front and rear."

"Loike scissors blades upon a snip o' paper," shouted Gahogan, in delight. Then he turned to Fitz Hugh, who happened to be nearest him, and added, "I tell ye he's got the God o' War in um. He's the burrnin' bussh of humanity, wid a God o' Battles inside on't."

"But how if they come down on our thin right wing?" asked a cautious officer, Taylor, of the Eighth. They might smash it and seize our line of retreat."

"Men who have taken up a strong position, a position obviously chosen for defence, rarely quit it promptly for an attack," replied Waldron. "There is not one chance in ten that these gentlemen will make a considerable forward movement early in the fight. Only the greatest geniuses jump from the defensive to the offensive. Besides, we must hold the wood. So long as we hold the wood in front of their centre we save the road."

Then came personal and detailed instructions. Each regimental commander was told whither he should march, the point where he should halt to form line, and the direction by which he should attack. The mass of the command was to advance in marching column toward a knoll where the highway entered and traversed the wood. Some time before reaching it Taylor was to deploy the Eighth to the right, throw out a strong skirmish line and open fire on the enemy's centre and left, supported by the battery of Parrotts, and, if pushed, by five companies of cavalry. The remaining troops would reach the knoll, file to the left under cover of the forest, skirt it for a mile as rapidly as possible, infold the right of the Confederate position, and then move upon it concentrically. Counting from the left, the Tenth, the Seventh, and the Fourteenth were to constitute the first line of battle, while five companies of cavalry, then the First, and then the Fifth formed the second line. Not until Gahogan might have time to wind into the enemy's right rear should Gildersleeve move out of the wood and commence the real attack.

"You will go straight at the front of their right," said Waldron, with a gay smile, to this latter Colonel. "Send up two companies as skirmishers. The moment they are clearly checked, lead up the other eight in line. It will be rough work. But keep pushing. You won't have fifteen minutes of it before Thomas, on your left, will be climbing the end of the ridge to take the rebels in flank. In fifteen minutes more Gahogan will be running in on their backs. Of course, they will try to change front and meet us. But they have extended their line a long way in order to cover the whole ridge. They will not be quick enough. We shall get hold of their right, and we shall roll them up. Then, Colonel Stilton, I shall expect to see the troopers jumping into the gaps and making prisoners."

"All right, Colonel," answered Stilton in that hoarse growl which is apt to mark the old cavalry officer. "Where shall we find you if we want a fresh order?"

"I shall be with Colburn, in rear of Gildersleeve. That is our centre. But never mind me; you know what the battle is to be, and you know how to fight it. The whole point with the infantry is to fold around the enemy's right, go in upon it concentrically, smash it, and roll up their line. The cavalry will watch against the infantry being flanked, and when the latter have seized the hill, will charge for prisoners. The artillery will reply to the enemy's guns with shell, and fire grape at any offensive demonstration. You all know your duties, now, gentlemen. Go to your commands, and march!"

The colonels saluted and started off at a gallop. In a few minutes twenty-five hundred men were in simultaneous movement. Five companies of cavalry wheeled into column of companies, and advanced at a trot through the fields, seeking to gain the shelter of the forest. The six infantry regiments slid up alongside of each other, and pushed on in six parallel columns of march, two on the right of the road and four on the left. The artillery, which alone left the highway, followed at a distance of two or three hundred yards. The remaining cavalry made a wide detour to the right as if to flank the enemy's left.

It was a mile and a quarter—it was a march of fully twenty minutes—to the edge of the woodland, the proposed cover of the column. Ten minutes before this point was reached a tiny puff of smoke showed on the brow of the hostile ridge; then, at an interval of several seconds, followed the sound of a distant explosion; then, almost immediately, came the screech of a rifled shell. Every man who heard it swiftly asked himself, "Will it strike *me?*" But even as the words were thought out it had passed, high in air, clean to the rear, and burst harmlessly. A few faces turned upward and a few eyes glanced backward, as if to see the invisible enemy. But there was no pause in the column; it flowed onward quietly, eagerly, and with business-like precision; it gave forth no sound but the trampling of feet and the muttering of the officers, "Steady, men! Forward, men!"

The Confederates, however, had got their range. A half minute later four puffs of smoke dotted the ridge, and a flight of hoarse humming shrieks tore the air. A little aureole cracked and splintered over the First, followed by loud cries of anguish and a brief, slight confusion. The voice of an officer rose sharply out of the flurry, "Close up, Company A! Forward, men!" The battalion column resumed its even formation in an instant, and tramped unitedly onward, leaving behind it two quivering corpses and a wounded man who tottered rearward.

Then came more screeches, and a shell exploded over the highroad, knocking a gunner lifeless from his carriage. The brigade commander glanced anxiously along his batteries, and addressed a few words to his chief of artillery. Presently the four Napoleons set forward at a gallop for the wood, while the four Parrotts wheeled to the right, deployed, and advanced across the fields, inclining toward the left of the enemy. Next, Taylor's regiment (the Eighth) halted, fronted, faced to the right, and filed off in column of march at a double-quick until it had gained the rear of the Parrotts, when it fronted again, and pushed on in support. A quarter of a mile further on these guns went into battery behind the brow of a little knoll, and opened fire. Four companies of the Eighth spread out to the right as skirmishers, and commenced stealing toward the ridge, from time to time measuring the distance with rifle-balls. The remainder of the regiment lay down in line between the Parrotts and the forest. Far away to the right, five companies of cavalry showed themselves, manœuvring as if they proposed to turn the left flank of the Southerners. The attack on this side was in form and in operation.

Meantime the Confederate fire had divided. Two guns pounded away at Taylor's feint, while two shelled the main column. The latter was struck repeatedly; more than twenty men dropped silent or groaning out of the hurrying files; but the survivors pushed on without faltering and without even caring for the wounded. At last a broad belt of green branches rose between the regiments and the ridge; and the rebel gunners, unable to see their foe, dropped suddenly into silence.

Here it appeared that the road divided. The highway traversed the forest, mounted the slope beyond and dissected the enemy's position, while a branch road turned to the left and skirted the exterior of the long curve of wooded hillocks. At the fork the battery of Napoleons had halted, and there it was ordered to remain for the present in quiet. There, too, the Fourteenth filed in among the dense greenery, threw out two companies of skirmishers toward the ridge, and pushed slowly after them into the shadows.

"Get sight of the enemy at once!" was Waldron's last word to Gildersleeve. "If they move down the slope, drive them back. But don't commence your attack under half an hour."

Next he filed the Fifth into the thickets, saying to Colburn, "I want you to halt a hundred yards to the left and rear of Gildersleeve. Cover his flank if he is attacked; but otherwise lie quiet. As soon as he charges, move forward to the edge of the wood, and be ready to support him. But make no assault yourself until further orders."

The next two regiments—the Seventh and First—he placed in *échelon,* in like manner, a quarter of a mile further along. Then he galloped forward to the cavalry, and a last word with Stilton. "You and Gahogan must take care of yourselves. Push on four or five hundred yards, and then face to the right. Whatever Gahogan finds let him go at it. If he can't shake it, help him. You two *must* reach the top of the ridge. Only, look out for your left flank. Keep a squadron or two in reserve on that side."

"Currnel, if we don't raich the top of the hill, it'll be because it hasn't got wan," answered Gahogan. Stilton only laughed and rode forward.

Waldron now returned toward the fork of the road. On the way he sent a staff officer to the Seventh with renewed orders to attack as soon as possible after Gildersleeve. Then another staff officer was hurried forward to Taylor with directions to push his feint strongly, and drive his skirmishers as far up the slope as they could get. A third staff officer set the Parrotts in rear of Taylor to firing with all their might. By the time that the commandant had returned to Colburn's ambushed ranks, no one was with him but his enemy, Fitz Hugh.

"You don't seem to trust me with duty, Colonel," said the young man.

"I shall use you only in case of extremity, Captain," replied Waldron. "We have business to settle to-morrow."

"I ask no favors on that account. I hope you will offer me none."

"In case of need I shall spare no one," declared Waldron.

Then he took out his watch, looked at it impatiently, put it to his ear, restored it to his pocket, and fell into an attitude of deep attention. Evidently his whole mind was on his battle, and he was waiting, watching, yearning for its outburst.

"If he wins this fight," thought Fitz Hugh, "how can I do him a harm? And yet," he added, "how can I help it?"

Minutes passed. Fitz Hugh tried to think of his injury, and to steel himself against his chief. But the roar of battle on the right, and the suspense and imminence of battle on the left, absorbed the attention of even this wounded and angry spirit, as, indeed, they might have absorbed that of any being not more or less than human. A private wrong, insupportable though it might be, seemed so small amid that deadly clamor and awful expectation! Moreover, the intellect which worked so calmly and vigorously by his side, and which alone of all things near appeared able to rule the coming crisis, began to dominate him, in spite of his sense of injury. A thought crossed him to the effect that the great among men are too valuable to be punished for their evil deeds. He turned to the absorbed brigade commander, now not only his ruler, but even his protector, with a feeling that he must accord him a word of peace, a proffer in some form of possible forgiveness and friendship. But the man's face was clouded and stern with responsibility and authority. He seemed at that moment too lofty to be approached with a message of pardon. Fitz Hugh gazed at him with a mixture of profound respect and smothered hate. He gazed, turned away, and remained silent.

Minutes more passed. Then a mounted orderly dashed up at full speed, with the words, "Colonel, Major Gahogan has fronted."

"Has he?" answered Waldron, with a smile which thanked the trooper and made him happy. "Ride on through the thicket here, my man, and tell Colonel Gildersleeve to push up his skirmishers."

With a thud of hoofs and a rustling of parting foliage the cavalryman disappeared amid the underwood. A minute or two later a thin, dropping rattle of musketry, five hundred yards or so to the front, announced that the sharpshooters of the Fourteenth were at work. Almost immediately there was an angry response, full of the threatenings and execution of death. Through the lofty leafage tore the screech of a shell, bursting with a sharp crash as it passed overhead, and scattering in humming slivers. Then came another, and another, and many more, chasing each other with hoarse hissings through the trembling air, a succession of flying serpents. The enemy doubtless believed that nearly the whole attacking force was massed in the wood around the road, and they had brought at least four guns to bear upon that point, and were working them with the utmost possible rapidity. Presently a large chestnut, not fifty yards from Fitz Hugh was struck by a shot. The solid trunk, nearly three feet in diameter, parted asunder as if it were the brittlest of vegetable matter. The upper portion started aside with a monstrous groan, dropped in a standing posture to the earth, and then toppled slowly, sublimely prostrate, its branches crashing and all its leaves wailing. Ere long, a little further to the front, another Anak of the forest went down; and, mingled with the noise of its sylvan agony, there arose sharp cries of human suffering. Then Colonel Colburn, a broad-chested and ruddy man of thirty-five, with a look of indignant anxiety in his iron-gray eyes, rode up to the brigade commander.

"This is very annoying, Colonel," he said. "I am losing my men without using them. That last tree fell into my command."

"Are they firing toward our left?" asked Waldron.

"Not a shot."

"Very good," said the chief, with a sigh of contentment. "If we can only keep them occupied in this direction! By the way, let your men lie down under the fallen tree, as far as it will go. It will protect them from others."

Colburn rode back to his regiment. Waldron looked impatiently at his watch. At that moment a fierce burst of line firing arose in front, followed and almost overborne by a long-drawn yell, the scream of charging men. Waldron put up his watch, glanced excitedly at Fitz Hugh, and smiled.

"I must forgive or forget," the latter could not help saying to himself. "All the rest of life is nothing compared with this."

"Captain," said Waldron, "ride off to the left at full speed. As soon as you hear firing at the shoulder of the ridge, return instantly and let me know."

Fitz Hugh dashed away. Three minutes carried him into perfect peace, beyond the whistling of ball or the screeching of shell. On the right was a tranquil, wide waving of foliage, and on the left a serene landscape of cultivated fields, with here and there an embowered farm-house. Only for the clamor of artillery and musketry far behind him, he could not have believed in the near presence of battle, of blood and suffering and triumphant death. But suddenly he heard to his right, assaulting and slaughtering the tranquillity of nature, a tumultuous outbreak of file firing, mingled with savage yells. He wheeled, drove spurs into his horse, and flew back to Waldron. As he re-entered the wood he met wounded men streaming through it, a few marching alertly upright, many more crouching and groaning, some clinging to their less injured comrades, but all haggard in face and ghastly.

"Are we winning?" he hastily asked of one man who held up a hand with three fingers gone and the bones projecting in sharp spikes through mangled flesh.

"All right, sir; sailing in," was the answer.

"Is the brigade commander all right?" he inquired

of another who was winding a bloody handkerchief around his arm.

"Straight ahead, sir; hurrah for Waldron!" responded the soldier, and almost in the same instant fell lifeless with a fresh ball through his head.

"Hurrah for him!" Fitz Hugh answered frantically, plunging on through the underwood. He found Waldron with Colburn, the two conversing tranquilly in their saddles amid hissing bullets and dropping branches.

"Move your regiment forward now," the brigade commander was saying; "but halt it in the edge of the wood."

"Shan't I relieve Gildersleeve if he gets beaten?" asked the subordinate officer eagerly.

"No. The regiments on the left will help him out. I want your men and Peck's for the fight on top of the hill. Of course the rebels will try to retake it; then I shall call for you."

Fitz Hugh now approached and said, "Colonel, the Seventh has attacked in force."

"Good!" answered Waldron, with that sweet smile of his which thanked people who brought him pleasant news. "I thought I heard his fire. Gahogan will be on their right rear in ten minutes. Then we shall get the ridge. Ride back now to Major Bradley, and tell him to bring his Napoleons through the wood, and set two of them to shelling the enemy's centre. Tell him my idea is to amuse them, and keep them from changing front."

Again Fitz Hugh galloped off as before on a comfortably safe errand, safer at all events than many errands of that day. "This man is sparing my life," he said to himself. "Would to God I knew how to spare his!"

He found Bradley lunching on a gun caisson, and delivered his orders. "Something to do at last, eh?" laughed the rosy-cheeked youngster. "The smallest favors thankfully received. Won't you take a bite of rebel chicken, Captain? This rebellion must be put down. No? Well, tell the Colonel I am moving on, and John Brown's soul not far ahead."

When Fitz Hugh returned to Waldron he found him outside of the wood, at the base of the long incline which rose into the rebel position. About the slope were scattered prostrate forms, most numerous near the bottom, some crawling slowly rearward, some quiescent. Under the brow of the ridge, decimated and broken into a mere skirmish line sheltered in knots and singly, behind rocks and knolls and bushes, lay the Fourteenth Regiment, keeping up a steady, slow fire. From the edge above, smokily dim against a pure, blue heaven, answered another rattle of musketry, incessant, obstinate, and spiteful. The combatants on both sides were lying down; otherwise neither party could have lasted ten minutes. From Fitz Hugh's point of view not a Confederate uniform could be seen. But the smoke of their rifles made a long gray line, which was disagreeably visible and permanent; and the sharp *whit! whit!* of their bullets continually passed him, and cheeped away in the leafage behind.

"Our men can't get on another inch," he ventured

to say to his commander. "Wouldn't it be well for me to ride up and say a cheering word?"

"Every battle consists largely in waiting," replied Waldron thoughtfully. "They have undoubtedly brought up a reserve to face Thomas. But when Gahogan strikes the flank of the reserve, we shall win."

"I wish you would take shelter," begged Fitz Hugh. "Everything depends on your life."

"My life has been both a help and a hurt to my fellow-creatures," sighed the brigade commander. "Let come what will to it."

He glanced upward with an expression of profound emotion; he was evidently fighting two battles, an outward and an inward one.

Presently he added, "I think the musketry is increasing on the left. Does it strike you so?"

He was all eagerness again, leaning forward with an air of earnest listening, his face deeply flushed and his eye brilliant. Of a sudden the combat above rose and swelled into higher violence. There was a clamor far away—it seemed nearly a mile away—over the hill. Then the nearer musketry—first Thomas's on the shoulder of the ridge, next Gildersleeve's in front—caught fire and raged with new fury.

Waldron laughed outright. "Gahogan has reached them," he said to one of his staff who had just rejoined him. "We shall all be up there in five minutes. Tell Colburn to bring on his regiment slowly."

Then, turning to Fitz Hugh, he added, "Captain, we will ride forward."

They set off at a walk, now watching the smoking brow of the eminence, now picking their way among dead and wounded. Suddenly there was a shout above them and a sudden diminution of the firing; and looking upward they saw the men of the Fourteenth running confusedly toward the summit. Without a word the brigade commander struck spurs into his horse and dashed up the long slope at a run, closely followed by his enemy and aid. What they saw when they overtook the straggling, running, panting, screaming pell-mell of the Fourteenth was victory!

The entire right wing of the Confederates, attacked on three sides at once, placed at enormous disadvantage, completely outgeneraled, had given way in confusion, was retreating, breaking, and flying. There were lines yet of dirty gray or butternut; but they were few, meagre, fluctuating, and recoiling, and there were scattered and scurrying men in hundreds. Three veteran and gallant regiments had gone all to wreck under the shock of three similar regiments far more intelligently directed. A strong position had been lost because the heroes who held it could not perform the impossible feat of forming successively two fresh fronts under a concentric fire of musketry. The inferior brain power had confessed the superiority of the stronger one.

On the victorious side there was wild, clamorous, fierce exultation. The hurrying, shouting, firing soldiers, who noted their commander riding among them, swung their rifles or their tattered hats at him, and screamed "Hurrah!" No one thought of the

Confederate dead underfoot, nor of the Union dead who dotted the slope behind. "What are you here for, Colonel?" shouted rough old Gildersleeve, one leg of his trousers dripping blood. "We can do it alone."

"It is a battle won," laughed Fitz Hugh, almost worshiping the man whom he had come to slay.

"It is a battle won, but not used," answered Waldron. "We haven't a gun yet, nor a flag. Where is the cavalry? Why isn't Stilton here? He must have got afoul of the enemy's horse, and been obliged to beat it off. Can anybody hear anything of Stilton?"

"Let him go," roared Old Grumps. "The infantry don't want any help."

"Your regiment has suffered, Colonel," answered Waldron, glancing at the scattered files of the Fourteenth. "Halt it and reorganize it, and let it fall in with the right of the First when Peck comes up. I shall replace you with the Fifth. Send your Adjutant back to Colburn and tell him to hurry along. Those fellows are making a new front over there," he added, pointing to the centre of the hill. "I want the Fifth, Seventh and Tenth in *échelon* as quickly as possible. And I want that cavalry. Lieutenant," turning to one of his staff, "ride off to the left and find Colonel Stilton. Tell him that I need a charge in ten minutes."

Presently cannon opened from that part of the ridge still held by the Confederates, the shell tearing through or over the dissolving groups of their right wing, and cracking viciously above the heads of the victorious Unionists. The explosions followed each other with stunning rapidity, and the shrill whirring of the splinters was ominous. Men began to fall again in the ranks or to drop out of them wounded. Of all this Waldron took no further note than to ride hastily to the brow of the ridge and look for his own artillery.

"See how he attinds to iverything himself," said Major Gahogan, who had cantered up to the side of Fitz Hugh. "It's just a matther of plain business, an' he looks after it loike a business man. Did ye see us, though, Captin, whin we come in on their right flank? By George, we murthered um. There's more'n a hundred lyin' in hapes back there. As for old Stilton, I just caught sight of um behind that wood to our left, an' he's makin' for the enemy's right rair. He'll have lots o' prisoners in half an hour."

When Waldron returned to the group he was told of his cavalry's whereabouts, and responded to the information with a smile of satisfaction.

"Bradley is hurrying up," he said, "and Taylor is pushing their left smartly. They will make one more tussle to recover their line of retreat; but we shall smash them from end to end and take every gun."

He galloped now to his infantry, and gave the word "Forward!" The three regiments which composed the *échelon* were the Fifth on the right, the Seventh fifty yards to the rear and left of the Fifth, the Tenth to the rear and left of the Seventh. It was behind the Fifth, that is the foremost battalion, that the brigade commander posted himself.

"Do *you* mean to stay here, Colonel?" asked Fitz Hugh, in surprise and anxiety.

"It is a certain victory now," answered Waldron, with a singular glance upward. "My life is no longer important. I prefer to do my duty to the utmost in the sight of all men."

"I shall follow you and do mine, sir," said the Captain, much moved, he could scarcely say by what emotions, they were so many and conflicting.

"I want you otherwheres. Ride to Colonel Taylor at once, and hurry him up the hill. Tell him the enemy have greatly weakened their left. Tell him to push up everything, infantry, and cavalry, and artillery, and to do it in haste."

"Colonel, this is saving my life against my will," remonstrated Fitz Hugh.

"Go!" ordered Waldron, imperiously. "Time is precious."

Fitz Hugh dashed down the slope to the right at a gallop. The brigade commander turned tranquilly, and followed the march of his *échelon*. The second and decisive crisis of the little battle was approaching, and to understand it we must glance at the ground on which it was to be fought. Two hostile lines were marching toward each other along the broad, gently rounded crest of the hill and at right angles to its general course. Between these lines, but much the nearest to the Union troops, a spacious road came up out of the forest in front, crossed the ridge, swept down the smooth decline in rear, and led to a single wooden bridge over a narrow but deep rivulet. On either hand the road was hedged in by a close board fence, four feet or so in height. It was for the possession of this highway that the approaching lines were about to shed their blood. If the Confederates failed to win it all their artillery would be lost, and their army captured or dispersed.

The two parties came on without firing. The soldiers on both sides were veterans, cool, obedient to orders, intelligent through long service, and able to reserve all their resources for a short-range and final struggle. Moreover, the fences as yet partially hid them from each other, and would have rendered all aim for the present vague and uncertain.

"Forward, Fifth!" shouted Waldron. "Steady. Reserve your fire." Then, as the regiment came up to the fence, he added, "Halt; right dress. Steady, men."

Meantime he watched the advancing array with an eager gaze. It was a noble sight, full of moral sublimity, and worthy of all admiration. The long, lean, sunburned, weather-beaten soldiers in ragged gray stepped forward, superbly, their ranks loose, but swift and firm, the men leaning forward in their haste, their tattered slouch hats pushed backward, their whole aspect business-like and virile. Their line was three battalions strong, far outflanking the Fifth, and at least equal to the entire *échelon*. When within thirty or forty yards of the further fence they increased their pace to nearly a double-quick, many of them stooping low in hunter fashion, and a few firing. Then Waldron rose in his stirrups and yelled, "Battalion! ready—aim—aim low. Fire!"

There was a stunning roar of three hundred and fifty rifles, and a deadly screech of bullets. But the smoke rolled out, the haste to reload was intense, and none could mark what execution was done. Whatever the Confederates may have suffered, they bore up under the volley, and they came on. In another minute each of those fences, not more than twenty-five yards apart, was lined by the shattered fragment of a regiment, each firing as fast as possible into the face of the other. The Fifth bled fearfully: it had five of its ten company commanders shot dead in three minutes; and its loss in other officers and in men fell scarcely short of this terrible ratio. On its left the Seventh and the Tenth were up, pouring in musketry, and receiving it in a fashion hardly less sanguinary. No one present had ever seen, or ever afterward saw, such another close and deadly contest.

But the strangest thing in this whole wonderful fight was the conduct of the brigade commander. Up and down the rear of the lacerated Fifth Waldron rode thrice, spurring his plunging and wounded horse close to the yelling and fighting file-closers, and shouting in a piercing voice encouragement to his men. Stranger still, considering the character which he had borne in the army, and considering the evil deed for which he was to account on the morrow, were the words which he was distinctly and repeatedly heard to utter. "Stand steady, men—God is with us!" was the extraordinary battle-cry of this backslidden clergyman, this sinner above many.

And it was a prophecy of victory. Bradley ran up his Napoleons on the right in the nick of time, and, although only one of them could be brought to bear, it was enough; the grape raked the Confederate left, broke it, and the battle was over. In five minutes more their whole array was scattered, and the entire position open to galloping cavalry, seizing guns, standards, and prisoners.

It was in the very moment of triumph, just as the stubborn Southern line reeled back from the fence in isolated clusters, that the miraculous immunity of Waldron terminated, and he received his death wound. A quarter of an hour later Fitz Hugh found a sorrowful group of officers gazing from a little distance upon their dying commander.

"Is the Colonel hit?" he asked, shocked and grieved, incredible as the emotion may seem.

"Don't go near him," called Gildersleeve, who, it will be remembered, knew or guessed his errand in camp. "The chaplain and surgeon are there. Let him alone."

"He's going to render his account," added Gahogan. "An' whativer he's done wrong, he's made it square to-day. Let um lave it to his brigade."

Adjutant Wallis, who had been blubbering aloud, who had cursed the rebels and the luck energetically, and who had also been trying to pray inwardly, groaned out, "This is our last victory. You see if it ain't. Bet you two to one."

"Hush, man!" replied Gahogan. "We'll win our share of um, though we'll have to work harder for it. We'll have to do more ourselves, an' get less done for us in the way of tactics."

"That's so, Major," whimpered a drummer, looking up from his duty of attending to a wounded comrade. "He knowed how to put his men in the right place, and his men knowed when they was in the right place. But it's goin' to be uphill through the steepest part of hell the rest of the way."

Soldiers, some of them weeping, some of them bleeding, arrived constantly to inquire after their commander, only to be sent quietly back to their ranks or to the rear. Around lay other men—dead men, and senseless, groaning men—all for the present unnoticed. Everything, except the distant pursuit of the cavalry, waited for Waldron to die. Fitz Hugh looked on silently with the tears of mingled emotions in his eyes, and with hopes and hatreds expiring in his heart. The surgeon supported the expiring victor's head, while Chaplain Colquhoun knelt beside him, holding his hand and praying audibly. Of a sudden the petition ceased, both bent hastily toward the wounded man, and after what seemed a long time exchanged whispers. Then the Chaplain rose, came slowly toward the now advancing group of officers, his hands outspread toward heaven in an attitude of benediction, and tears running down his haggard white face.

"I trust, dear friends," he said, in a tremulous voice, "that all is well with our brother and commander. His last words were, 'God is with us.'"

"Oh! but, man, *that* isn't well," broke out Gahogan, in a groan. "What did ye pray for his soul for? Why didn't ye pray for his loife?"

Fitz Hugh turned his horse and rode silently away. The next day he was seen journeying rearward by the side of an ambulance, within which lay what seemed a strangely delicate boy, insensible, and, one would say, mortally ill.

WHO WAS SHE?

BY BAYARD TAYLOR

James Bayard Taylor (born at Kennett Square, Pa., in 1825; died in 1878) was probably in his day the best American example of the all-round literary craftsman. He was poet, novelist, journalist, writer of books of travel, translator, and, in general, magazine writer. Says Albert H. Smith in the volume on Taylor in the "American Men of Letters" series: "He was a man of talent, and master of the mechanics of his craft. On all sides he touched the life of his time." Henry A. Beers, in his "Initial Studies in American Letters," says that in his short stories, as in his novels, "Taylor's pictorial skill is greater, on the whole, than his power of creating characters or inventing plots." In the present selection, however, he has both conceived an original type of character in the mysterious heroine, and invented an ingenious situation, if not plot, and so, in one instance at least, has achieved a short story classic.

❧

WHO WAS SHE?

BY BAYARD TAYLOR

COME, now, there may as well be an end of this! Every time I meet your eyes squarely, I detect the question just slipping out of them. If you had spoken it, or even boldly looked it; if you had shown in your motions the least sign of a fussy or fidgety concern on my account; if this were not the evening of my birthday, and you the only friend who remembered it; if confession were not good for the soul, though harder than sin to some people, of whom I am one—well, if all reasons were not at this instant converged into a focus, and burning me rather violently, in that region where the seat of emotion is supposed to lie, I should keep my trouble to myself.

Yes, I have fifty times had it on my mind to tell you the whole story. But who can be certain that his best friend will not smile—or, what is worse, cherish a kind of charitable pity ever afterward—when the external forms of a very serious kind of passion seem trivial, fantastic, foolish? And the worst of all is that the heroic part which I imagined I was playing proves to have been almost the reverse. The only comfort which I can find in my humiliation is that I am capable of feeling it. There isn't a bit of a paradox in this, as you will see; but I only mention it, now,

Reprinted by permission. From "The Atlantic Monthly" for September, 1874.

to prepare you for, maybe, a little morbid sensitiveness of my moral nerves.

The documents are all in this portfolio under my elbow. I had just read them again completely through when you were announced. You may examine them as you like afterward: for the present, fill your glass, take another Cabaña, and keep silent until my "ghastly tale" has reached its most lamentable conclusion.

The beginning of it was at Wampsocket Springs, three years ago last summer. I suppose most unmarried men who have reached, or passed, the age of thirty—and I was then thirty-three—experience a milder return of their adolescent warmth, a kind of fainter second spring, since the first has not fulfilled its promise. Of course, I wasn't clearly conscious of this at the time: who is? But I had had my youthful passion and my tragic disappointment, as you know: I had looked far enough into what Thackeray used to call the cryptic mysteries to save me from the Scylla of dissipation, and yet preserved enough of natural nature to keep me out of the Pharisaic Charybdis. My devotion to my legal studies had already brought me a mild distinction; the paternal legacy was a good nest-egg for the incubation of wealth—in short, I was a fair, respectable "party," desirable to the humbler mammas, and not to be despised by the haughty exclusives.

The fashionable hotel at the Springs holds three hundred, and it was packed. I had meant to lounge there for a fortnight and then finish my holidays at Long Branch; but eighty, at least, out of the three hundred were young and moved lightly in muslin. With my years and experience I felt so safe that to walk, talk, or dance with them became simply a luxury, such as I had never—at least so freely—possessed before. My name and standing, known to some families, were agreeably exaggerated to the others, and I enjoyed that supreme satisfaction which a man always feels when he discovers, or imagines, that he is popular in society. There is a kind of premonitory apology implied in my saying this, I am aware. You must remember that I am culprit, and culprit's counsel, at the same time.

You have never been at Wampsocket? Well, the hills sweep around in a crescent, on the northern side, and four or five radiating glens, descending from them, unite just above the village. The central one, leading to a waterfall (called "Minne-hehe" by the irreverent young people, because there is so little of it), is the fashionable drive and promenade; but the second ravine on the left, steep, crooked, and cumbered with bowlders which have tumbled from somewhere and lodged in the most extraordinary groupings, became my favorite walk of a morning. There was a footpath in it, well-trodden at first, but gradually fading out as it became more like a ladder than a path, and I soon discovered that no other city feet than mine were likely to scale a certain rough slope which seemed the end of the ravine. With the aid of the tough laurel-stems I climbed to the top, passed through a cleft as narrow as a doorway, and presently found myself in a little upper dell, as wild and sweet and strange as one of the pictures that haunts us on the brink of sleep.

There was a pond—no, rather a bowl—of water in the centre; hardly twenty yards across, yet the sky in it was so pure and far down that the circle of rocks and summer foliage inclosing it seemed like a little planetary ring, floating off alone through space. I can't explain the charm of the spot, nor the selfishness which instantly suggested that I should keep the discovery to myself. Ten years earlier I should have looked around for some fair spirit to be my "minister," but now—

One forenoon—I think it was the third or fourth time I had visited the place—I was startled to find the dent of a heel in the earth, half-way up the slope. There had been rain during the night and the earth was still moist and soft. It was the mark of a woman's boot, only to be distinguished from that of a walking-stick by its semicircular form. A little higher, I found the outline of a foot, not so small as to awake an ecstasy, but with a suggestion of lightness, elasticity, and grace. If hands were thrust through holes in a board-fence, and nothing of the attached bodies seen, I can easily imagine that some would attract and others repel us: with footprints the impression is weaker, of course, but we can not escape it. I am not sure whether I wanted to find the unknown wearer of the boot within my precious personal solitude: I was afraid I should see her, while passing through the rocky crevice, and yet was disappointed when I found no one.

But on the flat, warm rock overhanging the tarn—my special throne—lay some withering wild-flowers and a book! I looked up and down, right and left: there was not the slightest sign of another human life than mine. Then I lay down for a quarter of an hour, and listened: there were only the noises of bird and squirrel, as before. At last, I took up the book, the flat breadth of which suggested only sketches. There were, indeed, some tolerable studies of rocks and trees on the first pages; a few not very striking caricatures, which seemed to have been commenced as portraits, but recalled no faces I knew; then a number of fragmentary notes, written in pencil. I found no name, from first to last; only, under the sketches, a monogram so complicated and laborious that the initials could hardly be discovered unless one already knew them.

The writing was a woman's, but it had surely taken its character from certain features of her own: it was clear, firm, individual. It had nothing of that air of general debility which usually marks the manuscript of young ladies, yet its firmness was far removed from the stiff, conventional slope which all Englishwomen seem to acquire in youth and retain through life. I don't see how any man in my situation could have helped reading a few lines—if only for the sake of restoring lost property. But I was drawn on, and on, and finished by reading all: thence, since no further harm could be done, I reread, pondering over certain passages until they stayed with me. Here they are, as I set them down, that evening, on the back of a legal blank:

"It makes a great deal of difference whether we wear social forms as bracelets or handcuffs."

"Can we not still be wholly our independent selves, even while doing, in the main, as others do? I know two who are so; but they are married."

"The men who admire these bold, dashing young girls treat them like weaker copies of themselves. And yet they boast of what they call 'experience'!"

"I wonder if any one felt the exquisite beauty of the noon as I did to-day? A faint appreciation of sunsets and storms is taught us in youth, and kept alive by novels and flirtations; but the broad, imperial splendor of this summer noon!—and myself standing alone in it—yes, utterly alone!"

"The men I seek *must* exist: where are they? How make an acquaintance, when one obsequiously bows himself away, as I advance? The fault is surely not all on my side."

There was much more, intimate enough to inspire me with a keen interest in the writer, yet not sufficiently so to make my perusal a painful indiscretion. I yielded to the impulse of the moment, took out my pencil, and wrote a dozen lines on one of the blank pages. They ran something in this wise:

"IGNOTUS IGNOTÆ!—You have bestowed without intending it, and I have taken without your knowledge. Do not regret the accident which has enriched another. This concealed idyl of the hills was mine, as I supposed, but I acknowledge your equal right to it. Shall we share the possession, or will you banish me?"

There was a frank advance, tempered by a proper caution, I fancied, in the words I wrote. It was evident that she was unmarried, but outside of that certainty there lay a vast range of possibilities, some of them alarming enough. However, if any nearer acquaintance should arise out of the incident, the next step must be taken by her. Was I one of the men she sought? I almost imagined so—certainly hoped so.

I laid the book on the rock, as I had found it, bestowed another keen scrutiny on the lonely landscape, and then descended the ravine. That evening, I went early to the ladies' parlor, chatted more than usual with the various damsels whom I knew, and watched with a new interest those whom I knew not. My mind, involuntarily, had already created a picture of the unknown. She might be twenty-five, I thought; a reflective habit of mind would hardly be developed before that age. Tall and stately, of course; distinctly proud in her bearing, and somewhat reserved in her manners. Why she should have large dark eyes, with long dark lashes, I could not tell; but so I seemed to see her. Quite forgetting that I was (or had meant to be) *Ignotus*, I found myself staring rather significantly at one or the other of the young ladies, in whom I discovered some slight general resemblance to the imaginary character. My fancies, I must confess, played strange pranks with me. They had been kept in a coop so many years that now, when I suddenly turned them loose, their rickety attempts at flight quite bewildered me.

No! there was no use in expecting a sudden discovery. I went to the glen betimes, next morning: the book was gone and so were the faded flowers, but some of the latter were scattered over the top of another rock, a few yards from mine. Ha! this means that I am not to withdraw, I said to myself: she makes room for me! But how to surprise her?—for by this time I was fully resolved to make her acquaintance, even though she might turn out to be forty, scraggy, and sandy-haired.

I knew no other way so likely as that of visiting the glen at all times of the day. I even went so far as to write a line of greeting, with a regret that our visits had not yet coincided, and laid it under a stone on the top of *her* rock. The note disappeared, but there was no answer in its place. Then I suddenly remembered her fondness for the noon hours, at which time she was "utterly alone." The hotel *table d'hôte* was at one o'clock: her family, doubtless, dined later, in their own rooms. Why, this gave me, at least, her place in society! The question of age, to be sure, remained unsettled; but all else was safe.

The next day I took a late and large breakfast, and sacrificed my dinner. Before noon the guests had all straggled back to the hotel from glen and grove and lane, so bright and hot was the sunshine. Indeed, I could hardly have supported the reverberation of heat from the sides of the ravine, but for a fixed belief that I should be successful. While crossing the narrow meadow upon which it opened, I caught a glimpse of something white among the thickets higher up. A moment later it had vanished, and I quickened my pace, feeling the beginning of an absurd nervous excitement in my limbs. At the next turn, there it was again! but only for another moment. I paused, exulting, and wiped my drenched forehead. "She can not escape me!" I murmured between the deep draughts of cooler air I inhaled in the shadow of a rock.

A few hundred steps more brought me to the foot of the steep ascent, where I had counted on overtaking her. I was too late for that, but the dry, baked soil had surely been crumbled and dislodged, here and there, by a rapid foot. I followed, in reckless haste, snatching at the laurel branches right and left, and paying little heed to my footing. About one-third of the way up I slipped, fell, caught a bush which snapped at the root, slid, whirled over, and before I fairly knew what had happened, I was lying doubled up at the bottom of the slope.

I rose, made two steps forward, and then sat down with a groan of pain; my left ankle was badly sprained, in addition to various minor scratches and bruises. There was a revulsion of feeling, of course—instant, complete, and hideous. I fairly hated the Unknown. "Fool that I was!" I exclaimed, in the theatrical manner, dashing the palm of my hand softly against my brow: "lured to this by the fair traitress! But, no! —not fair: she shows the artfulness of faded, desperate spinsterhood; she is all compact of enamel, 'liquid bloom of youth' and hair dye!"

There was a fierce comfort in this thought, but it couldn't help me out of the scrape. I dared not sit still, lest a sunstroke should be added, and there was no resource but to hop or crawl down the rugged path, in the hope of finding a forked sapling from which I could extemporize a crutch. With endless pain and trouble I reached a thicket, and was feebly working on a branch with my pen-knife, when the sound of a heavy footstep surprised me.

A brown harvest-hand, in straw hat and shirt-sleeves, presently appeared. He grinned when he saw me, and the thick snub of his nose would have seemed like a sneer at any other time.

"Are you the gentleman that got hurt?" he asked. "Is it pretty tolerable bad?"

"Who said I was hurt?" I cried, in astonishment.

"One of your town-women from the hotel—I reckon she was. I was binding oats, in the field over the ridge; but I haven't lost no time in comin' here."

While I was stupidly staring at this announcement, he whipped out a big clasp-knife, and in a few minutes fashioned me a practicable crutch. Then, taking me by the other arm, he set me in motion toward the village.

Grateful as I was for the man's help, he aggravated me by his ignorance. When I asked if he knew the lady, he answered: "It's more'n likely *you* know her better." But where did she come from? Down from the hill, he guessed, but it might ha' been up the road. How did she look? was she old or young? what was the color of her eyes? of her hair? There, now, I was too much for him. When a woman kept one o' them speckled veils over her face, turned her head away, and held her parasol between, how were you to know her from Adam? I declare to you, I couldn't arrive at one positive particular. Even when he affirmed that she was tall, he added, the next instant: "Now I come to think on it, she stepped mighty quick; so I guess she must ha' been short."

By the time we reached the hotel, I was in a state of fever; opiates and lotions had their will of me for the rest of the day. I was glad to escape the worry of questions, and the conventional sympathy expressed in inflections of the voice which are meant to soothe, and only exasperate. The next morning, as I lay upon my sofa, restful, patient, and properly cheerful, the waiter entered with a bouquet of wild flowers.

"Who sent them?" I asked.

"I found them outside your door, sir. Maybe there's a card; yes, here's a bit o' paper."

I opened the twisted slip he handed me, and read: "From your dell—and mine." I took the flowers; among them were two or three rare and beautiful varieties which I had only found in that one spot. Fool, again! I noiselessly kissed, while pretending to smell them, had them placed on a stand within reach, and fell into a state of quiet and agreeable contemplation.

Tell me, yourself, whether any male human being is ever too old for sentiment, provided that it strikes him at the right time and in the right way! What did that bunch of wild flowers betoken? Knowledge, first; then, sympathy; and finally, encouragement, at least. Of course she had seen my accident, from above; of course she had sent the harvest laborer to aid me home. It was quite natural she should imagine some special, romantic interest in the lonely dell, on my part, and the gift took additional value from her conjecture.

Four days afterward, there was a hop in the large dining-room of the hotel. Early in the morning, a fresh bouquet had been left at my door. I was tired of my enforced idleness, eager to discover the fair unknown (she was again fair, to my fancy!), and I determined to go down, believing that a cane and a crimson velvet slipper on the left foot would provoke a glance of sympathy from certain eyes, and thus enable me to detect them.

The fact was, the sympathy was much too general and effusive. Everybody, it seemed, came to me with kindly greetings; seats were vacated at my approach, even fat Mrs. Huxter insisting on my taking her warm place, at the head of the room. But Bob Leroy—you know him—as gallant a gentleman as ever lived, put me down at the right point, and kept me there. He only meant to divert me, yet gave me the only place where I could quietly inspect all the younger ladies, as dance or supper brought them near.

One of the dances was an old-fashioned cotillon, and one of the figures, the "coquette," brought every one, in turn, before me. I received a pleasant word or two from those whom I knew, and a long, kind, silent glance from Miss May Danvers. Where had been my eyes? She was tall, stately, twenty-five, had large dark eyes, and long dark lashes! Again the changes of the dance brought her near me; I threw (or strove to throw) unutterable meanings into my eyes, and cast them upon hers. She seemed startled, looked suddenly away, looked back to me, and—blushed. I knew her for what is called "a nice girl"—that is, tolerably frank, gently feminine, and not dangerously intelligent. Was it possible that I had overlooked so much character and intellect?

As the cotillon closed, she was again in my neighborhood, and her partner led her in my direction. I was rising painfully from my chair, when Bob Leroy pushed me down again, whisked another seat from somewhere, planted it at my side, and there she was!

She knew who was her neighbor, I plainly saw; but instead of turning toward me, she began to fan herself in a nervous way and to fidget with the buttons of her gloves. I grew impatient.

"Miss Danvers!" I said, at last.

"Oh!" was all her answer, as she looked at me for a moment.

"Where are your thoughts?" I asked.

Then she turned, with wide, astonished eyes, coloring softly up to the roots of her hair. My heart gave a sudden leap.

"How can you tell, if I can not?" she asked.

"May I guess?"

She made a slight inclination of the head, saying nothing. I was then quite sure.

"The second ravine to the left of the main drive?"

This time she actually started; her color became deeper, and a leaf of the ivory fan snapped between her fingers.

"Let there be no more a secret!" I exclaimed.

"Your flowers have brought me your messages; I knew I should find you—"

Full of certainty, I was speaking in a low, impassioned voice. She cut me short by rising from her seat; I felt that she was both angry and alarmed. Fisher, of Philadelphia, jostling right and left in his haste, made his way toward her. She fairly snatched his arm, clung to it with a warmth I had never seen expressed in a ballroom, and began to whisper in his ear. It was not five minutes before he came to me, alone, with a very stern face, bent down, and said:

"If you have discovered our secret, you will keep silent. You are certainly a gentleman."

I bowed, coldly and savagely. There was a draught from the open window; my ankle became suddenly weary and painful, and I went to bed. Can you believe that I didn't guess, immediately, what it all meant? In a vague way, I fancied that I had been premature in my attempt to drop our mutual incognito, and that Fisher, a rival lover, was jealous of me. This was rather flattering than otherwise; but when I limped down to the ladies' parlor, the next day, no Miss Danvers was to be seen. I did not venture to ask for her; it might seem importunate, and a woman of so much hidden capacity was evidently not to be wooed in the ordinary way.

So another night passed by; and then, with the morning, came a letter which made me feel, at the same instant, like a fool and a hero. It had been dropped in the Wampsocket post-office, was legibly addressed to me and delivered with some other letters which had arrived by the night mail. Here it is; listen!

"NOTO IGNOTA!—Haste is not a gift of the gods, and you have been impatient, with the usual result. I was almost prepared for this, and thus am not wholly disappointed. In a day or two more you will discover your mistake, which, so far as I can learn, has done no particular harm. If you wish to find *me*, there is only one way to seek me; should I tell you what it is, I should run the risk of losing you—that is, I should preclude the manifestation of a certain quality which I hope to find in the man who may—or, rather, must—be my friend. This sounds enigmatical, yet you have read enough of my nature, as written in those random notes in my sketch-book, to guess, at least, how much I require. Only this let me add: mere guessing is useless.

"Being unknown, I can write freely. If you find me, I shall be justified; if not, I shall hardly need to blush, even to myself, over a futile experiment.

"It is possible for me to learn enough of your life, henceforth, to direct my relation toward you. This may be the end; if so, I shall know it soon. I shall also know whether you continue to seek me. Trusting in your honor as a man, I must ask you to trust in mine, as a woman."

I *did* discover my mistake, as the Unknown promised. There had been a secret betrothal between Fisher and Miss Danvers, and, singularly enough, the momentous question and answer had been given in the very ravine leading to my upper dell! The two meant to keep the matter to themselves; but therein, it seems, I thwarted them; there was a little opposition on the part of their respective families, but all was amicably settled before I left Wampsocket.

The letter made a very deep impression upon me. What was the one way to find her? What could it be but the triumph that follows ambitious toil—the manifestation of all my best qualities as a man? Be she old or young, plain or beautiful, I reflected, hers is surely a nature worth knowing, and its candid intelligence conceals no hazards for me. I have sought her rashly, blundered, betrayed that I set her lower, in my thoughts, than her actual self: let me now adopt the opposite course, seek her openly no longer, go back to my tasks, and, following my own aims vigorously and cheerfully, restore that respect which she seemed to be on the point of losing. For, consciously or not, she had communicated to me a doubt, implied in the very expression of her own strength and pride. She had meant to address me as an equal, yet, despite herself, took a stand a little above that which she accorded to me.

I came back to New York earlier than usual, worked steadily at my profession and with increasing success, and began to accept opportunities (which I had previously declined) of making myself personally known to the great, impressible, fickle, tyrannical public. One or two of my speeches in the hall of the Cooper Institute, on various occasions—as you may perhaps remember—gave me a good headway with the party, and were the chief cause of my nomination for the State office which I still hold. (There, on the table, lies a resignation, written to-day, but not yet signed. We'll talk of it afterward.) Several months passed by, and no further letter reached me. I gave up much of my time to society, moved familiarly in more than one province of the kingdom here, and vastly extended my acquaintance, especially among the women; but not one of them betrayed the mysterious something or other—really I can't explain precisely what it was!—which I was looking for. In fact, the more I endeavored quietly to study the sex, the more confused I became.

At last, I was subjected to the usual onslaught from the strong-minded. A small but formidable committee entered my office one morning and demanded a categorical declaration of my principles. What my views on the subject were, I knew very well; they were clear and decided; and yet, I hesitated to declare them! It wasn't a temptation of Saint Anthony—that is, turned the other way—and the belligerent attitude of the dames did not alarm me in the least; but *she!* What was *her* position? How could I best please her? It flashed upon my mind, while Mrs. —— was making her formal speech, that I had taken no step for months without a vague, secret reference to *her*. So I strove to be courteous, friendly, and agreeably noncommittal; begged for further documents, and promised to reply by letter in a few days.

I was hardly surprised to find the well-known hand on the envelope of a letter shortly afterward. I held it for a minute in my palm, with an absurd hope that I might sympathetically feel its character before breaking the seal. Then I read it with a great sense of relief.

"I have never assumed to guide a man, except toward the full exercise of his powers. It is not opinion in action, but opinion in a state of idleness or indifference, which repels me. I am deeply glad that you have gained so much since you left the country. If, in shaping your course, you have thought of me, I will frankly say that, *to that extent*, you have drawn nearer. Am I mistaken in conjecturing that you wish to know my relation to the movement concerning which you were recently interrogated? In this, as in other instances which may come, I must beg you to consider me only as a spectator. The more my own views may seem likely to sway your action, the less I shall be inclined to declare them. If you find this cold or unwomanly, remember that it is not easy!"

Yes! I felt that I had certainly drawn much nearer to her. And from this time on, her imaginary face and form became other than they were. She was twenty-eight—three years older; a very little above the middle height, but not tall; serene, rather than stately, in her movements; with a calm, almost grave face, relieved by the sweetness of the full, firm lips; and finally eyes of pure, limpid gray, such as we fancy belonged to the Venus of Milo. I found her thus much more attractive than with the dark eyes and lashes—but she did not make her appearance in the circles which I frequented.

Another year slipped away. As an official personage, my importance increased, but I was careful not to exaggerate it to myself. Many have wondered (perhaps you among the rest) at my success, seeing that I possess no remarkable abilities. If I have any secret, it is simply this—doing faithfully, with all my might, whatever I undertake. Nine-tenths of our politicians become inflated and careless, after the first few years, and are easily forgotten when they once lose place.

I am a little surprised now that I had so much patience with the Unknown. I was too important, at least, to be played with; too mature to be subjected to a longer test; too earnest, as I had proved, to be doubted, or thrown aside without a further explanation.

Growing tired, at last, of silent waiting, I bethought me of advertising. A carefully written "Personal," in which *Ignotus* informed *Ignota* of the necessity of his communicating with her, appeared simultaneously in the "Tribune," "Herald," "World," and "Times." I renewed the advertisement as the time expired without an answer, and I think it was about the end of the third week before one came, through the post, as before.

Ah, yes! I had forgotten. See! my advertisement is pasted on the note, as a heading or motto for the manuscript lines. I don't know why the printed slip should give me a particular feeling of humiliation as I look at it, but such is the fact. What she wrote is all I need read to you:

"I could not, at first, be certain that this was meant for me. If I were to explain to you why I have not written for so long a time, I might give you one of the few clews which I insist on keeping in my own hands. In your public capacity, you have been (so far as a woman may judge) upright, independent, wholly manly: in your relations with other men I learn nothing of you that is not honorable: toward women you are kind, chivalrous, no doubt, overflowing with the *usual* social refinements, but— Here, again, I run hard upon the absolute necessity of silence. The way to me, if you care to traverse it, is so simple, so very simple! Yet, after what I have written, I can not even wave my hand in the direction of it, without certain self-contempt. When I feel free to tell you, we shall draw apart and remain unknown forever.

"You desire to write? I do not prohibit it. I have heretofore made no arrangement for hearing from you, in turn, because I could not discover that any advantage would accrue from it. But it seems only fair, I confess, and you dare not think me capricious. So, three days hence, at six o'clock in the evening, a trusty messenger of mine will call at your door. If you have anything to give her for me, the act of giving it must be the sign of a compact on your part that you will allow her to leave immediately, unquestioned and unfollowed."

You look puzzled, I see: you don't catch the real drift of her words? Well, that's a melancholy encouragement. Neither did I, at the time: it was plain that I had disappointed her in some way, and my intercourse with or manner toward women had something to do with it. In vain I ran over as much of my later social life as I could recall. There had been no special attention, nothing to mislead a susceptible heart; on the other side, certainly no rudeness, no want of "chivalrous" (she used the word!) respect and attention. What, in the name of all the gods, was the matter?

In spite of all my efforts to grow clearer, I was obliged to write my letter in a rather muddled state of mind. I had *so* much to say! sixteen folio pages, I was sure, would only suffice for an introduction to the case; yet, when the creamy vellum lay before me and the moist pen drew my fingers toward it, I sat stock dumb for half an hour. I wrote, finally, in a half-desperate mood, without regard to coherency or logic. Here's a rough draft of a part of the letter, and a single passage from it will be enough:

"I can conceive of no simpler way to you than the knowledge of your name and address. I have drawn airy images of you, but they do not become incarnate, and I am not sure that I should recognize you in the brief moment of passing. Your nature is not of those which are instantly legible. As an abstract power, it has wrought in my life and it continually moves my heart with desires which are unsatisfactory because so vague and ignorant. Let me offer you, personally, my gratitude, my earnest friendship. you would laugh if I were *now* to offer more."

Stay! here is another fragment, more reckless in tone:

> "I want to find the woman whom I can love—who can love me. But this is a masquerade where the features are hidden, the voice disguised, even the hands grotesquely gloved. Come! I will venture more than I ever thought was possible to me. You shall know my deepest nature as I myself seem to know it. Then, give me the commonest chance of learning yours, through an intercourse which shall leave both free, should we not feel the closing of the inevitable bond!"

After I had written that, the pages filled rapidly. When the appointed hour arrived, a bulky epistle, in a strong linen envelope, sealed with five wax seals, was waiting on my table. Precisely at six there was an announcement: the door opened, and a little outside, in the shadow, I saw an old woman, in a threadbare dress of rusty black.

"Come in!" I said.

"The letter!" answered a husky voice. She stretched out a bony hand, without moving a step.

"It is for a lady—very important business," said I, taking up the letter; "are you sure that there is no mistake?"

She drew her hand under the shawl, turned without a word, and moved toward the hall door.

"Stop!" I cried: "I beg a thousand pardons! Take it—take it! You are the right messenger!"

She clutched it, and was instantly gone.

Several days passed, and I gradually became so nervous and uneasy that I was on the point of inserting another "Personal" in the daily papers, when the answer arrived. It was brief and mysterious; you shall hear the whole of it:

"I thank you. Your letter is a sacred confidence which I pray you never to regret. Your nature is sound and good. You ask no more than is reasonable, and I have no real right to refuse. In the one respect which I have hinted, *I* may have been unskilful or too narrowly cautious: I must have the certainty of this. Therefore, as a generous favor, give me six months more! At the end of that time I will write to you again. Have patience with these brief lines: another word might be a word too much."

You notice the change in her tone? The letter gave me the strongest impression of a new, warm, almost anxious interest on her part. My fancies, as first at Wampsocket, began to play all sorts of singular pranks: sometimes she was rich and of an old family, sometimes moderately poor and obscure, but always the same calm, reposeful face and clear gray eyes. I ceased looking for her in society, quite sure that I should not find her, and nursed a wild expectation of suddenly meeting her, face to face, in the most unlikely places and under startling circumstances. However, the end of it all was patience—patience for six months.

There's not much more to tell; but this last letter is hard for me to read. It came punctually, to a day. I knew it would, and at the last I began to dread the time, as if a heavy note were falling due, and I had no funds to meet it. My head was in a whirl when I broke the seal. The fact in it stared at me blankly, at once, but it was a long time before the words and sentences became intelligible.

"The stipulated time has come, and our hidden romance is at an end. Had I taken this resolution a year ago, it would have saved me many vain hopes, and you, perhaps, a little uncertainty. Forgive me, first, if you can, and then hear the explanation:

"You wished for a personal interview: *you have had, not one, but many.* We have met, in society, talked face to face, discussed the weather, the opera, toilettes, Queechy, Aurora Floyd, Long Branch and Newport, and exchanged a weary amount of fashionable gossip; and you never guessed that I was governed by any deeper interest! I have purposely uttered ridiculous platitudes, and you were as smilingly courteous as if you enjoyed them: I have let fall remarks whose hollowness and selfishness could not have escaped you, and have waited in vain for a word of sharp, honest, manly reproof. Your manner to me was unexceptionable, as it was to all other women: but there lies the source of my disappointment, of—yes—of my sorrow!

"You appreciate, I can not doubt, the qualities in woman which men value in one another—culture, independence of thought, a high and earnest apprehension of life; but you know not how to seek them. It is not true that a mature and unperverted woman is flattered by receiving only the general obsequiousness which most men give to the whole sex. In the man who contradicts and strives with her, she discovers a truer interest, a nobler respect. The empty-headed, spindle-shanked youths who dance admirably, understand something of billiards, much less of horses, and still less of navigation, soon grow inexpressibly wearisome to us; but the men who adopt their social courtesy, never seeking to arouse, uplift, instruct us, are a bitter disappointment.

"What would have been the end, had you really found me? Certainly a sincere, satisfying friendship. No mysterious magnetic force has drawn you to me or held you near me, nor has my experiment inspired me with an interest which can not be given up without a personal pang. I am grieved, for the sake of all men and all women. Yet, understand me! I mean no slightest reproach. I esteem and honor you for what you are. Farewell!"

There! Nothing could be kinder in tone, nothing more humiliating in substance. I was sore and offended for a few days; but I soon began to see, and ever more and more clearly, that she was wholly right. I was sure, also, that any further attempt to correspond with her would be vain. It all comes of taking society just as we find it, and supposing that conven-

MADEMOISELLE OLYMPE ZABRISKI

BY THOMAS BAILEY ALDRICH

I

WE are accustomed to speak with a certain light irony of the tendency which women have to gossip, as if the sin itself, if it is a sin, were of the gentler sex, and could by no chance be a masculine peccadillo. So far as my observation goes, men are as much given to small talk as women, and it is undeniable that we have produced the highest type of gossiper extant. Where will you find, in or out of literature, such another droll, delightful, chatty busybody as Samuel Pepys, Esq., Secretary to the Admiralty in the reigns of those fortunate gentlemen Charles II and James II of England? He is the king of tattlers, as Shakespeare is the king of poets.

If it came to a matter of pure gossip, I would back Our Club against the Sorosis or any women's club in existence. Whenever you see in your drawing-room four or five young fellows lounging in easy chairs, cigar in hand, and now and then bringing their heads together over the small round Japanese table which is always the pivot of these social circles, you may be sure that they are discussing Tom's engagement, or Dick's extravagance, or Harry's hopeless passion for the younger Miss Fleurdelys. It is here old Tippleton gets execrated for that everlasting *bon mot* of his which was quite a success at dinner-parties forty years ago; it is here the belle of the season passes under the scalpels of merciless young surgeons; it is here B's financial condition is handled in a way that would make B's hair stand on end; it is here, in short, that everything is canvassed—everything that happens in our set, I mean—much that never happens, and a great deal that could not possibly happen. It was at Our Club that I learned the particulars of the Van Twiller affair.

It was great entertainment to Our Club, the Van Twiller affair, though it was rather a joyless thing, I fancy, for Van Twiller. To understand the case fully, it should be understood that Ralph Van Twiller is one of the proudest and most sensitive men living. He is a lineal descendant of Wouter Van Twiller, the famous old Dutch governor of New York—Nieuw Amsterdam, as it was then; his ancestors have always been burgomasters or admirals or generals, and his mother is the Mrs. Vanrensselaer Vanzandt Van Twiller whose magnificent place will be pointed out to you on the right bank of the Hudson as you pass up the historic river toward Idlewild. Ralph is about twenty-five years old. Birth made him a gentleman, and the rise of real estate—some of it in the family since the old governor's time—made him a millionaire. It was a kindly fairy that stepped in and made him a good fellow also. Fortune, I take it, was in her most jocund mood when she heaped her

T. B. Aldrich.

gifts in this fashion on Van Twiller, who was, and will be again, when this cloud blows over, the flower of Our Club.

About a year ago there came a whisper—if the word "whisper" is not too harsh a term to apply to what seemed a mere breath floating gently through the atmosphere of the billiard-room—imparting the intelligence that Van Twiller was in some kind of trouble. Just as everybody suddenly takes to wearing square-toed boots, or to drawing his neckscarf through a ring, so it became all at once the fashion, without any preconcerted agreement, for everybody to speak of Van Twiller as a man in some way under a cloud. But what the cloud was, and how he got under it, and why he did not get away from it, were points that lifted themselves into the realm of pure conjecture. There was no man in the club with strong enough wing to his imagination to soar to the supposition that Van Twiller was embarrassed in money matters. Was he in love? That appeared nearly as improbable; for if he had been in love all the world—that is, perhaps a hundred first families—would have known all about it instantly.

"He has the symptoms," said Delaney, laughing. "I remember once when Jack Fleming—"

"Ned!" cried Flemming, "I protest against any allusion to that business."

This was one night when Van Twiller had wandered into the club, turned over the magazines absently in the reading-room, and wandered out again without speaking ten words. The most careless eye would have remarked the great change that had come over Van Twiller. Now and then he would play a game of billiards with De Peyster or Haseltine, or stop to chat a moment in the vestibule with old Duane; but he was an altered man. When at the club, he was usually to be found in the small smoking-room upstairs, seated on a fauteuil fast asleep, with the last number of "The Nation" in his hand. Once, if you went to two or three places of an evening, you were certain to meet Van Twiller at them all. You seldom met him in society now.

By and by came whisper number two—a whisper more emphatic than number one, but still untraceable to any tangible mouthpiece. This time the whisper said that Van Twiller *was* in love. But with whom? The list of possible Mrs. Van Twillers was carefully examined by experienced hands, and a check placed against a fine old Knickerbocker name here and there, but nothing satisfactory arrived at. Then that same still small voice of rumor, but now with an easily detected staccato sharpness to it, said that Van Twiller was in love—with an actress! Van Twiller, whom it had taken all these years and all this waste of raw material in the way of ancestors to bring to perfection—Ralph Van Twiller, the net result and flower of his race, the descendant of Wouter, the son of Mrs. Vanrensselaer Vanzandt Van Twiller—in love with an actress! That was too ridiculous to be believed—and so everybody believed it.

Six or seven members of the club abruptly discovered in themselves an unsuspected latent passion for the histrionic art. In squads of two or three they stormed successively all the theatres in town—Booth's, Wallack's, Daly's Fifth Avenue (not burned down then), and the Grand Opera House. Even the shabby homes of the drama over in the Bowery, where the Germanic Thespis has not taken out his naturalization papers, underwent rigid exploration. But no clew was found to Van Twiller's mysterious attachment. The *opéra bouffe,* which promised the widest field for investigation, produced absolutely nothing, not even a crop of suspicions. One night, after several weeks of this, Delaney and I fancied that we caught sight of Van Twiller in the private box of an uptown theatre, where some thrilling trapeze performance was going on, which we did not care to sit through; but we concluded afterward that it was only somebody who looked like him. Delaney, by the way, was unusually active in this search. I dare say he never quite forgave Van Twiller for calling him Muslin Delaney. Ned is fond of ladies' society, and that's a fact.

The Cimmerian darkness which surrounded Van Twiller's inamorata left us free to indulge in the wildest conjectures. Whether she was black-tressed Melpomene, with bowl and dagger, or Thalia, with the fair hair and the laughing face, was only to be guessed at. It was popularly conceded, however, that Van Twiller was on the point of forming a dreadful *mésalliance.*

Up to this period he had visited the club regularly. Suddenly he ceased to appear. He was not to be seen on Fifth Avenue, or in the Central Park, or at the houses he generally frequented. His chambers—and mighty comfortable chambers they were—on Thirty-fourth Street were deserted. He had dropped out of the world, shot like a bright particular star from his orbit in the heaven of the best society.

The following conversation took place one night in the smoking-room:

"Where's Van Twiller?"

"Who's seen Van Twiller?

"What has become of Van Twiller?"

Delaney picked up the "Evening Post," and read—with a solemnity that betrayed young Firkins into exclaiming, "By Jove, now!—"

"Married, on the 10th instant, by the Rev. Friar Laurence, at the residence of the bride's uncle, Montague Capulet, Esq., Miss Adrienne Le Couvreur to Mr. Ralph Van Twiller, both of this city. No cards."

"Free List suspended," murmured De Peyster.

"It strikes me," said Frank Livingstone, who had been ruffling the leaves of a magazine at the other end of the table, "that you fellows are in a great fever about Van Twiller."

"So we are."

"Well, he has simply gone out of town."

"Where?"

"Up to the old homestead on the Hudson."

"It's an odd time of year for a fellow to go into the country."

"He has gone to visit his mother," said Livingstone.

"In February?"

"I didn't know, Delaney, that there was any statute in force prohibiting a man from visiting his mother in February if he wants to."

Delaney made some light remark about the pleasure of communing with Nature with a cold in her head, and the topic was dropped.

Livingstone was hand in glove with Van Twiller, and if any man shared his confidence it was Livingstone. He was aware of the gossip and speculation that had been rife in the club, but he either was not at liberty or did not think it worth while to relieve our curiosity. In the course of a week or two it was reported that Van Twiller was going to Europe; and go he did. A dozen of us went down to the "Scythia" to see him off. It was refreshing to have something as positive as the fact that Van Twiller had sailed.

II

Shortly after Van Twiller's departure the whole thing came out. Whether Livingstone found the secret too heavy a burden, or whether it transpired through some indiscretion on the part of Mrs. Vanrensselaer Vanzandt Van Twiller, I can not say; but one evening the entire story was in the possession of the club.

Van Twiller had actually been very deeply interested—not in an actress, for the legitimate drama was not her humble walk in life, but — in Mademoiselle Olympe Zabriski, whose really perilous feats on the trapeze had astonished New York the year before, though they had failed to attract Delaney and me the night we wandered into the up-town theatre on the trail of Van Twiller's mystery.

That a man like Van Twiller should be fascinated even for an instant by a common circus-girl seems incredible; but it is always the incredible thing that happens. Besides, Mademoiselle Olympe was not a common circus-girl; she was a most daring and startling gymnaste, with a beauty and a grace of movement that gave to her audacious performance almost an air of prudery. Watching her wondrous dexterity and pliant strength, both exercised without apparent effort, it seemed the most natural proceeding in the world that she should do those unpardonable things. She had a way of melting from one graceful posture into another like the dissolving figures thrown from a stereopticon. She was a lithe, radiant shape out of the Grecian mythology, now poised up there above the gaslights, and now gleaming through the air like a slender gilt arrow.

I am describing Mademoiselle Olympe as she appeared to Van Twiller on the first occasion when he strolled into the theatre where she was performing. To me she was a girl of eighteen or twenty years of age (maybe she was much older, for pearl powder and distance keep these people perpetually young), slightly but exquisitely built, with sinews of silver wire; rather pretty, perhaps, after a manner, but showing plainly the effects of the exhaustive draughts she was making on her physical vitality. Now, Van Twiller was an enthusiast on the subject of calisthenics. "If

I had a daughter," Van Twiller used to say, "I wouldn't send her to a boarding school, or a nunnery; I'd send her to a gymnasium for the first five years. Our American women have no physique. They are lilies, pallid, pretty—and perishable. You marry an American woman, and what do you marry? A headache. Look at English girls. They are at least roses, and last the season through."

Walking home from the theatre that first night, it flitted through Van Twiller's mind that if he could give this girl's set of nerves and muscles to any one of the two hundred high-bred women he knew, he would marry her on the spot and worship her forever.

The following evening he went to see Mademoiselle Olympe again. "Olympe Zabriski," he soliloquized as he sauntered through the lobby—"what a queer name! Olympe is French and Zabriski is Polish. It is her *nom de guerre,* of course; her real name is probably Sarah Jones. What kind of creature can she be in private life, I wonder? I wonder if she wears that costume all the time, and if she springs to her meals from a horizontal bar. Of course she rocks the baby to sleep on the trapeze." And Van Twiller went on making comical domestic tableaux of Mademoiselle Zabriski, like the clever, satirical dog he was, until the curtain rose.

This was on a Friday. There was a matinée the next day, and he attended that, though he had secured a seat for the usual evening entertainment. Then it became a habit of Van Twiller's to drop into the theatre for half an hour or so every night, to assist at the interlude, in which she appeared. He cared only for her part of the programme, and timed his visits accordingly. It was a surprise to himself when he reflected, one morning, that he had not missed a single performance of Mademoiselle Olympe for nearly two weeks.

"This will never do," said Van Twiller. "Olympe"—he called her Olympe, as if she were an old acquaintance, and so she might have been considered by that time—"is a wonderful creature; but this will never do. Van, my boy, you must reform this altogether."

But half-past nine that night saw him in his accustomed orchestra chair, and so on for another week. A habit leads a man so gently in the beginning that he does not perceive he is led—with what silken threads and down what pleasant avenues it leads him! By and by the soft silk threads become iron chains, and the pleasant avenues Avernus!

Quite a new element had lately entered into Van Twiller's enjoyment of Mademoiselle Olympe's ingenious feats—a vaguely born apprehension that she might slip from that swinging bar; that one of the thin cords supporting it might snap, and let her go headlong from the dizzy height. Now and then, for a terrible instant, he would imagine her lying a glittering, palpitating heap at the foot-lights, with no color in her lips! Sometimes it seemed as if the girl were tempting this kind of fate. It was a hard, bitter life, and nothing but poverty and sordid misery at home could have driven her to it. What if she should end it all some night, by just unclasping that little hand? It looked so small and white from where Van Twiller sat!

This frightful idea fascinated while it chilled him, and helped to make it nearly impossible for him to keep away from the theatre. In the beginning his attendance had not interfered with his social duties or pleasures; but now he came to find it distasteful after dinner to do anything but read, or walk the streets aimlessly, until it was time to go to the play. When that was over, he was in no mood to go anywhere but to his rooms. So he dropped away by insensible degrees from his habitual haunts, was missed, and began to be talked about at the club. Catching some intimation of this, he ventured no more in the orchestra stalls, but shrouded himself behind the draperies of the private box in which Delaney and I thought we saw him on one occasion.

Now, I find it very perplexing to explain what Van Twiller was wholly unable to explain to himself. He was not in love with Mademoiselle Olympe. He had no wish to speak to her, or to hear her speak. Nothing could have been easier, and nothing further from his desire, than to know her personally. A Van Twiller personally acquainted with a strolling female acrobat! Good heavens! That was something possible only with the discovery of perpetual motion. Taken from her theatrical setting, from her lofty perch, so to say, on the trapeze-bar, Olympe Zabriski would have shocked every aristocratic fibre in Van Twiller's body. He was simply fascinated by her marvelous grace and *élan,* and the magnetic recklessness of the girl. It was very young in him and very weak, and no member of the Sorosis, or all the Sorosisters together, could have been more severe on Van Twiller than he was on himself. To be weak, and to know it, is something of a punishment for a proud man. Van Twiller took his punishment, and went to the theatre, regularly.

"When her engagement comes to an end," he meditated, "that will finish the business."

Mademoiselle Olympe's engagement finally did come to an end and she departed. But her engagement had been highly beneficial to the treasury-chest of the up-town theatre, and before Van Twiller could get over missing her she had returned from a short Western tour, and her immediate reappearance was underlined on the play-bills.

On a dead wall opposite the windows of Van Twiller's sleeping-room there appeared, as if by necromancy, an aggressive poster with MADEMOISELLE OLYMPE ZABRISKI on it in letters at least a foot high. This thing stared him in the face when he woke up one morning. It gave him a sensation as if she had called on him overnight and left her card.

From time to time through the day he regarded that poster with a sardonic eye. He had pitilessly resolved not to repeat the folly of the previous month. To say that this moral victory cost him nothing would be to deprive it of merit. It cost him many internal struggles. It is a fine thing to see a man seizing his temptation by the throat, and wrestling with it, and trampling it underfoot like St. Anthony. This was the spectacle Van Twiller was exhibiting to the angels.

The evening Mademoiselle Olympe was to make her reappearance, Van Twiller, having dined at the club, and feeling more like himself than he had felt for weeks, returned to his chamber, and, putting on dressing-gown and slippers, piled up the greater portion of his library about him, and fell to reading assiduously. There is nothing like a quiet evening at home with some slight intellectual occupation, after one's feathers have been stroked the wrong way.

When the lively French clock on the mantelpiece—a base of malachite surmounted by a flying bronze Mercury with its arms spread gracefully in the air, and not remotely suggestive of Mademoiselle Olympe in the act of executing her grand flight from the trapeze—when the clock, I repeat, struck nine, Van Twiller paid no attention to it. That was certainly a triumph. I am anxious to render Van Twiller all the justice I can, at this point of the narrative, inasmuch as when the half hour sounded musically, like a crystal ball dropping into a silver bowl, he rose from the chair automatically, thrust his feet into his walking-shoes, threw his overcoat across his arm, and strode out of the room.

To be weak and to scorn your weakness, and not to be able to conquer it, is, as has been said, a hard thing; and I suspect it was not with unalloyed satisfaction that Van Twiller found himself taking his seat in the back part of the private box night after night during the second engagement of Mademoiselle Olympe. It was so easy not to stay away!

In this second edition of Van Twiller's fatuity, his case was even worse than before. He not only thought of Olympe quite a number of times between breakfast and dinner, he not only attended the interlude regularly, but he began, in spite of himself, to occupy his leisure hours at night by dreaming of her. This was too much of a good thing, and Van Twiller regarded it so. Besides, the dream was always the same—a harrowing dream, a dream singularly adapted to shattering the nerves of a man like Van Twiller. He would imagine himself seated at the theatre (with all the members of Our Club in the parquette), watching Mademoiselle Olympe as usual, when suddenly that young lady would launch herself desperately from the trapeze, and come flying through the air like a firebrand hurled at his private box. Then the unfortunate man would wake up with cold drops standing on his forehead.

There is one redeeming feature in this infatuation of Van Twiller's which the sober moralist will love to look upon—the serene unconsciousness of the person who caused it. She went through her *rôle* with admirable aplomb, drew her salary, it may be assumed, punctually, and appears from first to last to have been ignorant that there was a miserable slave wearing her chains nightly in the left-hand proscenium box.

That Van Twiller, haunting the theatre with the persistency of an ex-actor, conducted himself so discreetly as not to draw the fire of Mademoiselle Olympe's blue eyes shows that Van Twiller, however deeply under a spell, was not in love. I say this, though I think if Van Twiller had not been Van Twiller, if he had been a man of no family and no position and no money, if New York had been Paris and Thirty-fourth Street a street in the Latin Quarter—but it is useless to speculate on what might have happened. What did happen is sufficient.

It happened, then, in the second week of Queen Olympe's second unconscious reign, that an appalling Whisper floated up the Hudson, effected a landing at a point between Spuyten Duyvil Creek and Cold Spring, and sought out a stately mansion of Dutch architecture standing on the bank of the river. The Whisper straightway informed the lady dwelling in this mansion that all was not well with the last of the Van Twillers; that he was gradually estranging himself from his peers, and wasting his nights in a play-house watching a misguided young woman turning unmaidenly somersaults on a piece of wood attached to two ropes.

Mrs. Vanrensselaer Vanzandt Van Twiller came down to town by the next train to look into this little matter.

She found the flower of the family taking an early breakfast at 11 A. M., in his cosey apartments on Thirty-fourth Street. With the least possible circumlocution she confronted him with what rumor had reported of his pursuits, and was pleased, but not too much pleased, when he gave her an exact account of his relations with Mademoiselle Zabriski, neither concealing nor qualifying anything. As a confession, it was unique, and might have been a great deal less entertaining. Two or three times in the course of the narrative, the matron had some difficulty in preserving the gravity of her countenance. After meditating a few minutes, she tapped Van Twiller softly on the arm with the tip of her parasol, and invited him to return with her the next day up the Hudson and make a brief visit at the home of his ancestors. He accepted the invitation with outward alacrity and inward disgust.

When this was settled, and the worthy lady had withdrawn, Van Twiller went directly to the establishment of Messrs. Ball, Black, and Company, and selected, with unerring taste, the finest diamond bracelet procurable. For his mother? Dear me, no! She had the family jewels.

I would not like to state the enormous sum Van Twiller paid for this bracelet. It was such a clasp of diamonds as would have hastened the pulsation of a patrician wrist. It was such a bracelet as Prince Camaralzaman might have sent to the Princess Badoura, and the Princess Badoura—might have been very glad to get.

In the fragrant Levant morocco case, where these happy jewels lived when they were at home, Van Twiller thoughtfully placed his card, on the back of which he had written a line begging Mademoiselle Olympe Zabriski to accept the accompanying trifle from one who had witnessed her graceful performances with interest and pleasure. This was not done inconsiderately. "Of course, I must inclose my card, as I would to any lady," Van Twiller had said to himself. "A Van Twiller can neither write an anonymous letter nor make an anonymous present." Blood entails its duties as well as its privileges.

The casket despatched to its destination, Van Twiller felt easier in his mind. He was under obligations to the girl for many an agreeable hour that might otherwise have passed heavily. He had paid the debt, and he had paid it *en prince,* as became a Van Twiller. He spent the rest of the day in looking at some pictures at Goupil's, and at the club, and in making a few purchases for his trip up the Hudson. A consciousness that this trip up the Hudson was a disorderly retreat came over him unpleasantly at intervals.

When he returned to his rooms late at night, he found a note lying on the writing-table. He started as his eyes caught the words "—— Theatre" stamped in carmine letters on one corner of the envelope. Van Twiller broke the seal with trembling fingers.

Now, this note some time afterward fell into the hands of Livingstone, who showed it to Stuyvesant, who showed it to Delaney, who showed it to me, and I copied it as a literary curiosity. The note ran as follows:

MR VAN TWILLER DEAR SIR—i am verry greatfull to you for that Bracelett. it come just in the nic of time for me. The Mademoiselle Zabriski dodg is about Plaid out. my beard is getting to much for me. i shall have to grow a mustash and take to some other line of busyness, i dont no what now, but will let you no. You wont feel bad if i sell that Bracelett. i have seen Abrahams Moss and he says he will do the square thing. Pleas accep my thanks for youre Beautifull and Unexpected present. Youre respectfull servent,

CHARLES MONTMORENCI WALTERS.

The next day Van Twiller neither expressed nor felt any unwillingness to spend a few weeks with his mother at the old homestead.

And then he went abroad.

BROTHER SEBASTIAN'S FRIENDSHIP

BY HAROLD FREDERIC

Harold Frederic (born at Utica, N. Y., August 19, 1856; died in 1898) was a novelist whose every book exceeded its predecessor in conception, general construction, and technique of detail. His death at the maturity of his powers was therefore a great loss to American literature. His posthumous novel, "The Market Place," indicates that Frederic, had he lived, might have outshone even Balzac in the fiction of business life. "Brother Sebastian's Friendship" is a clever short story of the days of his literary 'prenticeship. It was his introduction to the "Utica Observer," where he worked for several years.

BROTHER SEBASTIAN'S FRIENDSHIP

BY HAROLD FREDERIC

I WHO tell this story am called Brother Sebastian. This name was given me more than forty years ago, while Louis Philippe was still king. My other name has been buried so long that I have nearly forgotten it. I think that my people are dead. At least I have heard nothing from them in many years. My reputation has always been that of a misanthrope—if not that, then of a dreamer. In the seminary I had no intimates. In the order, for I am a Brother of the Christian Schools, my associates are polite—nothing more. I seem to be outside their social circles, their plans, their enjoyments. True, I am an old man now. But in other years it was the same. All my life I have been in solitude.

To this there is a single exception—one star shining in the blackness. And my career has been so bleak that, although it ended in deeper sadness than I had known before, I look back to the epsiode with gratitude. The bank of clouds which shut out this sole light of my life quickened its brilliancy before they submerged it.

After the terrible siege of '71, when the last German was gone, and our houses had breasted the ordeal of the Commune, I was sent to the South. The

By permission of the "Utica Observer."

Superior thought my cheeks were ominously hollow, and suspected threats of consumption in my cough. So I was to go to the Mediterranean, and try its milder air. I liked the change. Paris, with its gloss of noisy gayety and its substance of sceptical heartlessness, was repugnant to me. Perhaps it was because of this that Brother Sebastian had been mured up in the capital two-thirds of his life. If our surroundings are too congenial we neglect the work set before us. But no matter; to the coast I went.

My new home was a long-established house, spacious, venerable, and dreary. It was on the outskirts of an ancient town, which was of far more importance before our Lord was born than it has ever been since. We had little to do. There were nine brothers, a handful of resident orphans, and some threescore pupils. Ragged, stupid, big-eyed urchins they were, altogether different from the keen Paris boys. For that matter, every feature of my new home was odd. The heat of the summer was scorching in its intensity. The peasants were much more respectful to our cloth, and, as to appearance, looked like figures from Murillo's canvases. The foliage, the wine, the language, the manners of the people—everything was changed. This interested me, and my morbidness vanished. The Director was delighted with my improved condition. Poor man! he was positive that my cheeks had puffed out perceptibly after the first two months. So the winter came—a mild, wet, muggy winter, wholly unlike my favorite sharp season in the North.

We were killing time in the library one afternoon,

the Director and a Swiss Brother sitting by the lamp reading, I standing at one of the tall, narrow windows, drumming on the panes and dreaming. The view was not an inspiring one. There was a long horizontal line of pale yellow sky and another of flat, black land, out of which an occasional poplar raised itself solemnly. The great mass below the stripes was brown; above, gloomy gray. Close under the window two boys were playing in the garden of the house. I recall distinctly that they threw armfuls of wet fallen leaves at each other with a great shouting. While I stood thus, the Brother Servitor, Abonus, came in and whispered to the Director. He always whispered. It was not fraternal, but I did not like this Abonus.

"Send him up here," said the Director. Then I remembered that I had heard the roll of a carriage and the bell ring a few moments before. Abonus came in again. Behind him there was some one else, whose footsteps had the hesitating sound of a stranger's. Then I heard the Director's voice:

"You are from Algiers?"—"I am, Brother."

"Your name?"

"Edouard, Brother."

"Well, tell me more."

"I was under orders to be in Paris in January, Brother. As my health was poor, I received permission to come back to France this autumn. At Marseilles I was instructed to come here. So I am here. I have these papers from the Mother house, and from Etienne, Director, of Algiers."

Something in the voice seemed peculiar to me. I turned and examined the new-comer. He stood behind and to one side of the Director, who was laboriously deciphering some papers through his big horn spectacles. The light was not very bright, but there was enough to see a wonderfully handsome face, framed in dazzling black curls. Perhaps it looked the more beautiful because contrasted with the shaven gray poll and surly features of grim Abonus. But to me it was a dream of St. John the Evangel. The eyes of the face were lowered upon the Director, so I could only guess their brilliancy. The features were those of an extreme youth—round, soft, and delicate. The expression was one of utter fatigue, almost pain. It bore out the statement of ill-health.

The Director had finished his reading. He lifted his head now and surveyed the stranger in turn. Finally, stretching out his fat hand, he said:

"You are welcome, Brother Edouard. I see the letter says you have had no experience except with the youngest children. Brother Photius does that now. We will have you rest for a time. Then we will see about it. Meanwhile I will turn you over to the care of good Abonus, who will give you one of the north rooms."

So the two went out, Abonus shuffling his feet disagreeably. It was strange that he could do nothing to please me.

"Brother Sebastian," said the Director, as the door closed, "it is curious that they should have sent me a tenth man. Why, I lie awake now to invent pretences of work for those I have already. I will give up all show of teaching presently, and give out that I keep a hospital—a retreat for ailing brothers. Still, this Edouard is a pretty boy."

"Very."

"Etienne's letter says he is twenty and a Savoyard. He speaks like a Parisian."

"Very likely he is seminary bred," put in the Swiss.

"Whatever he is, I like his looks," said our Superior. This good man liked every one. His was the placid, easy Alsatian nature, prone to find goodness in all things—even crabbed Abonus. The Director, or, as he was known, Brother Elysee, was a stout, round little man, with a fine face and imperturbable good spirits. He was adored by all his subordinates. But I fancy he did not advance in favor at Paris very rapidly.

I liked Edouard from the first. The day after he came we were together much, and, when we parted after vespers, I was conscious of a vast respect for this new-comer. He was bright, ready spoken, and almost a man of the world. Compared with my dull career, his short life had been one of positive gayety. He had seen Frederic le Maitre at the Comédie Française. He had been at Court and spoken with the Prince Imperial. He was on terms of intimacy with Monsignori, and had been a protégé of the sainted Darboy. It was a rare pleasure to hear him talk of these things.

Before this, the ceaseless shifting of brothers from

one house to another had been indifferent to me. For the hundreds of strangers who came and went in the Paris house on Oudinot Street I cared absolutely nothing. I did not suffer their entrance nor their exit to excite me. This was so much the case that they called me a machine. But with Edouard this was different. I grew to love the boy from the first evening, when, as he left my room, I caught myself saying, "I shall be sorry when he goes." He seemed to be fond of me, too. For that matter most of the brothers petted him, Elysee especially. But I was flattered that he chose me as his particular friend. For the first time my heart had opened.

We were alone one evening after the holidays. It was cold without, but in my room it was warm and bright. The fire crackled merrily, and the candles gave out a mellow and pleasant light. The Director had gone up to Paris, and his mantle had fallen on me. Edouard sat with his feet stretched to the fender, his curly head buried in the great curved back of my invalid chair, the red fire-light reflected on his childish features. I took pleasure in looking at him. He looked at the coals and knit his brows as if in a puzzle. I often fancied that something weightier than the usual troubles of life weighed upon him. At last he spoke, just as I was about to question him:

"Are you afraid to die, Sebastian?"

Not knowing what else to say, I answered, "No, my child."

"I wonder if you enjoy life in community?"

This was still stranger. I could but reply that I

charged his nominal duties, his baby pupils (for Photius had gone to Peru) now became bewitched with him. He told them droll stories, incited their rivalry in study by instituting prizes for which they struggled monthly, and, in short, metamorphosed his department. The change spread to himself. His cheeks took on a ruddier hue, the sparkle of his black eyes mellowed into a calm and steady radiance. There was no trace of feverish elation which, in solitude, recoiled to the brink of despair. He sang to himself evenings in his dormitory, clearly and with joy. His step was as elastic as that of any schoolboy. I often thought upon this change, and meditated how beautiful an illustration of confession's blessings it furnished. Frequently we were alone, but he never referred again to that memorable evening, even by implication. At first I dreaded to have the door close upon us, feeling that he must perforce seek to take up the thread where he had broken it then. But he talked of other things, and so easily and naturally that I felt embarrassed. For weeks I could not shake off the feeling that, at our next talk, he would broach the subject. But he never did.

Elysee returned, bringing me kind words from the Mother house, and a half-jocular hint that Superior General Philippe had me much in his mind. No doubt there had been a time when the idea of becoming a Director would have stirred my pulses. Surely it was gone now. I asked for nothing but to stay beside Edouard, to watch him, and to be near to lend him a helping hand when his hour of trouble should come.

From that ordeal, which I saw approaching clearly and certainly, I shrank with all my nerves on edge. As the object of my misery grew bright-eyed and strong, I felt myself declining in health. My face grew thin, and I could not eat. I saw before my eyes always this wretched boy singing upon the brow of the abyss. Sometimes I strove not to see his fall—frightful and swift. His secret seemed to harass him no longer. To me it was heavier than lead.

The evening the Brother Director returned, we sat together in the reading-room, the entire community. Elysee had been speaking of the Mother house concerning which Brother Barnabas, an odd little Lorrainer who spoke better German than French, and who regarded Paris with the true provincial awe and veneration, exhibited much curiosity. We had a visitor, a gaunt, self-sufficient old Parisian, who had spent fourteen days in the Mazas prison during the Commune. I will call him Brother Albert, for his true name in religion is very well known.

"I heard a curious story in the Vaugirard house," said the Brother Director, refreshing himself with a pinch of snuff, "which made the more impression upon me that I once knew intimately one of the persons in it. Martin Delette was my schoolmate at Pfalsbourg in the old days. A fine, studious lad he was, too. He took orders and went to the north, where he lived for many years a quiet country curé. He had a niece, a charming girl who is not now more than twenty or one-and-twenty. She was an orphan, and lived with him, going to a convent to school and returning at vacations. She was not a bad girl, but a trifle wayward and easily led. She gave the Sisters much anxiety. Last spring she barely escaped compromising the house by an escapade with a young *miserable* of the town, named Banin."

"I know your story," said Albert, with an air which hinted that this was a sufficient reason why the rest should not hear it. "Banin is in prison."

Elysee proceeded: "The girl was reprimanded. Next week she disappeared. To one of her companions she had confided a great desire to see Paris. So good Father Delette was summoned, and, after a talk with the Superioress, started post-haste for the capital. He found no signs either of poor Renée or of Banin, who had also disappeared. The Curé was nearly heart-broken. Each day, they told me, added a year to his appearance. He did not cease to importune the police chiefs and to haunt the public places for a glimpse of his niece's face. But the summer came, and no Renée. The Curé began to cough and grow weak. But one day in August the Director, good Prosper, called him down to the reception-room to see a visitor.

" 'There is news for you,' " he whispered, pressing poor Martin's hand. In the room he found—"

"In the room he found—" broke in Albert, impertinently, but with a quiet tone of authority which cowed good Elysee, "a shabby man, looking like a poorly fed waiter. This person rose and said, 'I am a detective; do you know Banin—young man, tall, blond, squints, broken tooth upper jaw, hat back on his head, much talk, hails from Rheims?'

"'Ah,' said Delette, 'I have not seen him, but I know him too well.'

"The detective pointed with his thumb over his left shoulder. 'He is in jail. He is good for twenty years. I did it myself. My name is So-and-so. Good job. Procurator said you were interested—some woman in the case, parishioner of yours, eh?'

"'My niece,' gasped the Curé.

"'O ho! does you credit; pretty girl, curly head. good manners. Well, she's off. Good trick, too. She was the decoy. Banin stood in the shadow with club. She brought gentleman into alley, friend did work. That's Banin's story. Perhaps a lie. You have a brother in Algiers? Thought so. Girl went out there once? So I was told. Probably there now. African officers say not; but they're a sleepy lot. If I was a criminal I'd go to Algiers. Good hiding. The detective went. Delette stood where he was in silence. I went to him, and helped carry him upstairs. We put him in his bed. He died there."

Brother Albert stopped. He had told the story, dialogue and all, like a machine. We did not doubt its correctness. The memory of Albert had passed into a proverb years before.

Brother Albert raised his eyes again, and added, as if he had not paused, "He was ashamed to hold his head up. He might well be."

A strange, excited voice rose from the other end of the room. I looked and saw that it was Edouard who spoke. He had half arisen from his chair and scowled at Albert, throwing out his words with the tremulous haste of a young man first addressing an audience:

"Why should he be ashamed? Was he not a good man? Was the blame of his bad niece's acts his? From the story, she was well used and had no excuse. It is he who is to be pitied, not blamed!"

The Brother Director smiled benignly at the young enthusiast. "Brother Edouard is right," he said. "Poor Martin was to be compassioned. None the less, my heart is touched for the girl. In Banin's trial it appeared that he maltreated her, and forced her to do what she did by blows. They were really married. Her neighbors gave Renée a name for gentleness and a good heart. Poor thing!"

"And she never was found?" asked Abonus, eagerly. He spoke very rarely. He looked now at me as he spoke, and there was a strange, ungodly glitter in his eyes which made me shudder involuntarily.

"Never," replied the Director, "although there is a reward, 5,000 francs, offered for her recovery. Miserable child, who can tell what depths of suffering she may be in this moment?"

"It would be remarkable if she should be found now, after all this time," said Abonus, sharply. His wicked, squinting old eyes were still fastened upon me. This time, as by a flash of eternal knowledge, I read their meaning, and felt the ground slipping from under me.

I shall never forget the night that followed. I made no pretence of going to bed. Edouard's little dormitory was in another part of the house. I went once to see him, but dared not knock, since Abonus was stirring about just across the hall, in his own den. I scratched on a piece of paper "Fly!" in the dark, and pushed it under the door. Then I returned to walk my chamber, chafing like a wild beast. Ah, that night, that night!

With the first cock crow in the village below, long before the bell, I left my room. I wanted air to breathe. I passed Abonus on the broad stairway. He strode up with unwonted vigor, bearing a heavy caldron of water as if it had been straw. His gown was tumbled and dusty; his greasy *rabat* hung awry about his neck. I had it in my head to speak with him, but could not. So the early hours, with devotions which I went through in a dream, wore on in horrible suspense, and breakfast came.

We sat at the long table, five on a side, the Director—looking red-eyed and weary from the evening's unaccustomed dissipation—sitting at the head. Below us stood Brother Albert, reading from Tertullian in a dry, monotonous chant. I recall, as I write, how I found a certain comfort in those splendid, sonorous Latin sentences, though I was conscious of not comprehending a word. I dreaded the moment they should end. Edouard sat beside me. We had not exchanged a word during the morning. How could I speak? What should I say? I was in a nervous flutter, like unto those who watch the final pinioning of a criminal whose guillotine is awaiting him. I could not keep my eyes from the fair face beside me, with its delicately cut profile, made all the more cameo-like by its pallid whiteness. The lips were tightly compressed. I could see askant that the tiny nostrils were quivering with excitement. All else was impassive on Edouard's face. We two sat waiting for the axe to fall.

It is as distinct as a nightmare to me. Abonus came in with his great server laden with victuals. He stumbled as he approached. He too was excited. He drew near, and stood behind me. I seemed to feel his breath penetrate my skull; and yet I was forced to answer a whispered question of Brother John's with a smooth face. I saw Edouard suddenly reach for the milk glass in front of his plate, and hand it back to Abonus with the disdain of a duchess. He said, in a sharp, peremptory tone:

"Take it away and cleanse it. No one but a dirty monk would place such a glass on the table."

Albert ceased his reading. Abonus did not touch the glass. He shuffled hastily to the sideboard and deposited his burden. Then he came back with the same eager movement. He placed his fists on his hips, like a fish-woman, and hissed, in a voice choking with concentrated rage:

"No one but a woman would complain of it!"

The brothers stared at each other and the two speakers in mute surprise. But they saw nothing in the words beyond a personal wrangle—though even that was such a novelty as to arrest instant attention. I busied myself with my plate. The Director assumed his harshest tone, and asked the cause of the altercation. Abonus leaned over and whispered something in his ear. I remember next a room full of confusion, a babel of conflicting voices, and a whirling glimpse of uniforms. Then I fainted.

When I revived I was in my own room, stretched upon my pallet. I looked around in a dazed way and saw the Brother Director and a young gendarme by the closed door. Something black and irregular in the outline of the bed at my side attracted my eyes. I saw that it was Edouard's head buried in the drapery. As in a dream I laid my numb hand upon those crisp curls. I was an old man, she was a weak, wretched girl. She raised her face at my touch, and burned in my brain a vision of stricken agony, of horrible soul-pain, which we liken, for want of a better simile, to the anguish in the eyes of a dying doe. Her lips moved; she said something, I know not what. Then she went, and I was left alone with Elysee. His words—broken, stumbling words—I remember:

"She asked to see you, Sebastian, my friend. I could not refuse. Her papers were forged. She did come from Algiers, where her uncle is a Capuchin. I do not ask, I do not wish to know, how much you know of this. Before my Redeemer, I feel nothing but pity for the poor lamb. Lie still, my friend; try to sleep. We are both older men than we were yesterday."

There is little else to tell. Only twice have reflections of this episode in my old life reached me in the seclusion of a missionary post at the foot of the Andes. I learned a few weeks ago that the wretched

Abonus had bought a sailor's café on the Toulon wharves with his five thousand francs. And I know also that the heart of the Marshal-President was touched by the sad story of Renée, and that she left the prison La Salpetrière to lay herself in penitence at the foot of Mother Church. This is the story of my friendship.

A GOOD-FOR-NOTHING

BY HJALMAR HJORTH BOYESEN

Hjalmar Hjorth Boyesen (born at Frederiksværn, Norway, September 23, 1848; died in 1895) was a university graduate who came to this country in 1869 to take a professorship of languages in a small Ohio college. Soon after he was called to Cornell, and in 1882 he became Professor of German in Columbia. His proficiency in the English language was phenomenal. His mastery of scholarly English in the essay form was to be expected, but his ready command of the delicately shaded style required of a literary novelist has not been equaled by any other naturalized American author. Hence in this series he has received citizenship among those to the manner born. The story selected by his son, as representative of his work in brief fiction, is a fine study of character, with a pathetic ending, whose poignancy is due to its fidelity to truth.

A GOOD-FOR-NOTHING

BY HJALMAR HJORTH BOYESEN

I

RALPH GRIM was born a gentleman. He had the misfortune of coming into the world some ten years later than might reasonably have been expected. Colonel Grim and his lady had celebrated twelve anniversaries of their wedding-day, and had given up all hopes of ever having a son and heir, when this late comer startled them by his unexpected appearance. The only previous addition to the family had been a daughter, and she was then ten summers old.

Ralph was a very feeble child, and could only with great difficulty be persuaded to retain his hold of the slender thread which bound him to existence. He was rubbed with whiskey, and wrapped in cotton, and given mare's milk to drink, and God knows what not, and the Colonel swore a round oath of paternal delight when at last the infant stopped gasping in that distressing way and began to breathe like other human beings. The mother, who, in spite of her anxiety for the child's life, had found time to plot for him a career of future magnificence, now suddenly set him apart for literature, because that was the easiest road to fame, and disposed of him in marriage to one of the most distinguished families of the land. She cautiously suggested this to her husband when he came to take his seat at her bedside; but to her utter astonishment she found that he had been indulging a similar train of thought, and had already destined the infant prodigy for the army. She, however, could not give up her predilection for literature, and the Colonel, who could not bear to be contradicted in his own house, as he used to say, was getting every minute louder and more flushed, when, happily, the doctor's arrival interrupted the dispute.

As Ralph grew up from infancy to childhood, he began to give decided promise of future distinction. He was fond of sitting down in a corner and sucking his thumb, which his mother interpreted as the sign of that brooding disposition peculiar to poets and men of lofty genius. At the age of five, he had become sole master in the house. He slapped his sister Hilda in the face, or pulled her hair, when she hesitated to obey him, tyrannized over his nurse, and sternly refused to go to bed in spite of his mother's entreaties. On such occasions, the Colonel would hide his face behind his newspaper, and chuckle with delight; it was evident that nature had intended his son for a great military commander. As soon as Ralph himself was old enough to have any thoughts about his future destiny, he made up his mind that he would like to be a pirate. A few months later, having contracted an immoderate taste for candy, he contented himself with the comparatively humble position of a baker; but when he had read "Robinson Crusoe" he manifested a strong desire to go to sea in the hope of being wrecked on some desolate island. The parents spent long evenings gravely discussing these indications of uncommon genius, and each interpreted them in his or her own way.

"He is not like any other child I ever knew," said the mother.

"To be sure," responded the father, earnestly. "He is a most extraordinary child. I was a very remarkable child too, even if I do say it myself; but, as far as I remember, I never aspired to being wrecked on an uninhabited island."

The Colonel probably spoke the truth; but he forgot to take into account that he had never read "Robinson Crusoe."

Of Ralph's school-days there is but little to report, for, to tell the truth, he did not fancy going to school, as the discipline annoyed him. The day after his having entered the gymnasium, which was to prepare him for the Military Academy, the principal saw him waiting at the gate after his class had been dismissed. He approached him, and asked why he did not go home with the rest.

"I am waiting for the servant to carry my books," was the boy's answer.

"Give me your books," said the teacher.

Ralph reluctantly obeyed. That day the Colonel was not a little surprised to see his son marching up the street, and every now and then glancing behind him with a look of discomfort at the principal, who was following quietly in his train, carrying a parcel of school-books. Colonel Grim and his wife, divining the teacher's intention, agreed that it was a great outrage, but they did not mention the matter to Ralph. Henceforth, however, the boy refused to be accompanied by his servant. A week later he was impudent to the teacher of gymnastics, who whipped him in return. The Colonel's rage knew no bounds; he rode in great haste to the gymnasium, reviled the teacher for presuming to chastise *his* son, and committed the boy to the care of a private tutor.

At the age of sixteen, Ralph went to the capital with the intention of entering the Military Academy. He was a tall, handsome youth, slender of stature, and carried himself as erect as a candle. He had a light, clear complexion of almost feminine delicacy; blond, curly hair, which he always kept carefully brushed; a low forehead, and a straight, finely modeled nose. There was an expression of extreme sensitiveness about the nostrils, and a look of indolence in the dark-blue eyes. But the *ensemble* of his features was pleasing, his dress irreproachable, and his manners bore no trace of the awkward self-consciousness peculiar to his age. Immediately on his arrival in the capital he hired a suite of rooms in the aristocratic part of the city, and furnished them rather expensively, but in excellent taste. From a bosom friend, whom he met by accident in the restaurant's pavilion in the park, he learned that a pair of antlers, a stuffed eagle, or falcon, and a couple of swords, were indispensable to a well-appointed apartment. He accordingly bought these articles at a curiosity shop. During the first weeks of his residence in the city he made some feeble efforts to perfect himself in mathematics, in which he suspected he was somewhat deficient. But when the same officious friend laughed at him, and called him "green," he determined to trust to fortune, and henceforth devoted himself the more assiduously to the French ballet, where he had already made some interesting acquaintances.

The time for the examination came; the French ballet did not prove a good preparation; Ralph failed. It quite shook him for the time, and he felt humiliated. He had not the courage to tell his father; so he lingered on from day to day, sat vacantly gazing out of his window, and tried vainly to interest himself in the busy bustle down on the street. It provoked him that everybody else should be so light-hearted, when he was, or at least fancied himself, in trouble. The parlor grew intolerable; he sought refuge in his bedroom. There he sat one evening (it was the third day after the examination), and stared out upon the gray stone walls which on all sides inclosed the narrow courtyard. The round stupid face of the moon stood tranquilly dozing like a great Limburger cheese suspended under the sky.

Ralph, at least, could think of a no more fitting simile. But the bright-eyed young girl in the window hard by sent a longing look up to the same moon, and thought of her distant home on the fjords, where the glaciers stood like hoary giants, and caught the yellow moonbeams on their glittering shields of snow. She had been reading "Ivanhoe" all the afternoon, until the twilight had overtaken her quite unaware, and now she suddenly remembered that she had forgotten to write her German exercise. She lifted her face and saw a pair of sad, vacant eyes gazing at her from the next window in the angle of the court. She was a little startled at first, but in the next moment she thought of her German exercise and took heart.

"Do you know German?" she said; then immediately repented that she had said it.

"I do," was the answer.

She took up her apron and began to twist it with an air of embarrassment.

"I didn't mean anything," she whispered, at last. "I only wanted to know."

"You are very kind."

That answer roused her; he was evidently making sport of her.

"Well, then, if you do, you may write my exercise for me. I have marked the place in the book."

And she flung her book over to the window, and he caught it on the edge of the sill, just as it was falling.

"You are a very strange girl," he remarked, turning over the leaves of the book, although it was too dark to read. "How old are you?"

"I shall be fourteen six weeks before Christmas," answered she, frankly.

"Then I excuse you."

"No, indeed," cried she, vehemently. "You needn't excuse me at all. If you don't want to write my exercise, you may send the book back again. I am very sorry I spoke to you, and I shall never do it again."

"But you will not get the book back again without the exercise," replied he, quietly. "Good-night."

The girl stood long looking after him, hoping that he would return. Then, with a great burst of repentance, she hid her face in her lap, and began to cry.

"Oh, dear, I didn't mean to be rude," she sobbed. "But it was Ivanhoe and Rebecca who upset me."

The next morning she was up before daylight, and waited for two long hours in great suspense before the curtain of his window was raised. He greeted her politely; threw a hasty glance around the court to see if he was observed, and then tossed her book dexterously over into her hands.

"I have pinned the written exercise to the flyleaf," he said. "You will probably have time to copy it before breakfast."

"I am ever so much obliged to you," she managed to stammer.

He looked so tall and handsome, and grown-up, and her remorse stuck in her throat, and threatened to choke her. She had taken him for a boy as he sat there in his window the evening before.

"By the way, what is your name?" he asked, carelessly, as he turned to go.

"Bertha."

"Well, my dear Bertha, I am happy to have made your acquaintance."

And he again made her a polite bow, and entered his parlor.

"How provokingly familiar he is," thought she; "but no one can deny that he is handsome."

The bright roguish face of the young girl haunted Ralph during the whole next week. He had been in love at least ten times before, of course; but, like most boys, with young ladies far older than himself. He found himself frequently glancing over to her window in the hope of catching another glimpse of her face; but the curtain was always drawn down, and Bertha remained invisible. During the second week, however, she relented, and they had many a pleasant chat together. He now volunteered to write all her exercises, and she made no objections. He learned that she was the daughter of a well-to-do peasant in the sea-districts of Norway (and it gave him quite a shock to hear it), and that she was going to school in the city, and boarded with an old lady who kept a *pension* in the house adjoining the one in which he lived.

One day in the autumn Ralph was surprised by the sudden arrival of his father, and the fact of his failure in the examination could no longer be kept a secret. The old Colonel flared up at once when Ralph made his confession; the large veins upon his forehead swelled; he grew coppery-red in his face, and stormed up and down the floor, until his son became seriously alarmed; but, to his great relief, he was soon made aware that his father's wrath was not turned against him personally, but against the officials of the Military Academy who had rejected him. The Colonel took it as insult to his own good name and irreproachable standing as an officer; he promptly refused any other explanation, and vainly racked his brain to remember if any youthful folly of his could possibly have made him enemies among the teachers of the Academy. He at last felt satisfied that it was envy of his own greatness and rapid advancement which had induced the rascals to take vengeance on his son. Ralph reluctantly followed his father back to the country town where the latter was stationed, and the fair-haired Bertha vanished from his horizon. His mother's wish now prevailed, and he began, in his own easy way, to prepare himself for the University. He had little taste for Cicero, and still less for Virgil, but with the use of a "pony" he soon gained sufficient knowledge of these authors to be able to talk in a sort of patronizing way about them, to the great delight of his fond parents. He took quite a fancy, however, to the ode in Horace ending with the lines:

Dulce ridentem,
Dulce loquentem,
Lalagen amabo.

And in his thought he substituted for Lalage the fair-haired Bertha, quite regardless of the requirements of the metre.

To make a long story short, three years later Ralph returned to the capital, and, after having worn out several tutors, actually succeeded in entering the University.

The first year of college life is a happy time to every young man, and Ralph enjoyed its processions, its parliamentary gatherings, and its leisure, as well as the rest. He was certainly not the man to be sentimental over the loss of a young girl whom, moreover, he had only known for a few weeks. Nevertheless, he thought of her at odd times, but not enough to disturb his pleasure. The standing of his family, his own handsome appearance, and his immaculate linen opened to him the best houses of the city, and he became a great favorite in society. At lectures he was seldom seen, but more frequently in the theatres, where he used to come in during the middle of the first act, take his station in front of the orchestra box, and eye, through his lorgnette, by turns, the actresses and the ladies of the parquet.

II

Two months passed, and then came the great annual ball which the students give at the opening of the second semester. Ralph was a man of importance that evening; first, because he belonged to a great family; secondly, because he was the handsomest man of his year. He wore a large golden star on his breast (for his fellow-students had made him a Knight of the Golden Boar) and a badge of colored ribbons in his buttonhole.

The ball was a brilliant affair, and everybody was in excellent spirits, especially the ladies. Ralph danced incessantly, twirled his soft mustache, and uttered amiable platitudes. It was toward midnight, just as the company was moving out to supper, that he caught the glance of a pair of dark-blue eyes, which suddenly drove the blood to his cheeks and hastened the beating of his heart. But when he looked once more the dark-blue eyes were gone, and his unruly heart went on hammering against his side. He laid his hand on his breast and glanced furtively at his fair neighbor, but she looked happy and unconcerned, for the flavor of the ice cream was delicious. It seemed an endless meal, but, when it was done, Ralph rose, led his partner back to the ballroom, and hastily excused himself. His glance wandered round the wide hall, seeking the well-remembered eyes once more, and, at length, finding them in a remote corner, half hid behind a moving wall of promenaders. In another moment he was at Bertha's side.

"You must have been purposely hiding yourself, Miss Bertha," said he, when the usual greetings were exchanged. "I have not caught a glimpse of you all this evening, until a few moments ago."

"But I have seen you all the while," answered the girl, frankly. "I knew you at once as I entered the hall."

"If I had but known that you were here," resumed Ralph, as it were invisibly expanding with an agreeable sense of dignity, "I assure you, you would have been the very first one I should have sought."

She raised her large grave eyes to his, as if questioning his sincerity; but she made no answer.

"Good gracious!" thought Ralph. "She takes things terribly in earnest."

"You look so serious, Miss Bertha," said he, after a moment's pause. "I remember you as a bright-eyed, flaxen-haired little girl, who threw her German exercise-book to me across the yard, and whose merry laughter still rings pleasantly in my memory. I confess I don't find it quite easy to identify this grave young lady with my merry friend of three years ago."

"In other words, you are disappointed at not finding me the same as I used to be."

"No, not exactly that; but—"

Ralph paused and looked puzzled. There was something in the earnestness of her manner which made a facetious compliment seem grossly inappropriate, and in the moment no other escape suggested itself.

"But what?" demanded Bertha, mercilessly.

"Have you ever lost an old friend?" asked he, abruptly.

"Yes; how so?"

"Then," answered he, while his features lighted up with a happy inspiration—"then you will appreciate my situation. I fondly cherished my old picture of you in my memory. Now I have lost it, and I can not help regretting the loss. I do not mean, however, to imply that this new acquaintance—this second edition of yourself, so to speak—will prove less interesting."

She again sent him a grave, questioning look, and began to gaze intently upon the stone in her bracelet.

"I suppose you will laugh at me," began she, while a sudden blush flitted over her countenance. "But this is my first ball, and I feel as if I had rushed into a whirlpool, from which I have, since the first rash plunge was made, been vainly trying to escape. I feel so dreadfully forlorn. I hardly know anybody here except my cousin, who invited me, and I hardly think I know him either."

"Well, since you are irredeemably committed,"

replied Ralph, as the music, after some prefatory flourishes, broke into the delicious rhythm of a Strauss waltz, "then it is no use struggling against fate. Come, let us make the plunge together. Misery loves company."

He offered her his arm, and she rose, somewhat hesitatingly, and followed.

"I am afraid," she whispered, as they fell into line with the procession that was moving down the long hall, "that you have asked me to dance merely because I said I felt forlorn. If that is the case, I should prefer to be led back to my seat."

"What a base imputation!" cried Ralph.

There was something so charmingly *naïve* in this self-depreciation—something so altogether novel in his experience, and, he could not help adding, just a little bit countrified. His spirits rose; he began to relish keenly his position as an experienced man of the world, and, in the agreeable glow of patronage and conscious superiority, chatted with hearty *abandon* with his little rustic beauty.

"If your dancing is as perfect as your German exercises were," said she, laughing, as they swung out upon the floor, "then I promise myself a good deal of pleasure from our meeting."

"Never fear," answered he, quickly reversing his step, and whirling with many a capricious turn away among the thronging couples.

When Ralph drove home in his carriage toward morning he briefly summed up his impressions of Bertha in the following adjectives: intelligent, delightfully unsophisticated, a little bit verdant, but devilish pretty.

Some weeks later Colonel Grim received an appointment at the fortress of Aggershuus, and immediately took up his residence in the capital. He saw that his son cut a fine figure in the highest circles of society, and expressed his gratification in the most emphatic terms. If he had known, however, that Ralph was in the habit of visiting, with alarming regularity, at the house of a plebeian merchant in a somewhat obscure street, he would, no doubt, have been more chary of his praise. But the Colonel suspected nothing, and it was well for the peace of the family that he did not. It may have been cowardice in Ralph that he never mentioned Bertha's name to his family or to his aristocratic acquaintances; for, to be candid, he himself felt ashamed of the power she exerted over him, and by turns pitied and ridiculed himself for pursuing so inglorious a conquest. Nevertheless it wounded his egotism that she never showed any surprise at seeing him, that she received him with a certain frank unceremoniousness, which, however, was very becoming to her; that she invariably went on with her work heedless of his presence, and in everything treated him as if she had been his equal. She persisted in talking with him in a half sisterly fashion about his studies and his future career, warned him with great solicitude against some of his reprobate friends, of whose merry adventures he had told her; and if he ventured to compliment her on her beauty or her accomplishments, she would look up gravely from her sewing, or answer him in a way which seemed to banish the idea of love-making into the land of the impossible. He was constantly tormented by the suspicion that she secretly disapproved of him, and that from a mere moral interest in his welfare she was conscientiously laboring to make him a better man. Day after day he parted from her feeling humiliated, faint-hearted, and secretly indignant both at himself and her, and day after day he returned only to renew the same experience. At last it became too intolerable, he could endure it no longer. Let it make or break, certainty, at all risks, was at least preferable to this sickening suspense. That he loved her, he could no longer doubt; let his parents foam and fret as much as they pleased; for once he was going to stand on his own legs. And in the end, he thought, they would have to yield, for they had no son but him.

Bertha was going to return to her home on the seacoast in a week. Ralph stood in the little low-ceiled parlor, as she imagined, to bid her good-by. They had been speaking of her father, her brothers, and the farm, and she had expressed the wish that if he ever should come to that part of the country he might pay them a visit. Her words had kindled a vague hope in his breast, but in their very frankness and friendly regard there was something which slew the hope they had begotten. He held her hand in his, and her large confiding eyes shone with an emotion which was beautiful, but was yet not love.

"If you were but a peasant born like myself," said she, in a voice which sounded almost tender, "then

I should like to talk to you as I would to my own brother; but—"

"No, not brother, Bertha," cried he, with sudden vehemence; "I love you better than I ever loved any earthly being, and if you knew how firmly this love has clutched at the roots of my heart, you would perhaps—you would at least not look so reproachfully at me."

She dropped his hand, and stood for a moment silent.

"I am sorry that it should have come to this, Mr. Grim," said she, visibly struggling for calmness. "And I am perhaps more to blame than you."

"Blame," muttered he, "why are you to blame?"

"Because I do not love you; although I sometimes feared that this might come. But then again I persuaded myself that it could not be so."

He took a step toward the door, laid his hand on the knob, and gazed down before him.

"Bertha," began he, slowly, raising his head, "you have always disapproved of me, you have despised me in your heart, but you thought you would be doing a good work if you succeeded in making a man of me."

"You use strong language," answered she, hesitatingly; "but there is truth in what you say."

Again there was a long pause, in which the ticking of the old parlor clock grew louder and louder.

"Then," he broke out at last, "tell me before we part if I can do nothing to gain—I will not say your love—but only your regard? What would you do if you were in my place?"

"My advice you will hardly heed, and I do not even know that it would be well if you did. But if I were a man in your position, I should break with my whole past, start out into the world where nobody knew me, and where I should be dependent only upon my own strength, and there I would conquer a place for myself, if it were only for the satisfaction of knowing that I was really a man. Here cushions are sewed under your arms, a hundred invisible threads bind you to a life of idleness and vanity, everybody is ready to carry you on his hands, the road is smoothed for you, every stone carefully moved out of your path, and you will probably go to your grave without having ever harbored one earnest thought, without having done one manly deed."

Ralph stood transfixed, gazing at her with open mouth; he felt a kind of stupid fright, as if some one had suddenly seized him by the shoulders and shaken him violently. He tried vainly to remove his eyes from Bertha. She held him as by a powerful spell. He saw that her face was lighted with an altogether new beauty; he noticed the deep glow upon her cheek, the brilliancy of her eye, the slight quiver of her lip. But he saw all this as one sees things in a half-trance, without attempting to account for them; the door between his soul and his senses was closed.

"I know that I have been bold in speaking to you in this way," she said at last, seating herself in a chair at the window. "But it was yourself who asked me. And I have felt all the time that I should have to tell you this before we parted."

"And," answered he, making a strong effort to appear calm, "if I follow your advice, will you allow me to see you once more before you go?"

"I shall remain here another week, and shall, during that time, always be ready to receive you."

"Thank you. Good-by."

"Good-by."

Ralph carefully avoided all the fashionable thoroughfares; he felt degraded before himself, and he had an idea that every man could read his humiliation in his countenance. Now he walked on quickly, striking the sidewalk with his heels; now, again, he fell into an uneasy, reckless saunter, according as the changing moods inspired defiance of his sentence, or a qualified surrender. And, as he walked on, the bitterness grew within him, and he piteously reviled himself for having allowed himself to be made a fool of by "that little country goose," when he was well aware that there were hundreds of women of the best families of the land who would feel honored at receiving his attentions. But this sort of reasoning he knew to be both weak and contemptible, and his better self soon rose in loud rebellion.

"After all," he muttered, "in the main thing she was right. I am a miserable good-for-nothing, a hothouse plant, a poor stick, and if I were a woman myself, I don't think I should waste my affections on a man of that calibre."

Then he unconsciously fell to analyzing Bertha's character, wondering vaguely that a person who moved so timidly in social life, appearing so diffident, from an ever-present fear of blundering against the established forms of etiquette, could judge so quickly, and with such a merciless certainty, whenever a moral question, a question of right and wrong, was at issue. And, pursuing the same train of thought, he contrasted her with himself, who moved in the highest spheres of society as in his native element, heedless of moral scruples, and conscious of no loftier motive for his actions than the immediate pleasure of the moment.

As Ralph turned the corner of a street, he heard himself hailed from the other sidewalk by a chorus of merry voices.

"Ah, my dear Baroness," cried a young man, springing across the street and grasping Ralph's hand (all his student friends called him the Baroness), "in the name of this illustrious company, allow me to salute you. But why the deuce—what is the matter with you? If you have the *Katzenjammer*,* soda-water is the thing. Come along—it's my treat!"

The students instantly thronged around Ralph, who stood distractedly swinging his cane and smiling idiotically.

"I am not quite well," said he; "leave me alone."

"No, to be sure, you don't look well," cried a jolly youth, against whom Bertha had frequently warned him; "but a glass of sherry will soon restore you. It would be highly immoral to leave you in this condition without taking care of you."

---

* *Katzenjammer* is the sensation a man has the morning after a carousal.

Ralph again vainly tried to remonstrate; but the end was, that he reluctantly followed.

He had always been a conspicuous figure in the student world; but that night he astonished his friends by his eloquence, his reckless humor, and his capacity for drinking. He made a speech for "Woman," which bristled with wit, cynicism, and sarcastic epigrams. One young man, named Vinter, who was engaged, undertook to protest against his sweeping condemnation, and declared that Ralph, who was a universal favorite among the ladies, ought to be the last to revile them.

"If," he went on, "the Baroness should propose to six well-known ladies here in this city whom I could mention, I would wager six Johannisbergers, and an equal amount of champagne, that every one of them would accept him."

The others loudly applauded this proposal, and Ralph accepted the wager. The letters were written on the spot, and immediately despatched. Toward morning, the merry carousal broke up, and Ralph was conducted in triumph to his home.

III

Two days later, Ralph again knocked on Bertha's door. He looked paler than usual, almost haggard; his immaculate linen was a little crumpled, and he carried no cane; his lips were tightly compressed, and his face wore an air of desperate resolution.

"It is done," he said, as he seated himself opposite her. "I am going."

"Going!" cried she, startled at his unusual appearance. "How, where?"

"To America. I sail to-night. I have followed your advice, you see. I have cut off the last bridge behind me."

"But, Ralph," she exclaimed, in a voice of alarm. "Something dreadful must have happened. Tell me quick; I must know it."

"No; nothing dreadful," muttered he, smiling bitterly. "I have made a little scandal, that is all. My father told me to-day to go to the devil, if I chose, and my mother gave me five hundred dollars to help me along on the way. If you wish to know, here is the explanation."

And he pulled from his pocket six perfumed and carefully folded notes, and threw them into her lap.

"Do you wish me to read them?" she asked, with growing surprise.

"Certainly. Why not?"

She hastily opened one note after the other, and read.

"But, Ralph," she cried, springing up from her seat, while her eyes flamed with indignation, "what does this mean? What have you done?"

"I didn't think it needed any explanation," replied he, with feigned indifference. "I proposed to them all, and, you see, they all accepted me. I received all these letters to-day. I only wished to know whether the whole world regarded me as such a worthless scamp as you told me I was."

She did not answer, but sat mutely staring at him,

fiercely crumpling a rose-colored note in her hand. He began to feel uncomfortable under her gaze, and threw himself about uneasily in his chair.

"Well," said he, at length, rising, "I suppose there is nothing more. Good-by."

"One moment, Mr. Grim," demanded she, sternly. "Since I have already said so much, and you have obligingly revealed to me a new side of your character, I claim the right to correct the opinion I expressed of you at our last meeting."

"I am all attention."

"I did think, Mr. Grim," began she, breathing hard, and steadying herself against the table at which she stood, "that you were a very selfish man—an embodiment of selfishness, absolute and supreme, but I did not believe that you were wicked."

"And what convinced you that I was selfish, if I may ask?"

"What convinced me?" repeated she, in a tone of inexpressible contempt. "When did you ever act from any generous regard for others? What good did you ever do to anybody?"

"You might ask, with equal justice, what good I ever did to myself."

"In a certain sense, yes; because to gratify a mere momentary wish is hardly doing one's self good."

"Then I have, at all events, followed the Biblical precept, and treated my neighbor very much as I treat myself."

"I did think," continued Bertha, without heeding the remark, "that you were at bottom kind-hearted, but too hopelessly well-bred ever to commit an act of any decided complexion, either good or bad. Now I see that I have misjudged you, and that you are capable of outraging the most sacred feelings of a woman's heart in mere wantonness, or for the sake of satisfying a base curiosity, which never could have entered the mind of an upright and generous man."

The hard, benumbed look in Ralph's face thawed in the warmth of her presence, and her words, though stern, touched a secret spring in his heart. He made two or three vain attempts to speak, then suddenly broke down, and cried:

"Bertha, Bertha, even if you scorn me, have patience with me, and listen."

And he told her, in rapid, broken sentences, how his love for her had grown from day to day, until he could no longer master it; and how, in an unguarded moment, when his pride rose in fierce conflict against his love, he had done this reckless deed of which he was now heartily ashamed. The fervor of his words touched her, for she felt that they were sincere. Large mute tears trembled in her eyelashes as she sat gazing tenderly at him, and in the depth of her soul the wish awoke that she might have been able to return this great and strong love of his; for she felt that in this love lay the germ of a new, of a stronger and better man. She noticed, with a half-regretful pleasure, his handsome figure, his delicately shaped hands, and the noble cast of his features; an overwhelming pity for him rose within her, and she began to reproach herself for having spoken so harshly, and, as she now thought, so unjustly. Perhaps he read in her eyes the unspoken wish. He seized her hand, and his words fell with a warm and alluring cadence upon her ear.

"I shall not see you for a long time to come, Bertha," said he, "but if at the end of five or six years your hand is still free, and I return another man —a man to whom you could safely intrust your happiness—would you then listen to what I may have to say to you? For I promise, by all that we both hold sacred—"

"No, no," interrupted she, hastily. "Promise nothing. It would be unjust to yourself, and perhaps also to me; for a sacred promise is a terrible thing, Ralph. Let us both remain free; and, if you return and still love me, then come, and I shall receive you and listen to you. And even if you have outgrown your love, which is, indeed, more probable, come still to visit me wherever I may be, and we shall meet as friends and rejoice in the meeting."

"You know best," he murmured. "Let it be as you have said."

He arose, took her face between his hands, gazed long and tenderly into her eyes, pressed a kiss upon her forehead, and hastened away.

That night Ralph boarded the steamer for Hull, and three weeks later landed in New York.

IV

The first three months of Ralph's sojourn in America were spent in vain attempts to obtain a situation. Day after day he walked down Broadway, calling at various places of business, and night after night he returned to his cheerless room with a faint heart and declining spirits. It was, after all, a more serious thing than he had imagined, to cut the cable which binds one to the land of one's birth. There a hundred subtile influences, the existence of which no one suspects until the moment they are withdrawn, unite to keep one in the straight path of rectitude, or at least of external respectability; and Ralph's life had been all in society; the opinion of his fellow-men had been the one force to which he implicitly deferred, and the conscience by which he had been wont to test his actions had been nothing but the aggregate judgment of his friends. To such a man the isolation and the utter irresponsibility of a life among strangers was tenfold more dangerous; and Ralph found, to his horror, that his character contained innumerable latent possibilities which the easy-going life in his home probably never would have revealed to him. It often cut him to the quick, when, on entering an office in his daily search for employment, he was met by hostile or suspicious glances, or when, as it occasionally happened, the door was slammed in his face, as if he were a vagabond or an impostor. Then the wolf was often roused within him, and he felt a momentary wild desire to become what the people here evidently believed him to be. Many a night he sauntered irresolutely about the gambling places in obscure streets, and the glare of light, the rude shouts and clamors in the same moment repelled and attracted him. If he went to the devil, who would care? His father had himself pointed out the way to him; and nobody could blame him if he followed the advice. But then again a memory emerged from that chamber of his soul which still he held sacred; and Bertha's deep-blue eyes gazed upon him with their earnest look of tender warning and regret.

When the summer was half gone, Ralph had gained many a hard victory over himself, and learned many a useful lesson; and at length he swallowed his pride, divested himself of his fine clothes, and accepted a position as assistant gardener at a villa on the Hudson. And as he stood perspiring with a spade in his hand, and a cheap broad-brimmed straw hat on his head, he often took a grim pleasure in picturing to himself how his aristocratic friends at home would receive him if he should introduce himself to them in this new costume.

"After all, it was only my position they cared for," he reflected, bitterly; "without my father's name what would I be to them?"

Then, again, there was a certain satisfaction in knowing that, for his present situation, humble as it was, he was indebted to nobody but himself; and the thought that Bertha's eyes, if they could have seen him now, would have dwelt upon him with pleasure and approbation, went far to console him for his aching back, his sunburned face, and his swollen and blistered hands.

One day, as Ralph was raking the gravel-walks in the garden, his employer's daughter, a young lady of seventeen, came out and spoke to him. His culture and refinement of manner struck her with wonder, and she asked him to tell her his history; but then he suddenly grew very grave, and she forbore pressing him. From that time she attached a kind of romantic interest to him, and finally induced her father to obtain him a situation that would be more to his taste. And, before winter came, Ralph saw the dawn of a new future glimmering before him. He had wrestled bravely with fate, and had once more gained a victory. He began the career in which success and distinction awaited him as proofreader on a newspaper in the city. He had fortunately been familiar with the English language before he left home, and by the strength of his will he conquered all difficulties. At the end of two years he became attached to the editorial staff; new ambitious hopes, hitherto foreign to his mind, awoke within him; and with joyous tumult of heart he saw life opening its wide vistas before him, and he labored on manfully to repair the losses of the past, and to prepare himself for greater usefulness in times to come. He felt in himself a stronger and fuller manhood, as if the great arteries of the vast universal world-life pulsed in his own being. The drowsy, indolent existence at home appeared like a dull remote dream from which he had awaked, and he blessed the destiny which, by its very sternness, had mercifully saved him; he blessed her, too, who, from the very want of love for him, had, perhaps, made him worthier of love.

The years flew rapidly. Society had flung its doors open to him, and what was more, he had found some warm friends, in whose houses he could come and go at pleasure. He enjoyed keenly the privilege of daily association with high-minded and refined women; their eager activity of intellect stimulated him, their exquisite ethereal grace and their delicately chiseled beauty satisfied his æsthetic cravings, and the responsive vivacity of their nature prepared him ever new surprises. He felt a strange fascination in the presence of these women, and the conviction grew upon him that their type of womanhood was superior to any he had hitherto known. And by way of refuting his own argument, he would draw from his pocketbook the photograph of Bertha, which had a secret compartment there all to itself, and, gazing tenderly at it, would eagerly defend her against the disparaging reflections which the involuntary comparison had provoked. And still, how could he help seeing that her features, though well molded, lacked animation; that her eye, with its deep, trustful glance, was not brilliant, and that the calm earnestness of her face, when compared with the bright, intellectual beauty of his present friends, appeared pale and simple, like a violet in a bouquet of vividly colored roses? It gave him a quick pang, when, at times, he was forced to admit this; nevertheless, it was the truth.

After six years of residence in America, Ralph had gained a very high reputation as a journalist of rare culture and ability, and in 1867 he was sent to the World's Exhibition in Paris, as correspondent of the paper on which he had during all these years been employed. What wonder, then, that he started for Europe a few weeks before his presence was needed in the imperial city, and that he steered his course directly toward the fjord valley where Bertha had her home? It was she who had bidden him Godspeed when he fled from the land of his birth, and she, too, should receive his first greeting on his return.

V

The sun had fortified itself behind a citadel of flaming clouds, and the upper forest region shone with a strange ethereal glow, while the lower plains were wrapped in shadow; but the shadow itself had a strong suffusion of color. The mountain peaks rose cold and blue in the distance.

Ralph, having inquired his way of the boatman who had landed him at the pier, walked rapidly along the beach, with a small valise in his hand, and a light summer overcoat flung over his shoulder. Many half-thoughts grazed his mind, and ere the first had taken shape, the second and the third came and chased it away. And still they all in some fashion had reference to Bertha; for in a misty, abstract way, she filled his whole mind; but for some indefinable reason, he was afraid to give free rein to the sentiment which lurked in the remoter corners of his soul.

Onward he hastened, while his heart throbbed with the quickening tempo of mingled expectation and fear. Now and then one of those chill gusts of air, which seem to be careering about aimlessly in the atmosphere during early summer, would strike into his face, and recall him to a keener self-consciousness.

Ralph concluded, from his increasing agitation, that he must be very near Bertha's home. He stopped and looked around him. He saw a large maple at the roadside, some thirty steps from where he was standing, and the girl who was sitting under it, resting her head in her hand and gazing out over the sea, he recognized in an instant to be Bertha. He sprang up on the road, not crossing, however, her line of vision, and approached her noiselessly from behind.

"Bertha," he whispered.

She gave a little joyous cry, sprang up, and made a gesture as if to throw herself in his arms; then suddenly checked herself, blushed crimson, and moved a step backward.

"You came so suddenly," she murmured.

"But, Bertha," cried he (and the full bass of his voice rang through her very soul), "have I gone into exile and waited these many years for so cold a welcome?"

"You have changed so much, Ralph," she answered, with that old grave smile which he knew so well, and stretched out both her hands toward him. "And I have thought of you so much since you went away, and blamed myself because I had judged you so harshly, and wondered that you could listen to me so patiently, and never bear me any malice for what I said."

"If you had said a word less," declared Ralph, seating himself at her side on the greensward, "or if you had varnished it over with politeness, then you would probably have failed to produce any effect and I should not have been burdened with that heavy debt of gratitude which I now owe you. I was a pretty thick-skinned animal in those days, Bertha. You said the right word at the right moment; you gave me a bold and a good piece of advice, which my own ingenuity would never have suggested to me. I will not thank you, because, in so grave a case as this, spoken thanks sound like a mere mockery. Whatever I am, Bertha, and whatever I may hope to be, I owe it all to that hour."

She listened with rapture to the manly assurance of his voice; her eyes dwelt with unspeakable joy upon his strong, bronzed features, his full thick blond beard, and the vigorous proportions of his frame. Many and many a time during his absence had she wondered how he would look if he ever came back, and with that minute conscientiousness which, as it were, pervaded her whole character, she had held herself responsible before God for his fate, prayed for him, and trembled lest evil powers should gain the ascendency over his soul.

On their way to the house they talked together of many things, but in a guarded, cautious fashion, and without the cheerful abandonment of former years. They both, as it were, groped their way carefully in each other's minds, and each vaguely felt that there was something in the other's thought which it was not well to touch unbidden. Bertha saw that all her fears for him had been groundless, and his very appearance lifted the whole weight of responsibility from her breast; and still, did she rejoice at her deliverance from her burden? Ah, no; in this moment she knew that

that which she had foolishly cherished as the best and noblest part of herself had been but a selfish need of her own heart. She feared that she had only taken that interest in him which one feels in a thing of one's own making, and now, when she saw that he had risen quite above her; that he was free and strong, and could have no more need of her, she had, instead of generous pleasure at his success, but a painful sense of emptiness, as if something very dear had been taken from her.

Ralph, too, was loth to analyze the impression his old love made upon him. His feelings were of so complex a nature, he was anxious to keep his more magnanimous impulses active, and he strove hard to convince himself that she was still the same to him as she had been before they had ever parted. But, alas! though the heart be warm and generous, the eye is a merciless critic. And the man who had moved on the wide arena of the world, whose mind had housed the large thoughts of this century, and expanded with its invigorating breath—was he to blame because he had unconsciously outgrown his old provincial self, and could no more judge by its standards?

Bertha's father was a peasant, but he had, by his lumber trade, acquired what in Norway was called a very handsome fortune. He received his guest with dignified reserve, and Ralph thought he detected in his eyes a lurking look of distrust. "I know your errand," that look seemed to say, "but you had better give it up at once. It will be of no use for you to try."

And after supper, as Ralph and Bertha sat talking confidingly with each other at the window, he sent his daughter a quick, sharp glance, and then, without ceremony, commanded her to go to bed. Ralph's heart gave a great thump within him; not because he feared the old man, but because his words, as well as his glances, revealed to him the sad history of these long, patient years. He doubted no longer that the love which he had once so ardently desired was his at last; and he made a silent vow that, come what might, he would remain faithful.

As he came down to breakfast the next morning, he found Bertha sitting at the window, engaged in hemming what appeared to be a rough kitchen towel. She bent eagerly over her work, and only a vivid flush upon her cheek told him that she had noticed his coming. He took a chair, seated himself opposite her, and bade her "good-morning." She raised her head, and showed him a sweet, troubled countenance, which the early sunlight illumined with a high spiritual beauty. It reminded him forcibly of those pale, sweet-faced saints of Fra Angelico, with whom the frail flesh seems ever on the point of yielding to the ardent aspirations of the spirit. And still even in this moment he could not prevent his eyes from observing that one side of her forefinger was rough from sewing, and that the whiteness of her arm, which the loose sleeves displayed, contrasted strongly with the browned and sunburned complexion of her hands.

After breakfast they again walked together on the beach, and Ralph, having once formed his resolution, now talked freely of the New World—of his sphere of activity there; of his friends and of his plans for the future; and she listened to him with a mild, perplexed look in her eyes, as if trying vainly to follow the flight of his thoughts. And he wondered, with secret dismay, whether she was still the same strong, brave-hearted girl whom he had once accounted almost bold; whether the life in this narrow valley, amid a hundred petty and depressing cares, had not cramped her spiritual growth, and narrowed the sphere of her thought. Or was she still the same, and was it only he who had changed? At last he gave utterance to his wonder, and she answered him in those grave, earnest tones which seemed in themselves to be half a refutation of his doubts.

"It was easy for me to give you daring advice then, Ralph," she said. "Like most school-girls, I thought that life was a great and glorious thing, and that happiness was a fruit which hung within reach of every hand. Now I have lived for six years trying single-handed to relieve the want and suffering of the needy people with whom I come in contact, and their squalor and wretchedness have sickened me, and, what is still worse, I feel that all I can do is as a drop in the ocean, and, after all, amounts to nothing. I know I am no longer the same reckless girl who, with the very best intention, sent you wandering through the wide world; and I thank God that it proved to be for your good, although the whole now appears quite incredible to me. My thoughts have moved so long within the narrow circle of these mountains that they have lost their youthful elasticity, and can no more rise above them."

Ralph detected, in the midst of her despondency, a spark of her former fire, and grew eloquent in his endeavors to persuade her that she was unjust to herself, and that there was but a wider sphere of life needed to develop all the latent powers of her rich nature.

At the dinner-table, her father again sat eying his guest with that same cold look of distrust and suspicion. And when the meal was at an end, he rose abruptly and called his daughter into another room. Presently Ralph heard his angry voice resounding through the house, interrupted now and then by a woman's sobs, and a subdued, passionate pleading. When Bertha again entered the room, her eyes were very red, and he saw that she had been weeping. She threw a shawl over her shoulders, beckoned to him with her hand, and he arose and followed her. She led the way silently until they reached a thick copse of birch and alder near the strand. She dropped down upon a bench between two trees, and he took his seat at her side.

"Ralph," began she, with a visible effort, "I hardly know what to say to you; but there is something which I must tell you—my father wishes you to leave us at once."

"And *you*, Bertha?"

"Well—yes—I wish it too."

She saw the painful shock which her words gave him, and she strove hard to speak. Her lips trembled, her eyes became suffused with tears, which grew and grew, but never fell; she could not utter a word.

"Well, Bertha," answered he, with a little quiver in his voice, "if you, too, wish me to go, I shall not tarry. Good-by."

He rose quickly, and, with averted face, held out his hand to her; but as she made no motion to grasp the hand, he began distractedly to button his coat, and moved slowly away.

"Ralph."

He turned sharply, and, before he knew it, she lay sobbing upon his breast.

"Ralph," she murmured, while the tears almost choked her words, "I could not have you leave me thus. It is hard enough—it is hard enough—"

"What is hard, beloved?"

She raised her head abruptly, and turned upon him a gaze full of hope and doubt, and sweet perplexity.

"Ah, no, you do not love me," she whispered, sadly.

"Why should I come to seek you, after these many years, dearest, if I did not wish to make you my wife before God and men? Why should I—"

"Ah, yes, I know," she interrupted him with a fresh fit of weeping, "you are too good and honest to wish to throw me away, now when you have seen how my soul has hungered for the sight of you these many years, how even now I cling to you with a despairing clutch. But you can not disguise yourself, Ralph, and I saw from the first moment that you loved me no more."

"Do not be such an unreasonable child," he remonstrated, feebly. "I do not love you with the wild, irrational passion of former years; but I have the tenderest regard for you, and my heart warms at the sight of your sweet face, and I shall do all in my power to make you as happy as any man can make you who—"

"Who does not love me," she finished.

A sudden shudder seemed to shake her whole frame, and she drew herself more tightly up to him.

"Ah, no," she continued, after a while, sinking back upon her seat. "It is a hopeless thing to compel a reluctant heart. I will accept no sacrifice from you. You owe me nothing, for you have acted toward me honestly and uprightly, and I shall be a stronger or —at least—a better woman for what you gave me— and—for what you could not give me, even though you would."

"But, Bertha," exclaimed he, looking mournfully at her, "it is not true when you say that I owe you nothing. Six years ago, when first I wooed you, you could not return my love, and you sent me out into the world, and even refused to accept any pledge or promise for the future."

"And you returned," she responded, "a man, such as my hope had pictured you; but, while I had almost been standing still, you had outgrown me, and outgrown your old self, and, with your old self, outgrown its love for me, for your love was not of your new self, but of the old. Alas! it is a sad tale, but it is true."

She spoke gravely now, and with a steadier voice, but her eyes hung upon his face with an eager look of expectation, as if yearning to detect there some gleam of hope, some contradiction of the dismal truth. He read that look aright and it pierced him like a sharp sword. He made a brave effort to respond to its appeal, but his features seemed hard as stone, and he could only cry out against his destiny, and bewail his misfortune and hers.

Toward evening, Ralph was sitting in an open boat, listening to the measured oar-strokes of the boatmen who were rowing him out to the nearest stopping-place of the steamer. The mountains lifted their great placid heads up among the sun-bathed clouds, and the fjord opened its cool depths as if to make room for their vast reflections. Ralph felt as if he were floating in the midst of the blue infinite space, and, with the strength which this feeling inspired, he tried to face boldly the thought from which he had but a moment ago shrunk as from something hopelessly sad and perplexing.

And in that hour he looked fearlessly into the gulf which separates the New World from the Old. He had hoped to bridge it; but, alas! it can not be bridged.

THE IDYL OF RED GULCH

BY BRET HARTE

Francis Bret Harte (born at Albany, N.Y., August 25, 1839; died in 1902) wrought a revolution in the art of story-writing by his California tale, "The Luck of Roaring Camp," which appeared in 1868 in the second number of "The Overland Monthly," of which Harte was editor. This was followed by a number of stories of the same original quality, such as "The Outcasts of Poker Flat" and "The Idyl of Red Gulch," concerning which Parke Godwin wrote in "Putnam's Magazine," 1870: "Bret Harte has deepened and broadened our literary and moral sympathies; he has broken the sway of the artificial and conventional; he has substituted actualities for idealities—but actualities that manifest the grandeur of self-sacrifice, the beauty of love, the power of childhood, and the ascendency of nature."

THE IDYL OF RED GULCH

BY BRET HARTE

SANDY was very drunk. He was lying under an azalea-bush, in pretty much the same attitude in which he had fallen some hours before. How long he had been lying there he could not tell, and didn't care; how long he should lie there was a matter equally indefinite and unconsidered. A tranquil philosophy, born of his physical condition, suffused and saturated his moral being.

The spectacle of a drunken man, and of this drunken man in particular, was not, I grieve to say, of sufficient novelty in Red Gulch to attract attention. Earlier in the day some local satirist had erected a temporary tombstone at Sandy's head, bearing the inscription, "Effects of McCorkle's whiskey—kills at forty rods," with a hand pointing to McCorkle's saloon. But this, I imagine, was, like most local satire, personal; and was a reflection upon the unfairness of the process rather than a commentary upon the impropriety of the result. With this facetious exception, Sandy had been undisturbed. A wandering mule, released from his pack, had cropped the scant herbage beside him, and sniffed curiously at the prostrate man; a vagabond dog, with that deep sympathy which the species have for drunken men, had licked his dusty boots and curled himself up at his feet, and lay there, blinking one eye in the sunlight, with a simulation of dissipation that was ingenious and dog-like in its implied flattery of the unconscious man beside him.

Meanwhile the shadows of the pine-trees had slowly swung around until they crossed the road, and their trunks barred the open meadow with gigantic parallels of black and yellow. Little puffs of red dust, lifted by the plunging hoofs of passing teams, dispersed in a grimy shower upon the recumbent man. The sun sank lower and lower, and still Sandy stirred not. And then the repose of this philosopher was disturbed, as other philosophers have been, by the intrusion of an unphilosophical sex.

"Miss Mary," as she was known to the little flock that she had just dismissed from the log schoolhouse beyond the pines, was taking her afternoon walk. Observing an unusually fine cluster of blossoms on the azalea-bush opposite, she crossed the road to pluck it, picking her way through the red dust, not without certain fierce little shivers of disgust and some feline circumlocution. And then she came suddenly upon Sandy!

Of course she uttered the little staccato cry of her sex. But when she had paid that tribute to her physical weakness she became overbold and halted for a moment—at least six feet from this prostrate monster—with her white skirts gathered in her hand, ready for flight. But neither sound nor motion came from the bush. With one little foot she then overturned the satirical headboard, and muttered "Beasts!"—an epithet which probably, at that moment, conveniently classified in her mind the entire male population of Red Gulch. For Miss Mary, being possessed of certain rigid notions of her own, had not, perhaps, properly appreciated the demonstrative gallantry for which the Californian has been so justly celebrated by his brother Californians, and had, as a new-comer, perhaps fairly earned the reputation of being "stuck up."

As she stood there she noticed, also, that the slant sunbeams were heating Sandy's head to what she judged to be an unhealthy temperature, and that his hat was lying uselessly at his side. To pick it up and to place it over his face was a work requiring some courage, particularly as his eyes were open. Yet she did it and made good her retreat. But she was somewhat concerned, on looking back, to see that the hat was removed, and that Sandy was sitting up and saying something.

The truth was, that in the calm depths of Sandy's mind he was satisfied that the rays of the sun were beneficial and healthful; that from childhood he had objected to lying down in a hat; that no people but condemned fools, past redemption, ever wore hats; and that his right to dispense with them when he pleased was inalienable. This was the statement of his inner consciousness. Unfortunately, its outward expression was vague, being limited to a repetition of the following formula: "Su'shine all ri'! Wasser maär, eh? Wass up, su'shine?"

Miss Mary stopped, and, taking fresh courage from

her vantage of distance, asked him if there was anything that he wanted.

"Wass up? Wasser maär?" continued Sandy, in a very high key.

"Get up, you horrid man!" said Miss Mary, now thoroughly incensed; "get up and go home."

Sandy staggered to his feet. He was six feet high, and Miss Mary trembled. He started forward a few paces and then stopped.

"Wass I go home for?" he suddenly asked, with great gravity.

"Go and take a bath," replied Miss Mary, eying his grimy person with great disfavor.

To her infinite dismay, Sandy suddenly pulled off his coat and vest, threw them on the ground, kicked off his boots, and, plunging wildly forward, darted headlong over the hill in the direction of the river.

"Goodness heavens! the man will be drowned!" said Miss Mary; and then, with feminine inconsistency, she ran back to the schoolhouse and locked herself in.

That night, while seated at supper with her hostess, the blacksmith's wife, it came to Miss Mary to ask, demurely, if her husband ever got drunk. "Abner," responded Mrs. Stidger reflectively—"let's see! Abner hasn't been tight since last 'lection." Miss Mary would have liked to ask if he preferred lying in the sun on these occasions, and if a cold bath would have hurt him; but this would have involved an explanation, which she did not then care to give. So she contented herself with opening her gray eyes widely at the red-cheeked Mrs. Stidger—a fine specimen of Southwestern efflorescence—and then dismissed the subject altogether. The next day she wrote to her dearest friend in Boston: "I think I find the intoxicated portion of this community the least objectionable. I refer, my dear, to the men, of course. I do not know anything that could make the women tolerable."

In less than a week Miss Mary had forgotten this episode, except that her afternoon walks took thereafter, almost unconsciously, another direction. She noticed, however, that every morning a fresh cluster of azalea blossoms appeared among the flowers on her desk. This was not strange, as her little flock were aware of her fondness for flowers, and invariably kept her desk bright with anemones, syringas, and lupines; but, on questioning them, they one and all professed ignorance of the azaleas. A few days later, Master Johnny Stidger, whose desk was nearest to the window, was suddenly taken with spasms of apparently gratuitous laughter, that threatened the discipline of the school. All that Miss Mary could get from him was, that some one had been "looking in the winder." Irate and indignant, she sallied from her hive to do battle with the intruder. As she turned the corner of the schoolhouse she came plump upon the quondam drunkard, now perfectly sober, and inexpressibly sheepish and guilty-looking.

These facts Miss Mary was not slow to take a feminine advantage of, in her present humor. But it was somewhat confusing to observe, also, that the beast, despite some faint signs of past dissipation, was amiable-looking—in fact, a kind of blond Samson, whose corn-colored silken beard apparently had never yet known the touch of barber's razor or Delilah's shears. So that the cutting speech which quivered on her ready tongue died upon her lips, and she contented herself with receiving his stammering apology with supercilious eyelids and the gathered skirts of uncontamination. When she re-entered the schoolroom, her eyes fell upon the azaleas with a new sense of revelation; and then she laughed, and the little people all laughed, and they were all unconsciously very happy.

It was a hot day, and not long after this, that two short-legged boys came to grief on the threshold of the school with a pail of water, which they had laboriously brought from the spring, and that Miss Mary compassionately seized the pail and started for the spring herself. At the foot of the hill a shadow crossed her path, and a blue-shirted arm dexterously but gently relieved her of her burden. Miss Mary was both embarrassed and angry. "If you carried more of that for yourself," she said spitefully to the blue arm, without deigning to raise her lashes to its owner, "you'd do better." In the submissive silence that followed she regretted the speech, and thanked him so sweetly at the door that he stumbled. Which caused the children to laugh again—a laugh in which Miss Mary joined, until the color came faintly into her pale cheek. The next day a barrel was mysteriously placed beside the door, and as mysteriously filled with fresh spring-water every morning.

Nor was this superior young person without other

quiet attentions. "Profane Bill," driver of the Slumgullion Stage, widely known in the newspapers for his "gallantry" in invariably offering the box-seat to the fair sex, had excepted Miss Mary from this attention, on the ground that he had a habit of "cussin' on up grades," and gave her half the coach to herself. Jack Hamlin, a gambler, having once silently ridden with her in the same coach, afterward threw a decanter at the head of a confederate for mentioning her name in a barroom. The over-dressed mother of a pupil whose paternity was doubtful had often lingered near this astute Vestal's temple, never daring to enter its sacred precincts, but content to worship the priestess from afar.

With such unconscious intervals the monotonous procession of blue skies, glittering sunshine, brief twilights, and starlit nights passed over Red Gulch. Miss Mary grew fond of walking in the sedate and proper woods. Perhaps she believed, with Mrs. Stidger, that the balsamic odors of the firs "did her chest good," for certainly her slight cough was less frequent and her step was firmer; perhaps she had learned the unending lesson which the patient pines are never weary of repeating to heedful or listless ears. And so one day she planned a picnic on Buckeye Hill, and took the children with her. Away from the dusty road, the straggling shanties, the yellow ditches, the clamor of restless engines, the cheap finery of shop-windows, the deeper glitter of paint and colored glass, and the thin veneering which barbarism takes upon itself in such localities, what infinite relief was theirs! The last heap of ragged rock and clay passed, the last unsightly chasm crossed—how the waiting woods opened their long files to receive them! How the children—perhaps because they had not yet grown quite away from the breast of the bounteous Mother—threw themselves face downward on her brown bosom with uncouth caresses, filling the air with their laughter; and how Miss Mary herself—felinely fastidious and intrenched as she was in the purity of spotless skirts, collar, and cuffs—forgot all, and ran like a crested quail at the head of her brood, until, romping, laughing, and panting, with a loosened braid of brown hair, a hat hanging by a knotted ribbon from her throat, she came suddenly and violently, in the heart of the forest, upon the luckless Sandy!

The explanations, apologies, and not overwise conversation that ensued need not be indicated here. It would seem, however, that Miss Mary had already established some acquaintance with this ex-drunkard. Enough that he was soon accepted as one of the party; that the children, with that quick intelligence which Providence gives the helpless, recognized a friend, and played with his blond beard and long silken mustache, and took other liberties—as the helpless are apt to do. And when he had built a fire against a tree, and had shown them other mysteries of woodcraft, their admiration knew no bounds. At the close of two such foolish, idle, happy hours he found himself lying at the feet of the schoolmistress, gazing dreamily in her face as she sat upon the sloping hillside weaving wreaths of laurel and syringa, in very much the same attitude as he had lain when first they met. Nor was the similitude greatly forced. The weakness of an easy, sensuous nature, that had found a dreamy exaltation in liquor, it is to be feared was now finding an equal intoxication in love.

I think that Sandy was dimly conscious of this himself. I know that he longed to be doing something—slaying a grizzly, scalping a savage, or sacrificing himself in some way for the sake of this sallow-faced, gray-eyed schoolmistress. As I should like to present him in an heroic attitude, I stay my hand with great difficulty at this moment, being only withheld from introducing such an episode by a strong conviction that it does not usually occur at such times. And I trust that my fairest reader, who remembers that, in a real crisis, it is always some uninteresting stranger or unromantic policeman, and not Adolphus, who rescues, will forgive the omission.

So they sat there undisturbed—the woodpeckers chattering overhead and the voices of the children coming pleasantly from the hollow below. What they said matters little. What they thought—which might have been interesting—did not transpire. The woodpeckers only learned how Miss Mary was an orphan; how she left her uncle's house to come to California for the sake of health and independence; how Sandy was an orphan too; how he came to California for excitement; how he had lived a wild life, and how he was trying to reform; and other details, which, from a woodpecker's viewpoint, undoubtedly must have seemed stupid and a waste of time. But even in such trifles was the afternoon spent; and when the children were again gathered, and Sandy, with a delicacy which the schoolmistress well understood, took leave of them quietly at the outskirts of the settlement, it had seemed the shortest day of her weary life.

As the long, dry summer withered to its roots, the school term of Red Gulch—to use a local euphuism—"dried up" also. In another day Miss Mary would be free, and for a season, at least, Red Gulch would know her no more. She was seated alone in the schoolhouse, her cheek resting on her hand, her eyes half closed in one of those day-dreams in which Miss Mary, I fear, to the danger of school discipline, was lately in the habit of indulging. Her lap was full of mosses, ferns, and other woodland memories. She was so preoccupied with these and her own thoughts that a gentle tapping at the door passed unheard, or translated itself into the remembrance of far-off woodpeckers. When at last it asserted itself more distinctly, she started up with a flushed cheek and opened the door. On the threshold stood a woman, the self-assertion and audacity of whose dress were in singular contrast to her timid, irresolute bearing.

Miss Mary recognized at a glance the dubious mother of her anonymous pupil. Perhaps she was disappointed, perhaps she was only fastidious; but as she coldly invited her to enter, she half unconsciously settled her white cuffs and collar, and gathered closer her own chaste skirts. It was, perhaps, for this reason that the embarrassed stranger, after a moment's hesitation, left her gorgeous parasol open and sticking in the dust beside the door, and then sat down at the further end of a long bench. Her voice was husky as she began:

"I heerd tell that you were goin' down to the Bay to-morrow, and I couldn't let you go until I came to thank you for your kindness to my Tommy."

Tommy, Miss Mary said, was a good boy, and deserved more than the poor attention she could give him.

"Thank you, miss; thank ye!" cried the stranger, brightening even through the color which Red Gulch knew facetiously as her "war paint," and striving, in her embarrassment, to drag the long bench nearer the schoolmistress. "I thank you, miss, for that; and if I am his mother, there ain't a sweeter, dearer, better boy lives than him. And if I ain't much as says it, thar ain't a sweeter, dearer, angeler teacher lives than he's got."

Miss Mary, sitting primly behind her desk, with a ruler over her shoulder, opened her gray eyes widely at this, but said nothing.

"It ain't for you to be complimented by the like of me, I know," she went on hurriedly. "It ain't for me to be comin' here, in broad day, to do it, either; but I come to ask a favor—not for me, miss—not for me, but for the darling boy."

Encouraged by a look in the young schoolmistress's eye, and putting her lilac-gloved hands together, the fingers downward, between her knees, she went on, in a low voice:

"You see, miss, there's no one the boy has any claim

on but me, and I ain't the proper person to bring him up. I thought some, last year, of sending him away to Frisco to school, but when they talked of bringing a schoolma'am here, I waited till I saw you, and then I knew it was all right, and I could keep my boy a little longer. And, oh! miss, he loves you so much; and if you could hear him talk about you in his pretty way, and if he could ask you what I ask you now, you couldn't refuse him.

"It is natural," she went on rapidly, in a voice that trembled strangely between pride and humility—"it's natural that he should take to you, miss, for his father, when I first knew him, was a gentleman—and the boy must forget me, sooner or later—and so I ain't a-goin' to cry about that. For I come to ask you to take my Tommy—God bless him for the bestest, sweetest boy that lives—to—to—take him with you."

She had risen and caught the young girl's hand in her own, and had fallen on her knees beside her.

"I've money plenty, and it's all yours and his. Put him in some good school, where you can go and see him, and help him to—to—to forget his mother. Do with him what you like. The worst you can do will be kindness to what he will learn with me. Only take him out of this wicked life, this cruel place, this home of shame and sorrow. You will! I know you will—won't you? You will—you must not, you can not say no! You will make him as pure, as gentle as yourself; and when he has grown up, you will tell him his father's name—the name that hasn't passed my lips for years—the name of Alexander Morton, whom they call here Sandy! Miss Mary!—do not take your hand away! Miss Mary, speak to me! You will take my boy? Do not put your face from me. I know it ought not to look on such as me. Miss Mary!—my God, be merciful!—she is leaving me!"

Miss Mary had risen, and in the gathering twilight had felt her way to the open window. She stood there, leaning against the casement, her eyes fixed on the last rosy tints that were fading from the western sky. There was still some of its light on her pure young forehead, on her white collar, on her clasped white hands, but all fading slowly away. The suppliant had dragged herself, still on her knees, beside her.

"I know it takes time to consider. I will wait here all night; but I can not go until you speak. Do not deny me now. You will!—I see it in your sweet face—such a face as I have seen in my dreams. I see it in your eyes, Miss Mary!—you will take my boy!"

The last red beam crept higher, suffused Miss Mary's eyes with something of its glory, flickered, and faded, and went out. The sun had set on Red Gulch. In the twilight and silence Miss Mary's voice sounded pleasantly.

"I will take the boy. Send him to me to-night."

The happy mother raised the hem of Miss Mary's skirts to her lips. She would have buried her hot face in its virgin folds, but she dared not. She rose to her feet.

"Does—this man—know of your intention?" asked Miss Mary suddenly.

"No, nor cares. He has never seen the child to know it."

"Go to him at once—to-night—now! Tell him what you have done. Tell him I have taken his child, and tell him—he must never see—see—the child again. Wherever it may be, he must not come; wherever I may take it, he must not follow! There, go now, please—I'm weary, and—have much yet to do!"

They walked together to the door. On the threshold the woman turned.

"Good-night!"

She would have fallen at Miss Mary's feet. But at the same moment the young girl reached out her arms, caught the sinful woman to her own pure breast for one brief moment, and then closed and locked the door.

It was with a sudden sense of great responsibility that Profane Bill took the reins of the Slumgullion stage the next morning, for the schoolmistress was one of his passengers. As he entered the highroad, in obedience to a pleasant voice from the "inside," he suddenly reined up his horses and respectfully waited, as Tommy hopped out at the command of Miss Mary.

"Not that bush, Tommy—the next."

Tommy whipped out his new pocket-knife, and cutting a branch from a tall azalea-bush, returned with it to Miss Mary.

"All right now?"

"All right!"

And the stage-door closed on the Idyl of Red Gulch.

CRUTCH, THE PAGE

BY GEORGE ALFRED TOWNSEND

George Alfred Townsend (born at Georgetown, Del., January 30, 1841) has written over his signature of "Gath" more newspaper correspondence than any other living writer. In addition he has found time to write a number of books, one of which, "Tales of the Chesapeake," published in 1880, ranks among the notable collections of American short stories. It contains tales in the manner of Hawthorne, Poe, and Bret Harte, which critics have complimented as being equal to the work of these masters. Of the present selection, a story in which a famous Washington character, "Beau Hickman," is introduced, E. C. Stedman said: "It is good enough for Bret Harte or anybody."

CRUTCH, THE PAGE

BY GEORGE ALFRED TOWNSEND ("GATH")

I—CHIPS

THE Honorable Jeems Bee, of Texas, sitting in his committee-room half an hour before the convening of Congress, waiting for his negro familiar to compound a julep, was suddenly confronted by a small boy on crutches.

"A letter!" exclaimed Mr. Bee, "with the frank of Reybold on it—that Yankeest of Pennsylvania Whigs! Yer's familiarity! Wants me to appoint one U—U—U, what?"

"Uriel Basil," said the small boy on crutches, with a clear, bold, but rather sensitive voice.

"Uriel Basil, a page in the House of Representatives, bein' an infirm, deservin' boy, willin' to work to support his mother. Infirm boy wants to be a page, on the recommendation of a Whig, to a Dimmycratic committee. I say, gen'lemen, what do you think of that, heigh?"

This last addressed to some other members of the committee, who had meantime entered.

"Infum boy will make a spry page," said the Hon. Box Izard, of Arkansaw.

"Harder to get infum page than the Speaker's eye," said the orator, Pontotoc Bibb, of Georgia.

"Harder to get both than a 'pintment in these crowded times on a opposition recommendation when all ole Virginny is yaw to be tuk care of," said Hon. Fitzchew Smy, of the Old Dominion.

The small boy standing up on crutches, with large hazel eyes swimming and wistful, so far from being cut down by these criticisms, stood straighter, and only his narrow little chest showed feeling, as it breathed quickly under his brown jacket.

"I can run as fast as anybody," he said impetuously. "My sister says so. You try me!"

"Who's yo' sister, bub?"

"Joyce."

"Who's Joyce?"

"Joyce Basil—*Miss* Joyce Basil to you, gentlemen. My mother keeps boarders. Mr. Reybold boards there. I think it's hard when a little boy from the South wants to work, that the only body to help him find it is a Northern man. Don't you?"

"Good hit!" cried Jeroboam Coffee, Esq., of Alabama. "That boy would run, if he could!"

"Gentlemen," said another member of the committee, the youthful abstractionist from South Carolina, who was reputed to be a great poet on the stump, the Hon. Lowndes Cleburn—"gentlemen, that boy puts the thing on its igeel merits and brings it home to us. I'll ju my juty in this issue. Abe, wha's my julep?"

"Gentlemen," said the Chairman of the Committee, Jeems Bee, "it 'pears to me that there's a social p'int right here. Reybold, bein' the only Whig on the Lake and Bayou Committee, ought to have something if he sees fit to ask for it. That's courtesy! We, of all men, gentlemen, can't afford to forget it."

"No, by durn!" cried Fitzchew Smy.

"You're right, Bee!" cried Box Izard. "You give it a constitutional set."

"Reybold," continued Jeems Bee, thus encouraged, "Reybold is (to speak out) no genius! He never will rise to the summits of usefulness. He lacks the air, the swing, the *pose,* as the sculptors say; he won't treat, but he'll lend a little money, provided he knows where you goin' with it. If he ain't open-hearted, he ain't precisely mean!"

"You're right, Bee!" (General expression.)

"Further on, it may be said that the framers of the gov'ment never intended *all* the patronage to go to one side. Mr. Jeff'son put *that* on the steelyard principle: the long beam here, the big weight of being in the minority there. Mr. Jackson only threw it considabul more on one side, but even he, gentlemen, didn't take the whole patronage from the Outs; he always left 'em enough to keep up the courtesy of the thing, and we can't go behind *him.* Not and be true to our traditions. Do I put it right?"

"Bee," said the youthful Lowndes Cleburn, extending his hand, "you put it with the lucidity and spirituality of Kulhoon himself!"

"Thanks, Cleburn," said Bee; "this is a compliment not likely to be forgotten, coming from you. Then it is agreed, as the Chayman of yo' Committee, that I accede to the request of Mr. Reybold, of Pennsylvania?"

"Aye!" from everybody.

"And now," said Mr. Bee, "as we wair all up late at the club last night, I propose we take a second julep, and as Reybold is coming in he will jine us."

"I won't give you a farthing!" cried Reybold at the door, speaking to some one. "Chips, indeed! What shall I give you money to gamble away for? A gambling beggar is worse than an impostor! No, sir! Emphatically no!"

"A dollar for four chips for brave old Beau!" said the other voice. "I've struck 'em all but you. By the State Arms! I've got rights in this distreek! Everybody pays toll to brave old Beau! Come down!"

The Northern Congressman retreated before this pertinacious mendicant into his committee-room, and his pesterer followed him closely, nothing abashed, even into the privileged cloisters of the committee. The Southern members enjoyed the situation.

"Chips, Right Honorable! Chips for old Beau. Nobody this ten-year has run as long as you. I've laid for you, and now I've fell on you. Judge Bee, the fust business befo' yo' committee this mornin' is a assessment for old Beau, who's 'way down! Rheumatiz, bettin' on the black, failure of remittances from Fauqueeah, and other casualties by wind an' flood, have put ole Beau away down. He's a institution of his country and must be sustained!"

The laughter was general and cordial among the Southerners, while the intruder pressed hard upon Mr. Reybold. He was a singular object; tall, grim, half-comical, with a leer of low familiarity in his eyes, but his waxed mustache of military proportions, his patch of goatee just above the chin, his elaborately oiled hair and flaming necktie, set off his faded face with an odd gear of finery and impressiveness. His skin was that of an old *roué's,* patched up and chalked, but the features were those of a once handsome man of style and carriage.

He wore what appeared to be a cast-off spring overcoat, out of season and color on this blustering winter day, a rich buff waistcoat of an embossed pattern, such as few persons would care to assume, save, perhaps, a gambler, negro buyer, or fine "buck" barber. The assumption of a large and flashy pin stood in his frilled shirt-bosom. He wore watch-seals without the accompanying watch, and his pantaloons, though faded and threadbare, were once of fine material and cut in a style of extravagant elegance, and they covered his long, shrunken, but aristocratic limbs, and were strapped beneath his boots to keep them shapely. The boots themselves had been once of varnished kid or fine calf, but they were cracked and cut, partly by use, partly for comfort; for it was plain that their wearer had the gout, by his aristocratic hobble upon a gold-mounted cane, which was not the least inconsistent garniture of mendicancy.

"Boys," said Fitzchew Smy, "I s'pose we better come down early. There's a shillin', Beau. If I had one more such constituent as you, I should resign or die premachorely!"

"There's a piece o' tobacker," said Jeems Bee languidly, "all I can afford, Beau, this mornin'. I went to a chicken-fight yesterday and lost all my change."

"Mine," said Box Izard, "is a regulation pen-knife, contributed by the United States, with the regret, Beau, that I can't 'commodate you with a pine coffin for you to git into and git away down lower than you ever been."

"Yaw's a dollar," said Pontotoc Bibb; "it'll do for me an' Lowndes Cleburn, who's a poet and genius, and never has no money. This buys me off, Beau, for a month."

The gorgeous old mendicant took them all grimly and leering, and then pounced upon the Northern man, assured by their twinkles and winks that the rest expected some sport.

"And now, Right Honorable from the banks of the Susquehanna, Colonel Reybold—you see, I got your name; I ben a layin' for you!—come down handsome for the Uncle and ornament of this capital and country. What's yore's?"

"Nothing," said Reybold in a quiet way. "I can not give a man like you anything, even to get rid of him."

"You're mean," said the stylish beggar, winking to the rest. "You hate to put your hand down in yer pocket, mightily. I'd rather be ole Beau, and live on suppers at the faro banks, than love a dollar like you!"

"I'll make it a V for Beau," said Pontotoc Bibb, "if he gives him a rub on the raw like that another lick. Durn a mean man, Cleburn!"

"Come down, Northerner," pressed the incorrigible loafer again; "it don't become a Right Honorable to be so mean with old Beau."

The little boy on crutches, who had been looking at this scene in a state of suspense and interest for some time, here cried hotly:

"If you say Mr. Reybold is a mean man, you tell a story, you nasty beggar! He often gives things to me and Joyce, my sister. He's just got me work, which is the best thing to give; don't you think so, gentlemen?"

"Work," said Lowndes Cleburn, "is the best thing to give away, and the most onhandy thing to keep. I like play the best—Beau's kind o' play!"

"Yes," said Jeroboam Coffee; "I think I prefer to make the chips fly out of a table more than out of a log."

"I like to work!" cried the little boy, his hazel eyes shining, and his poor, narrow body beating with unconscious fervor, half suspended on his crutches, as if he were of that good descent and natural spirit which could assert itself without bashfulness in the presence of older people. "I like to work for my mother. If I was strong, like other little boys, I would make money for her, so that she shouldn't keep any boarders—except Mr. Reybold. Oh! she has to work a lot; but she's proud and won't tell anybody. All the money I get I mean to give her; but I wouldn't have it if I had to beg for it like that man!"

"O Beau," said Colonel Jeems Bee, "you've cotched it now! Reybold's even with you. Little Crutch has cooked your goose! Crutch is right eloquent when his wind will permit."

The fine old loafer looked at the boy, whom he had not previously noticed, and it was observed that the last shaft had hurt his pride. The boy returned his wounded look with a straight, undaunted, spirited glance, out of a child's nature. Mr. Reybold was impressed with something in the attitude of the two, which made him forget his own interest in the controversy.

Beau answered with a tone of nearly tender pacification:

"Now, my little man; come, don't be hard on the old veteran! He's down, old Beau is, sence the time he owned his blooded pacer and dined with the *Corps Diplomatique;* Beau's down sence then; but don't call the old feller hard names. We take it back, don't we? —we take *them* words back?"

"There's a angel somewhere," said Lowndes Cleburn, "even in a Washington bummer, which responds to a little chap on crutches with a clear voice. Whether the angel takes the side of the bummer or the little chap, is a p'int out of our jurisdiction. Abe, give Beau a julep. He seems to have been demoralized by little Crutch's last."

"Take them hard words back, Bub," whined the licensed mendicant, with either real or affected pain; "it's a p'int of honor I'm a-standin' on. Do, now, little Major!"

"I shan't!" cried the boy. "Go and work like me. You're big, and you called Mr. Reybold mean.

Haven't you got a wife or little girl, or nobody to work for? You ought to work for yourself, anyhow. Oughtn't he, gentlemen?"

Reybold, who had slipped around by the little cripple and was holding him in a caressing way from behind, looked over to Beau and was even more impressed with that generally undaunted worthy's expression. It was that of acute and suffering sensibility, perhaps the effervescence of some little remaining pride, or it might have been a twinge of the gout. Beau looked at the little boy, suspended there with the weak back and the narrow chest, and that scintillant, sincere spirit beaming out with courage born in the stock he belonged to. Admiration, conciliation, and pain were in the ruined vagrant's eyes. Reybold felt a sense of pity. He put his hand in his pocket and drew forth a dollar.

"Here, Beau," he said, "I'll make an exception. You seem to have some feeling. Don't mind the boy!"

In an instant the coin was flying from his hand through the air. The beggar, with a livid face and clinched cane, confronted the Congressman like a maniac.

"You bilk!" he cried. "You supper customer! I'll brain you! I had rather parted with my shoes at a dolly shop and gone gadding the hoof, without a doss to sleep on—a town pauper, done on the vag—than to have been made scurvy in the sight of that child and deserve his words of shame!"

He threw his head upon the table and burst into tears.

II—HASH

Mrs. Tryphonia Basil kept a boarding-house of the usual kind on Four-and-a-Half Street. Male clerks—there were no female clerks in the Government in 1854—to the number of half a dozen, two old bureau officers, an architect's assistant, Reybold, and certain temporary visitors made up the table. The landlady was the mistress; the slave was Joyce.

Joyce Basil was a fine-looking girl, who did not know it—a fact so astounding as to be fitly related only in fiction. She did not know it, because she had to work so hard for the boarders and her mother. Loving her mother with the whole of her affection, she had suffered all the pains and penalties of love from that repository. She was to-day upbraided for her want of coquetry and neatness; to-morrow, for proposing to desert her mother and elope with a person she had never thought of. The mainstay of the establishment, she was not aware of her usefulness. Accepting every complaint and outbreak as if she deserved it, the poor girl lived at the capital a beautiful scullion, an unsalaried domestic, and daily forwarded the food to the table, led in the chamber work, rose from bed unrested and retired with all her bones aching. But she was of a natural grace that hard work could not make awkward; work only gave her bodily power, brawn, and form. Though no more than seventeen years of age, she was a superb woman, her chest thrown forward, her back like the torso of a *Venus de Milo,* her head placed on the throat of a

Minerva, and the nature of a child molded in the form of a matron. Joyce Basil had black hair and eyes—very long, excessive hair, that in the mornings she tied up with haste so imperfectly that once Reybold had seen it drop like a cloud around her and nearly touch her feet. At that moment, seeing him, she blushed. He pleaded, for once, a Congressman's impudence, and without her objection wound that great crown of woman's glory around her head, and, as he did so, the perfection of her form and skin, and the overrunning health and height of the Virginia girl, struck him so thoroughly that he said:

"Miss Joyce, I don't wonder that Virginia is the mother of Presidents."

Between Reybold and Joyce there were already the delicate relations of a girl who did not know that she was a woman and a man who knew she was beautiful and worthy. He was a man vigilant over himself, and the poverty and menial estate of Joyce Basil were already insuperable obstacles to marrying her, but still he was attracted by her insensibility that he could ever have regarded her in the light of marriage. "Who was her father, the Judge?" he used to reflect. The Judge was a favorite topic with Mrs. Basil at the table.

"Mr. Reybold," she would say, "you commercial people of the Nawth can't hunt, I believe. Jedge Basil is now on the mountains of Fawquear hunting the plova. His grandfather's estate is full of plova."

If, by chance, Reybold saw a look of care on Mrs.

Basil's face, he inquired for the Judge, her husband, and found he was still shooting on the Occequan.

"Does he never come to Washington, Mrs. Basil?" asked Reybold one day, when his mind was very full of Joyce, the daughter.

"Not while Congress is in session," said Mrs. Basil. "It's a little too much of the *oi polloi* for the Judge. His family, you may not know, Mr. Reybold, air of the Basils of King George. They married into the Tayloze of Mount Snaffle. The Tayloze of Mount Snaffle have Ingin blood in their veins—the blood of Pokyhuntus. They dropped the name of Taylor, which had got to be common through a want of Ingin blood, and spelled it with a E. It used to be Taylor, but now it's Tayloze."

On another occasion, at sight of Joyce Basil cooking over the fire, against whose flame her molded arms took momentary roses upon their ivory, Reybold said to himself: "Surely there is something above the common in the race of this girl." And he asked the question of Mrs. Basil:

"Madame, how was the Judge, your husband, at the last advices?"

"Hunting the snipe, Mr. Reybold. I suppose you do not have the snipe in the Nawth. It is the aristocratic fowl of the Old Dominion. Its bill is only shorter than its legs, and it will not brown at the fire, to perfection, unless upon a silver spit. Ah! when the Jedge and myself were young, before his land troubles overtook us, we went to the springs with our own silver and carriages, Mr. Reybold."

Looking up at Mrs. Basil, Reybold noticed a pallor and flush alternately, and she evaded his eye.

Once Mrs. Basil borrowed a hundred dollars from Reybold in advance of board, and the table suffered in consequence.

"The Judge," she had explained, "is short of taxes on his Fawquear lands. It's a desperate moment with him." Yet in two days the Judge was shooting blue-winged teal at the mouth of the Accotink, and his entire indifference to his family set Reybold to thinking whether the Virginia husband and father was anything more than a forgetful savage. The boarders, however, made very merry over the absent unknown. If the beefsteak was tough, threats were made to send for "the Judge," and let him try a tooth on it; if scant, it was suggested that the Judge might have paid a gunning visit to the premises and inspected the larder. The daughter of the house kept such an even temper, and was so obliging within the limitations of the establishment, that many a boarder went to his department without complaint, though with an appetite only partly satisfied. The boy, Uriel, also was the guardsman of the household, old-faced as if with the responsibility of taking care of two women. Indeed, the children of the landlady were so well behaved and prepossessing that, compared with Mrs. Basil's shabby *hauteur* and garrulity, the legend of the Judge seemed to require no other foundation than offspring of such good spirit and intonation.

Mrs. Tryphonia Basil was no respecter of persons. She kept boarders, she said, as a matter of society, and to lighten the load of the Judge. He had very little idea that she was making a mercantile matter of hospitality, but, as she feelingly remarked, "the old families are misplaced in such times as these yer, when the departments are filled with Dutch, Yankees, Crackers, Pore Whites, and other foreigners." Her manner was, at periods, insolent to Mr. Reybold, who seldom protested, out of regard to the daughter and the little Page; he was a man of quite ordinary appearance, saying little, never making speeches or soliciting notice, and he accepted his fare and quarters with little or no complaint.

"Crutch," he said one day to the little boy, "did you ever see your father?"

"No, I never saw him, Mr. Reybold, but I've had letters from him."

"Don't he ever come to see you when you are sick?"

"No. He wanted to come once when my back was very sick, and I laid in bed weeks and weeks, sir, dreaming, oh! such beautiful things. I thought mamma and sister and I were all with papa in that old home we are going to some day. He carried me up and down in his arms, and I felt such rest that I never knew anything like it, when I woke up, and my back began to ache again. I wouldn't let mamma send for him, though, because she said he was working for us all to make our fortunes, and get doctors for me, and clothes and school for dear Joyce. So I sent him my love, and told papa to work, and he and I would bring the family out all right."

"What did your papa seem like in that dream, my little boy?"

"Oh! sir, his forehead was bright as the sun. Sometimes I see him now when I am tired at night after running all day through Congress."

Reybold's eyes were full of tears as he listened to the boy, and, turning aside, he saw Joyce Basil weeping also.

"My dear girl," he said to her, looking up significantly, "I fear he will see his great Father very soon."

Reybold had few acquaintances, and he encouraged the landlady's daughter to go about with him when she could get a leisure hour or evening. Sometimes they took a seat at the theatre, more often at the old Ascension Church, and once they attended a President's reception. Joyce had the bearing of a well-bred lady, and the purity of thought of a child. She was noticed as if she had been a new and distinguished arrival in Washington.

"Ah! Reybold," said Pontotoc Bibb, "I understand, ole feller, what keeps you so quiet now. You've got a wife unbeknown to the Kemittee! and a happy man I know you air."

It pleased Reybold to hear this, and deepened his interest in the landlady's family. His attention to her daughter stirred Mrs. Basil's pride and revolt together.

"My daughter, Colonel Reybold," she said, "is designed for the army. The Judge never writes to me but he says: 'Tryphonee, be careful that you impress upon my daughter the importance of the military profession. My mother, grandmother, and great-grandmother married into the army, and no girl of the Basil stock shall descend to civil life while I can keep the Fawquear estates.' "

"Madame," said the Congressman, "will you permit me to make the suggestion that your daughter is already a woman and needs a father's care, if she is ever to receive it. I beseech you to impress this subject upon the Judge. His estates can not be more precious to his heart, if he is a man of honor; nay, what is better than honor, his duty requires him to come to the side of these children, though he be ever so constrained by business or pleasure to attend to more worldly concerns."

"The Judge," exclaimed Mrs. Basil, much miffed, "is a man of hereditary ijees, Colonel Reybold. He is now in pursuit of the—ahem!—the Kinvas-back on his ancestral waters. If he should hear that you suggest a pacific life and the groveling associations of he capital for him, he might call you out, sir!"

Reybold said no more; but one evening when Mrs. Basil was absent, called across the Potomac, as happened frequently, at the summons of the Judge—and on such occasions she generally requested a temporary loan or a slight advance of board—Reybold found Joyce Basil in the little parlor of the dwelling. She was alone and in tears, but the little boy Uriel slept before the chimney-fire on a rug, and his pale, thin face, catching the glow of the burning wood, looked beautified as Reybold addressed the young woman.

"Miss Joyce," he said, "our little brother works

too hard. Is there never to be relief for him? His poor, withered body, slung on those crutches for hours and hours, racing up the aisles of the House with stronger pages, is wearing him out. His ambition is very interesting to see, but his breath is growing shorter and his strength is frailer every week. Do you know what it will lead to?"

"O my Lord!" she said, in the negrofied phrase natural to her latitude, "I wish it was no sin to wish him dead."

"Tell me, my friend," said Reybold, "can I do nothing to assist you both? Let me understand you. Accept my sympathy and confidence. Where is Uriel's father? What is this mystery?"

She did not answer.

"It is for no idle curiosity that I ask," he continued. "I will appeal to him for his family, even at the risk of his resentment. Where is he?"

"Oh, do not ask!" she exclaimed. "You want me to tell you only the truth. He is *there!*"

She pointed to one of the old portraits in the room —a picture fairly painted by some provincial artist— and it revealed a handsome face, a little voluptuous, but aristocratic, the shoulders clad in a martial cloak, the neck in ruffles, and a diamond in the shirt bosom. Reybold studied it with all his mind.

"Then it is no fiction," he said, "that you have a living father, one answering to your mother's description. Where have I seen that face? Has some irreparable mistake, some miserable controversy, alienated him from his wife? Has he another family?"

She answered with spirit:

"No, sir. He is my father and my brother's only. But I can tell you no more."

"Joyce," he said, taking her hand, "this is not enough. I will not press you to betray any secret you may possess. Keep it. But of yourself I must know something more. You are almost a woman. You are beautiful."

At this he tightened his grasp, and it brought him closer to her side. She made a little struggle to draw away, but it pleased him to see that when the first modest opposition had been tried she sat quite happily, though trembling, with his arm around her.

"Joyce," he continued, "you have a double duty: one to your mother and this poor invalid, whose journey toward that Father's house not made with hands is swiftly hastening; another duty toward your nobler self—the future that is in you and your woman's heart. I tell you again that you are beautiful, and the slavery to which you are condemning yourself forever is an offence against the creator of such perfection. Do you know what it is to love?"

"I know what it is to feel kindness," she answered after a time of silence. "I ought to know no more. Your goodness is very dear to me. We never sleep, brother and I, but we say your name together, and ask God to bless you."

Reybold sought in vain to suppress a confession he had resisted. The contact of her form, her large dark eyes now fixed upon him in emotion, the birth of the conscious woman in the virgin and her affection still in the leashes of a slavish sacrifice, tempted him onward to the conquest.

"I am about to retire from Congress," he said. "It is no place for me in times so insubstantial. There is darkness and beggary ahead for all your Southern race. There is a crisis coming which will be followed by desolation. The generation to which your parents belong is doomed! I open my arms to you, dear girl, and offer you a home never yet gladdened by a wife. Accept it, and leave Washington with me and with your brother. I love you wholly."

A happy light shone in her face a moment. She was weary to the bone with the day's work and had not the strength, if she had the will, to prevent the Congressman drawing her to his heart. Sobbing there, she spoke with bitter agony:

"Heaven bless you, dear Mr. Reybold, with a wife good enough to deserve you! Blessings on your generous heart. But I can not leave Washington. I love another here!"

III—DUST

The Lake and Bayou Committee reaped the reward of a good action. Crutch, the page, as they all called Uriel Basil, affected the sensibility of the whole committee to the extent that profanity almost ceased there, and vulgarity became a crime in the presence of a child. Gentle words and wishes became the rule; a glimmer of reverence and a thought of piety were not unknown in that little chamber.

"Dog my skin!" said Jeems Bee, "if I ever made

a 'pintment that give me sech satisfaction! I feel as if I had sot a nigger free!"

The youthful abstractionist, Lowndes Cleburn, expressed it even better. "Crutch," he said, "is like a angel reduced to his bones. Them air wings or pinions, that he might have flew off with, being a pair of crutches, keeps him here to tarry awhile in our service. But, gentlemen, he's not got long to stay. His crutches is growing too heavy for that expandin' sperit. Some day we'll look up and miss him through our tears."

They gave him many a present; they put a silver watch in his pocket, and dressed him in a jacket with gilt buttons. He had a bouquet of flowers to take home every day to that marvelous sister of whom he spoke so often; and there were times when the whole committee, seeing him drop off to sleep as he often did through frail and weary nature, sat silently watching lest he might be wakened before his rest was over. But no persuasion could take him off the floor of Congress. In that solemn old Hall of Representatives, under the semicircle of gray columns, he darted with agility from noon to dusk, keeping speed upon his crutches with the healthiest of the pages, and racing into the document-room, and through the dark and narrow corridors of the old Capitol loft, where the House library was lost in twilight. Visitors looked with interest and sympathy at the narrow back and body of this invalid child, whose eyes were full of bright, beaming spirit. He sometimes nodded on the steps by the Speaker's chair; and these spells of dreaminess and fatigue increased as his disease advanced upon his wasting system. Once he did not awaken at all until adjournment. The great Congress and audience passed out, and the little fellow still slept, with his head against the Clerk's desk, while all the other pages were grouped around him, and they finally bore him off to the committee-room in their arms, where, among the sympathetic watchers, was old Beau. When Uriel opened his eyes the old mendicant was looking into them.

"Ah! little Major," he said, "poor Beau has been waiting for you to take those bad words back. Old Beau thought it was all bob with his little cove."

"Beau," said the boy, "I've had such a dream! I thought my dear father, who is working so hard to bring me home to him, had carried me out on the river in a boat. We sailed through the greenest marshes, among white lilies, where the wild ducks were tame as they can be. All the ducks were diving and diving, and they brought up long stalks of celery from the water and gave them to us. Father ate all his. But mine turned into lilies and grew up so high that I felt myself going with them, and the higher I went the more beautiful grew the birds. Oh! let me sleep and see if it will be so again."

The outcast raised his gold-headed cane and hobbled up and down the room with a laced handkerchief at his eyes.

"Great God!" he exclaimed, "another generation is going out, and here I stay without a stake, playing a lone hand forever and forever."

"Beau," said Reybold, "there's hope while one can feel. Don't go away until you have a good word from our little passenger."

The outstretched hand of the Northern Congressman was not refused by the vagrant, whose eccentric sorrow yet amused the Southern Committeemen.

"Ole Beau's jib-boom of a mustache 'll put his eye out," said Pontotoc Bibb, "ef he fetches another groan like that."

"Beau's very shaky around the hams an' knees," said Box Izard; "he's been a good figger, but even figgers can lie ef they stand up too long."

The little boy unclosed his eyes and looked around on all those kindly, watching faces.

"Did anybody fire a gun?" he said. "Oh! no. I was only dreaming that I was hunting with father, and he shot at the beautiful pheasants that were making such a whirring of wings for me. It was music. When can I hunt with father, dear gentlemen?"

They all felt the tread of the mighty hunter before the Lord very near at hand—the hunter whose name is Death.

"There are little tiny birds along the beach," muttered the boy. "They twitter and run into the surf and back again, and I am one of them! I must be, for I feel the water cold, and yet I see you all, so kind to me! Don't whistle for me now; for I don't get much play, gentlemen! Will the Speaker turn me out if I play with the beach birds just once? I'm only a little boy working for my mother."

"Dear Uriel," whispered Reybold, "here's Old

Beau, to whom you once spoke angrily. Don't you see him?"

The little boy's eyes came back from far-land somewhere, and he saw the ruined gamester at his feet.

"Dear Beau," he said, "I can't get off to go home with you. They won't excuse me, and I give all my money to mother. But you go to the back gate. Ask for Joyce. She'll give you a nice warm meal every day. Go with him, Mr. Reybold! If you ask for him it will be all right; for Joyce—dear Joyce!—she loves you."

The beach birds played again along the strand; the boy ran into the foam with his companions and felt the spray once more. The Mighty Hunter shot his bird—a little cripple that twittered the sweetest of them all. Nothing moved in the solemn chamber of the committee but the voice of an old forsaken man, sobbing bitterly.

IV—CAKE

The funeral was over, and Mr. Reybold marveled much that the Judge had not put in an appearance. The whole committee had attended the obsequies of Crutch and acted as pall-bearers. Reybold had escorted the page's sister to the Congressional cemetery, and had observed even old Beau to come with a wreath of flowers and hobble to the grave and deposit them there. But the Judge, remorseless in death as frivolous in life, never came near his mourning wife and daughter in their severest sorrow. Mrs. Tryphonia Basil, seeing that this singular want of behavior on the Judge's part was making some ado, raised her voice above the general din of meals.

"Jedge Basil," she exclaimed, "has been on his Tennessee purchase. These Christmas times there's no getting through the snow in the Cumberland Gap. He's stopped off thaw to shoot the—ahem!—the wild torkey—a great passion with the Jedge. His half-uncle, Gineral Johnson, of Awkinso, was a torkey-killer of high celebrity. He was a Deshay on his Maw's side. I s'pose you haven't the torkey in the Dutch country, Mr. Reybold?"

"Madame," said Reybold, in a quieter moment, "have you written to the Judge the fact of his son's death?"

"Oh, yes—to Fawquear."

"Mrs. Basil," continued the Congressman, "I want you to be explicit with me. Where is the Judge, your husband, at this moment?"

"Excuse me, Colonel Reybold, this is a little of a assumption, sir. The Jedge might call you out, sir, for intruding upon his incog. He's very fine on his incog., you air awair."

"Madame," exclaimed Reybold straightforwardly, "there are reasons why I should communicate with your husband. My term in Congress is nearly expired. I might arouse your interest, if I chose, by recalling to your mind the memorandum of about seven hundred dollars in which you are my debtor. That would be a reason for seeing your husband anywhere north of the Potomac, but I do not intend to mention it. Is he aware—are you?—that Joyce Basil is in love with some one in this city?"

Mrs. Basil drew a long breath, raised both hands, and ejaculated: "Well, I declaw!"

"I have it from her own lips," continued Reybold. "She told me as a secret, but all my suspicions are awakened. If I can prevent it, madame, that girl shall not follow the example of hundreds of her class in Washington, and descend, through the boarding-house or the lodging quarter, to be the wife of some common and unambitious clerk, whose penury she must some day sustain by her labor. I love her myself, but I will never take her until I know her heart to be free. Who is this lover of your daughter?"

An expression of agitation and cunning passed over Mrs. Basil's face.

"Colonel Reybold," she whined, "I pity your blasted hopes. If I was a widow, they should be comfoted. 'Alas! my daughter is in love with one of the Fitz-chews of Fawqueeah. His parents is cousins of the Jedge, and attached to the military."

The Congressman looked disappointed, but not yet satisfied.

"Give me at once the address of your husband," he spoke. "If you do not, I shall ask your daughter for it, and she can not refuse me."

The mistress of the boarding-house was not without alarm, but she dispelled it with an outbreak of anger.

"If my daughter disobeys her mother," she cried, "and betrays the Jedge's incog., she is no Basil, Colonel Reybold. The Basils repudiate her, and she may jine the Dutch and other foreigners at her pleasure."

"That is her only safety," exclaimed Reybold. "I hope to break every string that holds her to yonder barren honor and exhausted soil."

He pointed toward Virginia, and hastened away to the Capitol. All the way up the squalid and muddy avenue of that day he mused and wondered: "Who is Fitzhugh? Is there such a person any more than a Judge Basil? And yet there *is* a Judge, for Joyce has told me so. *She*, at least, can not lie to me. At last," he thought, "the dream of my happiness is over. Invincible in her prejudice as all these Virginians, Joyce Basil has made her bed among the starveling First Families, and there she means to live and die. Five years hence she will have her brood around her. In ten years she will keep a boarding-house and borrow money. As her daughters grow up to the stature and grace of their mother, they will be proud and poor again and breed in and out, until the race will perish from the earth."

Slow to love, deeply interested, baffled but unsatisfied, Reybold made up his mind to cut his perplexity short by leaving the city for the county of Fauquier. As he passed down the avenue late that afternoon, he turned into E Street, near the theatre, to engage a carriage for his expedition. It was a street of livery stables, gambling dens, drinking houses, and worse; murders had been committed along its sidewalks. The more pretentious *canaille* of the city harbored there to prey on the hotels close at hand and aspire to the chance acquaintance of gentlemen. As Reybold stood in an archway of this street, just as the evening shadows deepened above the line of sunset, he saw something pass which made his heart start to his throat and fastened him to the spot. Veiled and walking fast, as if escaping detection or pursuit, the figure of Joyce Basil flitted over the pavement and disappeared in a door about at the middle of this Alsatian quarter of the capital.

"What house is that?" he asked of a constable passing by, pointing to the door she entered.

"Gambling den," answered the officer. "It used to be old Phil Pendleton's."

Reybold knew the reputation of the house: a resort for the scions of the old tidewater families, where hospitality thinly veiled the paramount design of plunder. The connection established the truth of Mrs. Basil's statement. Here, perhaps, already married to the dissipated heir of some unproductive estate, Joyce Basil's lot was cast forever. It might even be that she had been tempted here by some wretch whose villany she knew not of. Reybold's brain took fire at the thought, and he pursued the fugitive into the doorway. A negro steward unfastened a slide and peeped at Reybold knocking in the hall; and, seeing him of respectable appearance, bowed ceremoniously as he let down a chain and opened the door.

"Short cards in the front saloon," he said; "supper and faro back. Chambers on the third floor. Walk up."

Reybold only tarried a moment at the gaming tables,

where the silent, monotonous deal from the tin box, the lazy stroke of the markers, and the transfer of ivory "chips" from card to card of the sweat-cloth, impressed him as the dullest form of vice he had ever found. Treading softly up the stairs, he was attracted by the light of a door partly ajar, and a deep groan, as of a dying person. He peeped through the crack of the door and beheld Joyce Basil leaning over an old man, whose brow she moistened with her handkerchief. "Dear father," he heard her say, and it brought consolation to more than the sick man. Reybold threw open the door and entered into the presence of Mrs. Basil and her daughter. The former arose with surprise and shame, and cried:

"Jedge Basil, the Dutch have hunted you down. He's here—the Yankee creditor."

Joyce Basil held up her hand in imploration, but Reybold did not heed the woman's remark. He felt a weight rising from his heart, and the blindness of many months lifted from his eyes. The dying mortal upon the bed, over whose face the blue billow of death was rolling rapidly, and whose eyes sought in his daughter's the promise of mercy from on high, was the mysterious parent who had never arrived—the Judge from Fauquier. In that old man's long waxed mustache, crimped hair, and threadbare finery the Congressman recognized old Beau, the outcast gamester and mendicant, and the father of Joyce and Uriel Basil.

"Colonel Reybold," faltered that old wreck of manly beauty and of promise long departed, "old Beau's passing in his checks. The chant coves will be telling to-morrow what they know of his life in the papers, but I've dropped a cold deck on 'em these twenty years. Not one knows old Beau, the Bloke, to be Tom Basil, cadet at West Point in the last generation. I've kept nothing of my own but my children's good names. My little boy never knew me to be his father. I tried to keep the secret from my daughter, but her affection broke down my disguises. Thank God! the old rounder's deal has run out at last. For his wife he'll flash her diles no more, nor be taken on the vag."

"Basil," said Reybold, "what trust do you leave to me in your family?"

Mrs. Basil strove to interpose, but the dying man raised his voice:

"Tryphonee can go home to Fauquier. She was always welcome there—without me. I was disinherited. But here, Colonel! My last drop of blood is in the girl. She loves you."

A rattle arose in the sinner's throat. He made an effort, and transferred his daughter's hand to the Congressman's. Not taking it away, she knelt with her future husband at the bedside and raised her voice:

"Lord, when Thou comest into Thy kingdom, remember him!"

IN EACH OTHER'S SHOES

BY GEORGE PARSONS LATHROP

George Parsons Lathrop (born in Hawaii, August 25, 1851; died in 1898) was literally wedded to American literature, in that he married Rose, the second daughter of Nathaniel Hawthorne. She had inspired his youthful poems, and now collaborated with him in several prose works, as well as helped him materially in his master work, a biographical edition of the works of Hawthorne. The fantastic conception of the present story is reminiscent of the imaginative tales of his father-in-law, but there is lacking the glamour of mysticism that Hawthorne would have thrown around it. However, in aiming directly at the moral sense of his readers, instead of approaching this through the æsthetic sense, the obvious treatment of Lathrop gains in human interest more than it loses in literary quality.

IN FACH OTHER'S SHOES

BY GEORGE PARSONS LATHROP

I

JOHN CROMBIE had taken a room at the new apartment building, The Lorne; having advanced so far in his experience of New York as to be aware that if he could once establish himself in a house associated by name with foreign places and titles his chance of securing "position" would be greatly increased. He did not, however, take his meals in the expensive café of that establishment, finding it more economical to go to an outlandish little French restaurant, some distance away, which had been nicknamed among those of his acquaintance who resorted to it "The Fried Cat." This designation, based on a supposed resemblance to the name of the proprietor, Fricat, was also believed to have value as a sarcasm.

It was with no pleasant sensations, therefore, that Crombie, waking on a gray and drizzling morning of November, remembered that he must hie him to "The Fried Cat" for an early breakfast. He was in a hurry that day; he had a great deal to do. His room was very small and dark; he bounced up and dressed himself, in an obscure sort of way, surreptitiously opening the door and reaching vaguely for his shoes, which stood just outside, ready blacked. Nor did it add to his comfort to know that the shoes were very defective as to their soles, and would admit the water freely from the accumulated puddles of the sidewalks. In fact, he had been ashamed to expose their bad condition to the porter when he put them out every night, as he was forced to do, since they were his only pair. Drawing them on hastily, in order to conceal his mortification from even his own mind, he sallied forth; and though at the moment of putting them on a dim sense of something unfamiliar crossed his mind, it was not until he reached "The Fried Cat" that he became fully aware that he had carried off some one else's shoes. He turned up the soles, privately, underneath the low-hanging tablecloth, and by a brief examination convinced himself that the gaiters did not belong to him. The test was simple: his feet were unaccountably dry, and there were none of those breaks in the lower surface of their leather covering which he had so often been obliged to contemplate.

He saw at once that the porter of The Lorne had made a mistake, and must have deposited at another apartment his own very insufficient foot-gear; but there was no chance now to remedy the confusion. Crombie had barely time to reach the office where he was employed.

On an ordinary occasion he would perhaps have gone back to The Lorne and effected an honorable exchange. This particular day, however, was by no means an ordinary occasion. Crombie had made up his mind to take a momentous step; and it was therefore essential that he should appear at his desk exactly on time.

He was a clerk in an important engraving company. For several years he had occupied that post, without any opportunity having presented itself for a promotion. At the best, even should he rise, what could he expect? To be cashier, perhaps, or possibly, under exceptional circumstances, a confidential private secretary. This prospect did not satisfy him; he was determined to strike for something higher.

It will naturally be inferred that he was ambitious. I am not in a position to deny this; but all I can be certain of is, that he was in love—which is often about the same thing.

Several times at The Lorne he had met in the hallways or in the elevator a young lady, who was in no small degree beautiful, and charmed him still more by her generous presence, which conveyed the idea of a harmonious and lovely character. She had light hair and blue eyes, but these outward attributes were joined with a serenity and poise of manner that indicated greater stability than is attributed, as a rule, to individuals of her type.

Once he happened to arrive at the main entrance just as this vision of beauty emerged to take her place in a coupé which was waiting by the curbstone. She dropped her card-case upon the sidewalk, and Crombie's heart throbbed with delight as he picked it up, gave it to her, and received her smiling thanks for his little service. Another time, as he was descending in the elevator, a door opposite the shaft, on the second floor, stood open, and he caught a glimpse of the apartment to which it gave access. The room was finished in soft tints, and was full of upholstery and hangings that lent it a dim golden atmosphere. In the middle of it stood the young girl, clad in the palest blue, above which her hair shone like a golden cloud on some dim evening sky.

Slight occurrences of this sort had affected him. He learned that she was the daughter of Littimer, the rich, widowed banker: her name was Blanche.

II

In these new, stout shoes that did not belong to him Crombie trod with a buoyancy and assurance strongly in contrast with the limp and half-hearted pace to which his old, shabby gaiters had formerly inclined him. He rattled down the stairs of the elevated station with an alacrity almost bumptious; and the sharp, confident step that announced his entrance into the company's office made the other clerks quite ashamed of their own want of spirit.

He worked at his desk until noon; but when the bells of Trinity rang twelve in solemn music over the busy streets, he dropped his pen, walked with a decisive air the length of the room, and, opening a door at the other end, presented himself before Mr. Blatchford, the treasurer, who was also an influential director. "Crombie, eh? Well, what is it?"

"I want to speak with you a moment, sir."

"Anything important? I'm busy."

"Yes, sir; quite important—to me. Possibly it may be to you."

"Fire away, then; but cut it short." Mr. Blatchford's dense, well-combed gray side-whiskers were directed toward the young man in an aggressive way, as if they had been some sort of weapon.

Crombie nonchalantly settled himself in a chair, at ease.

"I am tired of being a clerk," he said. "I'm going to be a director in this company."

"I guess you're going to be an inmate of a lunatic asylum," Mr. Blatchford remarked with astonished cheerfulness.

"That seems as unlikely to me as the other thing does to you," said Crombie.

Hereupon Mr. Blatchford became sarcastically deferential. "And just about when do you propose to become a director?" he asked.

"In the course of a month. The election, I believe, takes place in December."

"Quite right," said his senior, whose urbanity was meant to be crushing. "Meanwhile, you will need leisure to attend to this little matter. Suppose I oblige you by saying that the company has no further need of your services?"

"Suppose you do. What then?"

Mr. Blatchford gave way to his anger. "What then? Why, then you would have to go; that's all. You would be thrown out of employment. You would have to live on your principal, as long as there was any; and afterward you would be obliged to find some other work, or beg, or borrow, or—"

"That's enough," said Crombie, rising with dignity.

"No, it isn't," the treasurer declared, "for you

don't seem to understand even now. I discharge you, Mr. Crombie, on the company's behalf, and you may leave this office at once."

Crombie bowed and went out. "I'm going to be a director, all the same," he told Mr. Blatchford before he closed the door. Then he collected the few articles that belonged to him from his desk, and departed, a free man. He had his future to himself; or else he had no future worth speaking of; he wasn't sure which. Nevertheless, he felt quite happy. Such a result as this had seemed to him, in the prospect, hardly possible; but now that it had arrived he was not discomfited. Unbounded courage seemed to rise from the stout soles of the alien boots, percolating through his whole system. He was surprised at himself. He had intended to use more diplomacy with Mr. Blatchford, and it was no joke to him to lose his place. But instead of feeling despondent, or going at once in search of new employment, he cheerfully went about making calls on several gentlemen who, he thought, might be induced to aid in his ambitious project. His manner was that of a person sure of his powers and enjoying a well-earned leisure. It had its effect. Two or three stockholders of the company joined in agreeing with him that improved methods could be introduced into its management, and that it would be a good thing to have in the board, say, two young, fresh, active men—of whom Crombie, by reason of his experience and training, should be one.

"I own a little stock," said the deposed clerk, who had taken the precaution to obtain a couple of shares by great effort in saving. "Besides, not having any other engrossing interests at present, I could give my whole attention to the company's affairs."

"Quite so," said the merchant whom he was addressing, comfortably. "We must see if we can get together a majority; no time to be lost, you know."

"No, sir. I shall go right to work; and perhaps you will speak to some of your friends, and give me some names."

"Certainly. Come in again pretty soon; will you?"

Crombie saw that he had a good foundation to build upon already. Blatchford was not popular, even among the other directors; and sundry stockholders, as well as people having business with the company, had conceived a strong dislike of him on account of his overbearing manners. Therefore it would not be hard to enlist sympathy for a movement obnoxious to him. But it was imperative that the self-nominated candidate should acquire more of the stock; and to do this capital must be had. Crombie did not see quite how it was to be got; he had no sufficient influence with the bankers.

The afternoon was nearly spent, and he trudged uptown, thinking of the ways and means. But though the problem was far from solved, he still continued in a state of extraordinary buoyancy. Those shoes, those shoes! He was so much impressed by their comfort and the service they had done him in making a good appearance that he resolved to get a new pair of his own. He stopped and bought them; then kept on toward The Lorne, carrying his purchase under his arm without embarrassment. The cold drizzle had ceased, and the sunset came out clear and golden, dipping its bright darts into the shallow pools of wet on the pavement, and somehow mingling with his financial dreams a dream of that fair hair that gave a glory to Miss Blanche's face.

On regaining his modest apartment he sent for the boot-boy, and inquired the whereabouts of his missing shoes.

"Couldn't tell you, sir," said the servant. "Pretty near all the men's boots in the house has gone out, you see, and they'll only be coming back just about now. I'll look out for 'em, sir, and nab 'em as soon as they show up."

"All right. Whose are these that I've been wearing?"

The boy took them, turned them over, and examined them with the eye of a connoisseur in every part. "Them? I should say, sir, them was Mr. Littimer's."

Crombie blushed with mortification. Of all the dwellers in The Lorne, this was the very one with whom it was the most embarrassing to have such a complication occur; and yet, strange inconsistency! he had been longing for any accident, no matter how absurd or fantastic, that could bring him some chance of an acquaintance with Blanche.

"Take these boots, dry them right away, and give 'em a shine. Then carry them up to Mr. Littimer's rooms." He gave the boy a quarter: he was becoming reckless.

Now that he had embarked upon a new career, he

perceived the impropriety of a future director in the Engraving Company going to dine at "The Fried Cat," and so resolved to take his dinner in the gorgeous café of The Lorne. While he was waiting for the proper moment to descend thither, he could not get the shoe question out of his mind. Surely, the boot-boy could not have been so idiotic as to have left that ancient, broken-down pair at Littimer's threshold! And yet it was possible. Crombie felt another flush of humility upon his cheeks. Then he wandered off into reverie upon the multifarious errands of all the pairs of boots and shoes that had gone forth from the great apartment house that day. Patter, patter, patter! tramp, tramp!—he imagined he heard them all walking, stamping, shuffling along toward different parts of the city, with many different objects, and sending back significant echoes. Whither had his own ruinous Congress gaiters gone?—to what destination which they would never have reached had he been in them? Had they carried their temporary possessor into any such worriment and trouble as he himself had often traveled through on their worn but faithful soles?

Breaking off from these idle fancies at length, he went down to the café; and there he had the pleasure of dining at a table not far from Blanche Littimer. But, to his surprise, she was alone. Her father did not appear during the meal.

III

The fact was that the awful possibility, mere conjecture of which had frightened Crombie, had occurred. Littimer had received the young man's shoes in place of his own.

They happened to fit him moderately well; so that he, likewise, did not notice the exchange until he had started for his office. He believed in walking the entire distance, no matter what the weather; and to this practice he made rare exceptions. But he had not progressed very far before he became annoyed by an unaccustomed intrusion of dampness that threatened him with a cold. He looked down, carefully surveyed the artificial casing of his extremities, and decided to hail the first unoccupied coupé he should meet. It was some time before he found one; and when finally he took his seat in the luxurious little bank parlor at Broad Street, his feet were quite wet.

His surprise at this occurrence was doubled when, on taking off the shoes and scrutinizing them more closely, he ascertained that they were the work of his usual maker. What had happened to him? Was he dreaming? It seemed to him that he had gone back many years; that he was a poor young man again, entering upon his first struggle for a foothold in the crowded, selfish, unhomelike metropolis. He remembered the day when *he* had worn shoes like these.

He sent out for an assortment of new ones, from which, with unnecessary lavishness, he chose and kept three or four pairs. All the rest of the day, nevertheless, those sorry Congress boots of Crombie's, which he had directed his office-boy to place beside the soft-coal fire, for drying, faced him with a sort of haunting look. However much he might be occupied with weightier matters, he could not keep his eyes from straying in that direction; and whenever they rested on that battered "right" and that way-worn "left," turned up in that mute, appealing repose and uselessness at the fender, his thoughts recurred to his early years of trial and poverty. Ah! how greatly he had changed since then! On some accounts he could almost wish that he were poor again. But when he remembered Blanche, he was glad, for her sake, that he was rich.

But if for her sake, why not for others? Perhaps he had been rather selfish, not only about Blanche, but toward her. His conscience began to reproach him. Had he made for her a large life? Since her mother's premature death, had he instilled into her sympathies, tastes, companionships that would make her existence the richer? Had he not kept her too much to himself? On the other hand, he had gratified all her material wants; she could wear what she pleased, she could go where she chose, she had acquaintances of a sort becoming to the daughter of a wealthy man. Yet there was something lacking. What did she know about old, used-up boots and all that pertains to them? What did she know about indigence, real privation, and brave endurance, such as a hundred thousand fellow-creatures all around her were undergoing?

Somehow it dawned upon the old banker that if she knew about all these things and had some share in them, albeit only through sympathy and helping, she might be happier, more truly a woman, than she was now.

As he sat alone, in revery, he actually heaved a deep sigh. A sigh is often as happy a deliverance as a laugh, in this world of sorrows. It was the first that had escaped Littimer in years. Let us say that it was a breathing space, which gave him time for reflection; it marked the turning of a leaf; it was the beginning of a new chapter in his life.

Before he left the bank he locked the door of the private parlor, and was alone for two or three minutes. The office boy was greatly puzzled the next morning, when he found all the new pairs of shoes ranged intact in the adjoining cupboard. The old ones were missing.

Littimer had gone away in them, furtively. He was ashamed of his own impulse.

This time he resolutely remained afoot instead of hiring a carriage. He despatched a messenger to Blanche, saying that sudden business would prevent his returning to dinner, and continued indefinitely on his way—whither? As to that he was by no means certain; he knew only that he must get out of the beaten track, out of the ruts. For an hour or two he must cease to be Littimer, the prosperous moneyed man, and must tread once more the obscure paths through which he had made his way to fortune. He could hardly have explained the prompting which he obeyed. Could it have had anything to do with the treacherous holes in the bottoms of those old shoes?

As it chanced, he passed by "The Fried Cat"; and, dingy though the place was, he felt an irresistible desire to enter it. Seating himself, he ordered the regular dinner of the day. The light was dim; the tablecloth was dirty; the attendance was irregular and distracted. Littimer took one sip of the sour wine—which had a flavor resembling vinegar and carmine ink in equal parts—and left the further contents of his bottle untasted. The soup, the stew, and the faded roast that were set before him, he could scarcely swallow; but a small cup of coffee at the end of the wellnigh Barmecide repast came in very palatably.

In default of prandial attractions, Littimer tried to occupy himself by looking at the people around him. The omnifarious assembly included pale, prim-whiskered young clerks; shabby, lonely, sallow young women, whose sallowness and shabbiness stamped them with the mark of integrity; other females whose specious splendor was not nearly so reassuring; old men, broken-down men, middle-aged men of every description, except the well-to-do.

"Some of them," Littimer reflected, "are no worse than I am. But are any of them really any better?"

He could not convince himself that they were; yet his sympathies, somehow, went out toward this motley crowd. It appeared to him very foolish that he should sympathize, but he could not help it. "And, after all," was the next thought that came to him, "are we to give pity to people, or withhold it, simply because they are better or worse than ourselves? No; there is something more in it than that."

Leaving "The Fried Cat" abruptly, he betook himself to an acquaintance who, he knew, was very active in charities—a man who worked practically, and gave time to the work.

"Do you visit any of your distress cases to-night?" he asked.

"Yes, I shall make a few calls," answered the man of charity. "Would you like to go along?"

"Very much."

So the two started out together. The places they went to were of various kinds, and revealed a considerable diversity of misfortune. Sometimes they entered tenement houses of the most wretched character; but in other instances they went to small and cheap but decent lodgings over the shops on West Side avenues, or even penetrated into boarding-houses of such good appearance that the banker was surprised to find his friend's mission carrying him thither. All the cases, however, had been studied, and were vouched for; and several were those of young men and women having employment, but temporarily disabled, and without friends who could help them.

"You do well to help these beginners, at critical times," said the banker, with satisfaction. "I take a special interest in them."

It was almost the same as if he were receiving relief himself. Who knows? Perhaps he was; but to the outward eye it appeared merely that, with his friend's sanction, he was dispensing money and offers of goodwill to the needy. What a strange freak it was, though, in Littimer! He kept on with the work until quite late in the evening, regardless of the risk he ran by continuing out-of-doors when so ill shod.

I think he had some idea in his mind that he was performing an act of penance.

IV

Having waited a reasonable length of time after dinner, Crombie again left his room, resolved to make a call upon Mr. Littimer, on the plea of apologizing for having marched away with his shoes.

He would not run the risk, by sending his card, of being denied as a stranger; so, notwithstanding much hesitation and tremor, he approached the door which he had once seen standing open, and knocked. A voice which he now heard for the second time in his life, but which was so sweet and crept so naturally into the centre of his heart that the thought of it seemed always to have been there, answered: "Come in." And he did come in.

"Is Mr. Lit—is your father at home?" It seemed to bring him a little nearer to her to say "your father."

Blanche had risen from the chair where she was reading, and looked very much surprised. "Oh," she exclaimed, with girlish simplicity, "I thought it was the waiter! N-no; he hasn't come home yet."

"I beg pardon. Then perhaps I'd better call later." Crombie made a feeble movement toward withdrawal.

"Did you want to see him on business? Who shall I tell him?"

"Mr. Crombie, please. It's nothing very important."

"Oh," said Blanche, with a little blush at her own deception, "haven't I seen you in the house before? Are you staying here?"

She remembered distinctly the incident of the card-case, and how very nice she had thought him, both on that occasion and every time she had seen him. But as for him, his heart sank at the vague impersonality with which she seemed to regard him.

"Yes, I'm here, and can easily come in again."

"I expect my father almost any moment," she said. "Would you like to wait?"

What an absurd question, to one in his frame of mind! "Well, really, it is such a very small matter," he began, examining his hat attentively. Then he glanced up at her again, and smiled: "I only wanted to—to make an apology."

"An apology!" echoed Blanche, becoming rather more distant. "Oh, dear! I'm very sorry, I'm sure. I didn't know there'd been any trouble." She began to look anxious, and turned her eyes upon the smouldering fire in the grate. So this was to be the end of her pleasant, cheerful reveries about this nice young man. And the reveries had been more frequent than she had been aware of until now.

"There has been no trouble," he assured her, eagerly. "Just a little mistake that occurred; and, in fact, I was hardly responsible for it."

Blanche's eyes began to twinkle with a new and amusing interpretation. "Ah!" she cried, "are you the gentleman who—" Then she stopped short.

Crombie was placed in an unexpected embarrassment. How could he possibly drag into his conversation with this lovely young creature so commonplace and vulgar a subject as shoe-leather! Ignoring her unfinished question, he asked: "Do you know, Miss Littimer, whether the—a—one of the servants here has brought up anything for your father—that is, a parcel, a—"

"A pair of shoes?" Blanche broke in, her eyes dancing, while her lips parted in a smile.

"Yes, yes; that's what I meant."

"They came up just after dinner," Blanche returned. "Then you *are* the gentleman."

"I'm afraid I am," Crombie owned, and they both laughed.

Blanche quietly, and with no apparent intention, resumed her chair; and this time Crombie took a seat without waiting to be invited again. Thus they fell to talking in the friendliest way.

"I can't imagine what has become of papa," said Blanche. "He sent word, in the most mysterious manner, that he had an engagement; and it is so unusual! Perhaps it's something about the new house he's building—up-town, you know. Dear me! it does make so much trouble, and I don't believe I shall like it half as well as these little, cosey rooms."

The little, cosey rooms were as the abode of giants compared with Crombie's contracted quarters; but he drew comfort from what she said, thinking how such sentiments might make it possible to win even so unattainable an heiress into some modest home of his own.

"You don't know till you try it," he replied. "Just think of having a place all to yourself, belonging to you."

Blanche lifted her eyebrows, and a little sigh escaped her. She was reflecting, perhaps, that a place all to herself would be rather lonely.

"You have never met my father?" she asked.

"No. I have seen him."

"Well, I think you will like him when you know him."

"I don't doubt it!" Crombie exclaimed with fervor, worshiping the very furniture that surrounded Blanche.

"I hope we may become better acquainted."

"Only I think, Mr. Crombie, he will owe *you* an apology now."

"Why?"

"For keeping your shoes out so late."

"*My* shoes!" said the young man, in vehement surprise.

"Why, yes. Didn't you know they came to him? The porter said so."

Crombie grew red with the sense of his disgrace in having his poverty-stricken boots come to the knowledge of the banker. Really, his mortification was so great that the accident seemed to him to put an end to all his hopes of further relations with Blanche and her father.

"Oh, I assure you," he said, rising, "that makes no difference at all! I'm sorry I mentioned the matter. Pray tell Mr. Littimer not to think of it. I—I believe I'd better go now, Miss Littimer."

Blanche rose too, and Crombie was on the point of bowing a good-night, when the door opened, and a weary figure presented itself on the threshold; the figure of a short man with a spare face, and whiskers in which gray mingled with the sandy tint. He had a pinched, half-growling expression, was draped in a light, draggled overcoat, and carried an umbrella, the ribs of which hung loose around the stick.

"There's papa this moment!" cried Blanche.

Crombie perceived that escape was impossible, and, in a few words, the reason of his presence there was made known to the old gentleman.

Littimer examined the visitor swiftly, from head to foot—especially the foot. He advanced to the fire, toasted first one and then the other of the damp gaiters he had on, and at length broke out, in a tone bordering on reproach: "So you are the owner, are you? Then my sympathy has all been wasted! Why, I supposed, from the condition of these machines that I've been lugging around with me half the day that you must be in the greatest distress. And, lo and behold! I find you a young fellow in prime health, spruce and trim, doing well, I should say, and perfectly happy."

"I can't help that, sir," retorted Crombie, nettled, but speaking with respect. "I confess I was very happy until a moment or two ago."

"What do you mean by that?" the other demanded, with half-yielding pugnacity. "Till I came in—is that the idea?"

"Oh, papa!" said Banche, softly.

"Well, honey-bee, what's the matter?" her father asked, trying to be gruff. "Can't I say what I like, here?" But he surrendered at once by adding: "You may be sure I don't want to offend any one. Sit down, Mr. Crombie, and wait just a few moments while I go into the other room and rejuvenate my hoofs, so to speak—for I fear I've made a donkey of myself."

He disappeared into an adjoining room with Blanche, who there informed him artlessly of Crombie's consideration and attentiveness in restoring the errant shoes. When they came back Littimer insisted upon having the young man remain a little longer and drink a glass of port with him. Before taking his departure, however, Crombie, who felt free to speak since Blanche had retired, made a brief statement in satisfaction of conscience.

"You hinted," he said, "that you judged me to be doing well. I don't want to leave you with a false impression. The truth is, I am not doing well. I have no money to speak of, and to-day I lost the position on which I depended."

"You don't tell me!" Littimer's newly roused charitable impulses came to the fore. "Why, now you begin to be really interesting, Mr. Crombie."

"Thanks," said Crombie; "I'm not ambitious to interest people in that way, I told you only because I thought it fair."

"Don't be touchy, my dear sir," answered the banker. "I meant what I said. Come, let's see what can be done. Have you any scheme in view?"

"Yes, I have," said Crombie, with decision.

Littimer gave a grunt. He was afraid of people with schemes, and was disappointed with the young man's want of helplessness. Dependence would have been an easier thing to deal with.

"Well," said he, "we must talk it over. Come and see me at the bank to-morrow. You know the address."

V

The next day Crombie called at the bank; but Littimer was not there. He was not very well, it was said; had not come down-town. Crombie did what he could toward organizing his fight for a directorship, and then returned to The Lorne, where he punctually inquired after Mr. Littimer's health, and learned that the banker's ardor in making the rounds among distressed people the night before had been followed by reaction into a bad cold, with some threat of pneumonia. Blanche was plainly anxious. The attack lasted three or four days, and Crombie, though the affair of the directorship was pressing for attention, could not forbear to remain as near as possible to Blanche, offering every aid within his power, so far as he might without overstepping the lines of his very recent acquaintance. But the Littimers did not, according to his observation, number any very intimate companions in their circle, or at least had not many friends who would be assiduous in such an emergency. Perhaps their friends were too busy with social engagements. Consequently, he saw a good deal of Blanche, and became to her an object of reliance.

Well, it was simply one of those things that happen

only in fairy tales or in romances—or in real life. Littimer recovered without any serious illness, and, after a brief conference with Crombie, entered heartily into the young man's campaign. Crombie showed him just what combinations could be formed, how success could be achieved, and what lucrative results might be made to ensue. He conquered by figures and by lucid common-sense. Littimer agreed to buy a number of shares in the Engraving Company, which he happened to know could be purchased, and to advance Crombie a good sum with which to procure a portion of the same lot. But before this agreement could be consummated, Crombie, with his usual frankness, said to the banker:

"I will conceal nothing from you, Mr. Littimer. I fell in love with Blanche before I knew her, and if this venture of mine succeeds, I shall ask her to become my wife."

"Let us attend to business," said Littimer, severely. "Sentiment can take care of itself."

Their manœuvre went on so vigorously that Blatchford became alarmed, and sent an ambassador to arrange a compromise; but by this time Crombie had determined to oust Blatchford himself and elect an entirely new set of men, to compose more than half the Board, and so control everything.

He succeeded.

But Littimer did not forget the charitable enthusiasm which had been awakened by a circumstance on the surface so trivial as the mistake of a boot-boy. He did not desist from his interest in aiding disabled or unfortunate people who could really be aided. Some time after Crombie had achieved his triumph in the Engraving Company, and had repaid Littimer's loan, he was admitted to a share in the banking business; and eventually the head of the house was able to give a great deal of attention to perfecting his benevolent plans.

When the details of their wedding were under discussion, Crombie said to Blanche: "Oughtn't we to have an old shoe thrown after the carriage as we drive away?"

She smiled; looked him full in the eyes with a peculiar tenderness in which there was a bright, delicious sparkle of humor. "No; old shoes are much too useful to be wasted that way."

Somehow she had possessed herself of that particular, providential pair; and, though I don't want anybody to laugh at my two friends, I must risk saying that I suspect Mrs. Crombie of preserving it somewhere to this day, in the big new house up-town.

THE DENVER EXPRESS

BY A. A. HAYES

Augustus Allen Hayes (born in New England in 1837, died in 1892) was the author of two works relating to the Far West which have placed on permanent record an interesting phase, now forever past, of the development of civilization in that region. "New Colorado and the Santa Fe Trail" is a descriptive book yielding the information of fact concerning the pioneer period of settlement in that region; and "The Denver Express" is a stirring piece of fiction vividly reproducing the spirit of those days when the forces of social order introduced by the railroad were battling with the primitive elements of vice and crime. The latter story, which is here reproduced, appeared in an English magazine, "Belgravia," where it was most favorably received by readers whose appetite for such fiction had already been whetted by the tales of Bret Harte.

THE DENVER EXPRESS

BY A. A. HAYES

ANY one who has seen an outward-bound clipper ship getting under way, and heard the "shanty-songs" sung by the sailors as they toiled at capstan and halliards, will probably remember that rhymeless but melodious refrain—

"I'm bound to see its muddy waters,
Yeo ho! that rolling river;
Bound to see its muddy waters,
Yeo ho! the wild Missouri."

Only a happy inspiration could have impelled Jack to apply the adjective "wild" to that ill-behaved and disreputable river which, tipsily bearing its enormous burden of mud from the far Northwest, totters, reels, runs its tortuous course for hundreds on hundreds of miles; and which, encountering the lordly and thus far well-behaved Mississippi at Alton, and forcing its company upon this splendid river (as if some drunken fellow should lock arms with a dignified pedestrian), contaminates it all the way to the Gulf of Mexico.

At a certain point on the banks of this river, or rather—as it has the habit of abandoning and destroying said banks—at a safe distance therefrom, there is a town from which a railroad takes its departure, for its long climb up the natural incline of the Great Plains,

From "Belgravia" for January, 1884.

to the base of the mountains; hence the importance to this town of the large but somewhat shabby building serving as terminal station. In its smoky interior, late in the evening and not very long ago, a train was nearly ready to start. It was a train possessing a certain consideration. For the benefit of a public easily gulled and enamored of grandiloquent terms, it was advertised as the "Denver Fast Express"; sometimes, with strange unfitness, as the "Lightning Express"; "elegant" and "palatial" cars were declared to be included therein; and its departure was one of the great events of the twenty-four hours in the country round about. A local poet described it in the "live" paper of the town, cribbing from an old Eastern magazine and passing off as original the lines—

> "Again we stepped into the street,
> A train came thundering by,
> Drawn by the snorting iron steed
> Swifter than eagles fly.
> Rumbled the wheels, the whistle shrieked,
> Far rolled the smoky cloud,
> Echoed the hills, the valleys shook,
> The flying forests bowed."

The trainmen, on the other hand, used no fine phrases. They called it simply "Number Seventeen"; and, when it started, said it had "pulled out."

On the evening in question, there it stood, nearly ready. Just behind the great hissing locomotive, with its parabolic headlight and its coal-laden tender, came the baggage, mail, and express cars; then the passenger coaches, in which the social condition of the occupants seemed to be in inverse ratio to their distance from the engine. First came emigrants, "honest miners," "cowboys," and laborers; Irishmen, Germans, Welshmen, Mennonites from Russia, quaint of garb and speech, and Chinamen. Then came long cars full of people of better station, and last the great Pullman "sleepers," in which the busy black porters were making up the berths for well-to-do travelers of diverse nationalities and occupations.

It was a curious study for a thoughtful observer, this motley crowd of human beings sinking all differences of race, creed, and habits in the common purpose to move westward—to the mountain fastnesses, the sage-brush deserts and the Golden Gate.

The warning bell had sounded, and the fireman leaned far out for the signal. The gong struck sharply the conductor shouted, "All aboard," and raised his hand; the tired ticket-seller shut his window, and the train moved out of the station, gathered way as it cleared the outskirts of the town, rounded a curve, entered on an absolutely straight line, and, with one long whistle from the engine, settled down to its work. Through the night hours it sped on, past lonely ranches and infrequent stations, by and across shallow streams fringed with cottonwood trees, over the greenish-yellow buffalo grass near the old trail where many a poor emigrant, many a bold frontiersman, many a brave soldier, had laid his bones but a short time before.

Familiar as they may be, there is something strangely impressive about all-night journeys by rail, and those forming part of an American transcontinental trip are almost weird. From the windows of a night express in Europe or the older portions of the United States, one looks on houses and lights, cultivated fields, fences, and hedges; and, hurled as he may be through the darkness, he has a sense of companionship and semi-security. Far different is it when the long train is running over those two rails which, seen before night set in, seem to meet on the horizon. Within all is as if between two great seaboard cities; the neatly dressed people, the uniformed officials, the handsome fittings, the various appliances for comfort. Without are now long dreary levels, now deep and wild canyons, now an environment of strange and grotesque rock-formations, castles, battlements, churches, statues. The antelope fleetly runs, and the coyote skulks away from the track, and the gray wolf howls afar off. It is for all the world, to one's fancy, as if a bit of civilization, a family or community, its belongings and surroundings complete, were flying through regions barbarous and inhospitable.

From the cab of Engine No. 32, the driver of the Denver Express saw, showing faintly in the early morning, the buildings grouped about the little station ten miles ahead, where breakfast awaited his passengers. He looked at his watch; he had just twenty minutes in which to run the distance, as he had run it often before. Something, however, traveled faster than he. From the smoky station out of which the train passed the night before, along the slender wire stretched on rough poles at the side of the track, a spark of that mysterious something which we call electricity flashed at the moment he returned the watch to his pocket; and in five minutes' time the station-master came out on the platform, a little more thoughtful than his wont, and looked eastward for the smoke of the train. With but three of the passengers in that train has this tale especially to do, and they were all in the new and comfortable Pullman "City of Cheyenne." One was a tall, well-made man of about thirty—blond, blue-eyed, bearded, straight, sinewy, alert. Of all in the train he seemed the most thoroughly at home, and the respectful greeting of the conductor, as he passed through the car, marked him as an officer of the road. Such was he—Henry Sinclair, assistant engineer, quite famed on the line, high in favor with the directors, and a rising man in all ways. It was known on the road that he was expected in Denver, and there were rumors that he was to organize the parties for the survey of an important "extension." Beside him sat his pretty young wife. She was a New Yorker—one could tell at first glance—from the feather of her little bonnet, matching the gray traveling dress, to the tips of her dainty boots; and one, too, at whom old Fifth Avenue promenaders would have turned to look. She had a charming figure, brown hair, hazel eyes, and an expression at once kind, intelligent, and spirited. She had cheerfully left a luxurious home to follow the young engineer's fortunes; and it was well known that those fortunes had been materially advanced by her tact and cleverness.

The third passenger in question had just been in conversation with Sinclair and the latter was telling his wife of their curious meeting. Entering the toilet-room at the rear of the car, he said, he had begun his ablutions by the side of another man, and it was as they were sluicing their faces with water that he heard the cry:

"Why, Major, is that you? Just to think of meeting you here!"

A man of about tweny-eight years of age, slight, muscular, wiry, had seized his wet hand and was wringing it. He had black eyes, keen and bright, swarthy complexion, black hair and mustache. A keen observer might have seen about him some signs of a *jeunesse orageuse,* but his manner was frank and pleasing. Sinclair looked him in the face, puzzled for a moment.

"Don't you remember Foster?" asked the man.

"Of course I do," replied Sinclair. "For a moment I could not place you. Where have you been and what have you been doing?"

"Oh," replied Foster, laughing, "I've braced up and turned over a new leaf. I'm a respectable member of society, have a place in the express company, and am going to Denver to take charge."

"I am very glad to hear it, and you must tell me your story when we have had our breakfast."

The pretty young woman was just about to ask who Foster was, when the speed of the train slackened, and the brakeman opened the door of the car and cried out in stentorian tones:

"Pawnee Junction; twenty minutes for refreshments!"

II

When the celebrated Rocky Mountain gold excitement broke out, more than twenty years ago, and people painted "PIKE'S PEAK OR BUST" on the canvas covers of their wagons and started for the diggings, they established a "trail" or "trace" leading in a southwesterly direction from the old one to California.

At a certain point on this trail a frontiersman named Barker built a forlorn ranch-house and *corral,* and offered what is conventionally called "entertainment for man and beast."

For years he lived there, dividing his time between fighting the Indians and feeding the passing emigrants and their stock. Then the first railroad to Denver was built, taking another route from the Missouri, and Barker's occupation was gone. He retired with his gains to St. Louis and lived in comfort.

Years passed on, and the "extension" over which our train is to pass was planned. The old pioneers were excellent natural engineers and their successors could find no better route than they had chosen. Thus it was that "Barker's" became, during the construction period, an important point, and the frontiersman's name came to figure on time-tables. Meanwhile the place passed through a process of evolution which would have delighted Darwin. In the party of engineers which first camped there was Sinclair and it was by his advice that the contractors selected it for division headquarters. Then came drinking "saloons" and gambling houses—alike the inevitable concomitant and the bane of Western settlements; then scattered houses and shops and a shabby so-called hotel, in which the letting of miserable rooms (divided from each other by canvas partitions) was wholly subordinated to the business of the bar. Before long, Barker's had acquired a worse reputation than even other towns of its type, the abnormal and uncanny aggregations of squalor and vice which dotted the plains in those days; and it was at its worst when Sinclair returned thither and took up his quarters in the engineers' building. The passion for gambling was raging, and to pander thereto were collected as choice a lot of desperadoes as ever "stacked" cards or loaded dice. It came to be noticed that they were on excellent terms with a man called "Jeff" Johnson, who was lessee of the hotel; and to be suspected that said Johnson, in local parlance, "stood in with" them. With this man had come to Barker's his daughter Sarah, commonly known as "Sally," a handsome girl, with a straight, lithe figure, fine features, reddish auburn hair, and dark-blue eyes. It is but fair to say that even the "toughs" of a place like Barker's show some respect for the other sex, and Miss Sally's case was no exception to the rule. The male population admired her; they said she "put on heaps of style"; but none of them had seemed to make any progress in her good graces.

On a pleasant afternoon just after the track had been laid some miles west of Barker's, and construction trains were running with some regularity to and from the end thereof, Sinclair sat on the rude veranda of the engineers' quarters, smoking his well-colored meerschaum and looking at the sunset. The atmosphere had been so clear during the day that glimpses were had of Long's and Pike's peaks, and as the young engineer gazed at the gorgeous cloud display he was thinking of the miners' quaint and pathetic idea that the dead "go over the Range."

"Nice-looking, ain't it, Major?" asked a voice at his elbow, and he turned to see one of the contractors' officials taking a seat near him.

"More than nice-looking to my mind, Sam," he replied. "What is the news to-day?"

"Nothin' much. There's a sight of talk about the doin's of them faro an' keno sharps. The boys is gettin' kind o' riled, fur they allow the game ain't on the square wuth a cent. Some of 'em down to the tie-camp wuz a-talkin' about a vigilance committee, an' I wouldn't be surprised ef they meant business. Hev yer heard about the young feller that come in a week ago from Laramie an' set up a new faro-bank?"

"No. What about him?"

"Wa'al, yer see he's a feller thet's got a lot of sand an' ain't afeared of nobody, an' he's allowed to hev the deal to his place on the square every time. Accordin' to my idee, gamblin's about the wust racket a feller kin work, but it takes all sorts of men to make a world, an' ef the boys is bound to hev a game, I calkilate they'd like to patronize his bank. Thet's made the old crowd mighty mad an' they're a-talkin' about puttin' up a job of cheatin' on him an' then stringin' him up. Besides, I kind o' think there's some cussed jealousy on another lay as comes in. Yer see the young feller—Cyrus Foster's his name—is sweet on thet gal of Jeff Johnson's. Jeff wuz to Laramie before he come here, an' Foster knowed Sally up thar. I allow he moved here to see her. Hello! Ef thar they ain't a-coming now."

Down a path leading from the town past the railroad buildings, and well on the prairie, Sinclair saw the girl walking with the "young feller." He was talking earnestly to her and her eyes were cast down. She looked pretty and, in a way, graceful; and there was in her attire a noticeable attempt at neatness, and a faint reminiscence of bygone fashions. A smile came to Sinclair's lips as he thought of a couple walking up Fifth Avenue during his leave of absence not many months before, and of a letter many times read, lying at that moment in his breast-pocket.

"Papa's bark is worse than his bite," ran one of its sentences. "Of course he does not like the idea of my leaving him and going away to such dreadful and remote places as Denver and Omaha and I don't know what else; but he will not oppose me in the end, and when you come on again—"

"By thunder!" exclaimed Sam; "ef thar ain't one of them cussed sharps a-watchin' 'em."

Sure enough a rough-looking fellow, his hat pulled over his eyes, half concealed behind a pile of lumber, was casting a sinister glance toward the pair.

"The gal's well enough," continued Sam; "but I don't take a cent's wuth of stock in thet thar father of her'n. He's in with them sharps, sure pop, an' it don't suit his book to hev Foster hangin' round. It's ten to one he sent that cuss to watch 'em. Wa'al, they're a queer lot, an' I'm afeared thar's plenty of trouble ahead among 'em. Good luck to you, Major," and he pushed back his chair and walked away.

After breakfast next morning, when Sinclair was sitting at the table in his office, busy with maps and plans, the door was thrown open, and Foster, panting for breath, ran in.

"Major Sinclair," he said, speaking with difficulty, "I've no claim on you, but I ask you to protect me. The other gamblers are going to hang me. They are more than ten to one. They will track me here; unless you harbor me, I'm a dead man."

Sinclair rose from his chair in a second and walked to the window. A party of men were approaching the building. He turned to Foster:

"I do not like your trade," said he; "but I will not see you murdered if I can help it. You are welcome here." Foster said "Thank you," stood still a moment, and then began to pace the room, rapidly clinching his hands, his whole frame quivering, his eyes flashing fire—"for all the world," Sinclair said, in telling the story afterward, "like a fierce caged tiger."

"My God!" he muttered, with concentrated intensity, "to be *trapped,* TRAPPED like this!"

Sinclair stepped quickly to the door of his bedroom and motioned Foster to enter. Then there came a knock at the outer door, and he opened it and stood on the threshold erect and firm. Half a dozen "toughs" faced him.

"Major," said their spokesman, "we want that man."

"You can not have him, boys."

"Major, we're a-goin' to take him."

"You had better not try," said Sinclair, with perfect ease and self-possession, and in a pleasant voice. "I have given him shelter, and you can only get him over my dead body. Of course you can kill me, but you won't do even that without one or two of you going down; and then you know perfectly well, boys, what will happen. You *know* that if you lay your finger on a railroad man it's all up with you. There are five hundred men in the tie-camp, not five miles away, and you don't need to be told that in less than one hour after they get word there won't be a piece of one of you big enough to bury."

The men made no reply. They looked him straight in the eyes for a moment. Had they seen a sign of flinching they might have risked the issue, but there was none. With muttered curses, they slunk away. Sinclair shut and bolted the door, then opened the one leading to the bedroom.

"Foster," he said, "the train will pass here in half an hour. Have you money enough?"

"Plenty, Major."

"Very well; keep perfectly quiet and I will try to get you safely off." He went to an adjoining room and called Sam, the contractor's man. He took in the situation at a glance.

"Wa'al, Foster," said he, "kind o' 'close call' for yer, warn't it? Guess yer'd better be gittin' up an' gittin' pretty lively. The train boys will take yer through an' yer kin come back when this racket's worked out."

Sinclair glanced at his watch, then he walked to the window and looked out. On a small *mesa,* or elevated plateau, commanding the path to the railroad, he saw a number of men with rifles.

"Just as I expected," said he. "Sam, ask one of the boys to go down to the track and, when the train arrives, tell the conductor to come here."

In a few minutes the whistle was heard and the conductor entered the building. Receiving his instructions, he returned, and immediately on engine, tender, and platform appeared the trainmen, with *their* rifles covering the group on the bluff. Sinclair put on his hat.

"Now, Foster," said he, "we have no time to lose. Take Sam's arm and mine, and walk between us."

The trio left the building and walked deliberately to the railroad. Not a word was spoken. Besides the men in sight on the train, two behind the window-blinds of the one passenger coach, and unseen, kept their fingers on the triggers of their repeating carbines. It seemed a long time, counted by anxious seconds, until Foster was safe in the coach.

"All ready, conductor," said Sinclair. "Now, Foster, good-by. I am not good at lecturing, but if I were you, I would make this the turning-point in my life."

Foster was much moved.

"I will do it, Major," said he; "and I shall never

forget what you have done for me to-day. I am sure we shall meet again."

With another shriek from the whistle the train started. Sinclair and Sam saw the men quietly returning the firearms to their places as it gathered way. Then they walked back to their quarters. The men on the *mesa*, balked of their purpose, had withdrawn.

Sam accompanied Sinclair to his door, and then sententiously remarked: "Major, I think I'll light out and find some of the boys. You ain't got no call to know anything about it, but I allow it's about time them cusses was bounced."

Three nights after this, a powerful party of *Vigilantes*, stern and inexorable, made a raid on all the gambling dens, broke the tables and apparatus, and conducted the men to a distance from the town, where they left them with an emphatic and concise warning as to the consequences of any attempt to return. An exception was made in Jeff Johnson's case—but only for the sake of his daughter—for it was found that many a "little game" had been carried on in his house.

Ere long he found it convenient to sell his business and retire to a town some miles to the eastward, where the railroad influence was not as strong as at Barker's. At about this time, Sinclair made his arrangements to go to New York, with the pleasant prospect of marrying the young lady in Fifth Avenue. In due time he arrived at Barker's with his young and charming wife and remained for some days. The changes were astounding. Commonplace respectability had replaced abnormal lawlessness. A neat station stood where had been the rough contractor's buildings. At a new "Windsor" (or was it "Brunswick"?) the performance of the kitchen contrasted sadly (alas! how common is such contrast in these regions) with the promise of the *menu.* There was a tawdry theatre yclept "Academy of Music," and there was not much to choose in the way of ugliness between two "meeting-houses."

"Upon my word, my dear," said Sinclair to his wife, "I ought to be ashamed to say it, but I prefer Barker's *au naturel.*"

One evening, just before the young people left the town, and as Mrs. Sinclair sat alone in her room, the frowzy waitress announced "a lady," and was requested to bid her enter. A woman came with timid mien into the room, sat down, as invited, and removed her veil. Of course the young bride had never known Sally Johnson, the whilom belle of Barker's, but her husband would have noticed at a glance how greatly she was changed from the girl who walked with Foster past the engineers' quarters. It would be hard to find a more striking contrast than was presented by the two women as they sat facing each other: the one in the flush of health and beauty, calm, sweet, self-possessed; the other still retaining some of the shabby finery of old days, but pale and haggard, with black rings under her eyes, and a pathetic air of humiliation.

"Mrs. Sinclair," she hurriedly began, "you do not know me, nor the like of me. I've got no right to speak to you, but I couldn't help it. Oh! please be lieve me, I am not real downright bad. I'm Sally Johnson, daughter of a man whom they drove out of the town. My mother died when I was little, and I *never* had a show; and folks think because I live with my father, and he makes me know the crowd he travels with, that I must be in with them, and be of their sort. I never had a woman speak a kind word to me, and I've had so much trouble that I'm just drove wild, and like to kill myself; and then I was at the station when you came in, and I saw your sweet face and the kind look in your eyes, and it came in my heart that I'd speak to you if I died for it." She leaned eagerly forward, her hands nervously closing on the back of a chair. "I suppose your husband never told you of me; like enough he never knew me; but I'll never forget him as long as I live. When he was here before, there was a young man"—here a faint color came in the wan cheeks—"who was fond of me, and I thought the world of him, and my father was down on him, and the men that father was in with wanted to kill him; and Mr. Sinclair saved his life. He's gone away, and I've waited and waited for him to come back—and perhaps I'll never see him again. But oh! dear lady, I'll never forget what your husband did. He's a good man, and he deserves the love of a dear good woman like you, and if I dared I'd pray for you both, night and day."

She stopped suddenly and sank back in her seat, pale as before, and as if frightened by her own emotion. Mrs. Sinclair had listened with sympathy and increasing interest.

"My poor girl," she said, speaking tenderly (she had a lovely, soft voice) and with slightly heightened color, "I am delighted that you came to see me, and that my husband was able to help you. Tell me, can we not do more for you? I do not for one moment believe you can be happy with your present surroundings. Can we not assist you to leave them?"

The girl rose, sadly shaking her head. "I thank you for your words," she said. "I don't suppose I'll ever see you again, but I'll say, God bless you!"

She caught Mrs. Sinclair's hand, pressed it to her lips, and was gone.

Sinclair found his wife very thoughtful when he came home, and he listened with much interest to her story.

"Poor girl!" said he; "Foster is the man to help her. I wonder where he is? I must inquire about him."

The next day they proceeded on their way to San Francisco, and matters drifted on at Barker's much as before. Johnson had, after an absence of some months, come back and lived without molestation amid the shifting population. Now and then, too, some of the older residents fancied they recognized, under slouched sombreros, the faces of some of his former "crowd" about the "Ranchman's Home," as his gaudy saloon was called.

Late on the very evening on which this story opens, and they had been "making up" the Denver Express in the train-house on the Missouri, "Jim" Watkins, agent and telegrapher at Barker's, was sitting in his little office, communicating with the station rooms by the ticket window. Jim was a cool, silent, efficient man, and not much given to talk about such episodes in his past life as the "wiping out" by Indians of the construction party to which he belonged, and his own rescue by the scouts. He was smoking an old and favorite pipe, and talking with one of "the boys" whose head appeared at the wicket. On a seat in the station sat a woman in a black dress and veil, apparently waiting for a train.

"Got a heap of letters and telegrams there, ain't yer, Jim?" remarked the man at the window.

"Yes," replied Jim; "they're for Engineer Sinclair, to be delivered to him when he passes through here. He left on No. 17, to-night." The inquirer did not notice the sharp start of the woman near him.

"Is that good-lookin' wife of his'n a-comin' with him?" asked he.

"Yes, there's letters for her, too."

"Well, good-night, Jim. See yer later," and he went out. The woman suddenly rose and ran to the window.

"Mr. Watkins," cried she, "can I see you for a few moments where no one can interrupt us? It's a matter of life and death." She clutched the sill with her thin hands, and her voice trembled. Watkins recognized Sally Johnson in a moment. He unbolted a door, motioned her to enter, closed and again bolted it, and also closed the ticket window. Then he pointed to a chair, and the girl sat down and leaned eagerly forward.

"If they knew I was here," she said in a hoarse

whisper, "my life wouldn't be safe five minutes. I was waiting to tell you a terrible story, and then I heard who was on the train due here to-morrow night. Mr. Watkins, don't, for God's sake, ask me how I found out, but I hope to die if I ain't telling you the living truth! They're going to wreck that train—No. 17—at Dead Man's Crossing, fifteen miles east, and rob the passengers and the express car. It's the worst gang in the country, *Perry's*. They're going to throw the train off the track, the passengers will be maimed and killed—and Mr. Sinclair and his wife on the cars! Oh! my God! Mr. Watkins, send them warning!"

She stood upright, her face deadly pale, her hands clasped. Watkins walked deliberately to the railroad map which hung on the wall and scanned it. Then he resumed his seat, laid his pipe down, fixed his eyes on the girl's face, and began to question her. At the same time his right hand, with which he had held the pipe, found its way to the telegraph key. None but an expert could have distinguished any change in the *clicking* of the instrument, which had been almost incessant; but Watkins had "called" the head office on the Missouri. In two minutes the "sounder" rattled out "*All right! What is it?*"

Watkins went on with his questions, his eyes still fixed on the poor girl's face, and all the time his fingers, as it were, playing with the key. If he were imperturbable, so was *not* a man sitting at a receiving instrument nearly five hundred miles away. He had "taken" but a few words when he jumped from his chair and cried:

"Shut that door, and call the superintendent and be quick! Charley, brace up—lively—and come and write this out!" With his wonderful electric pen, the handle several hundreds of miles long, Watkins, unknown to his interlocutor, was printing in the Morse alphabet this startling message:

"Inform'n rec'd. Perry gang going to throw No. 17 off track near —xth mile-post, this division, about nine to-morrow (Thursday) night, kill passengers, and rob express and mail. Am alone here. No chance to verify story, but believe it to be on square. Better make arrangements from your end to block game. No Sheriff here now. Answer."

The superintendent, responding to the hasty summons, heard the message before the clerk had time to write it out. His lips were closely compressed as he put his own hand on the key and sent these laconic sentences: *"O. K. Keep perfectly dark. Will manage from this end."*

Watkins, at Barker's, rose from his seat, opened the door a little way, saw that the station was empty, and then said to the girl, brusquely, but kindly:

"Sally, you've done the square thing, and saved that train. I'll take care that you don't suffer and that you get well paid. Now come home with me, and my wife will look out for you."

"Oh! no," cried the girl, shrinking back, "I must run away. You're mighty kind, but I daren't go with you." Detecting a shade of doubt in his eye, she added: "Don't be afeared; I'll die before they'll know I've given them away to you!" and she disappeared in the darkness.

At the other end of the wire, the superintendent had

quietly impressed secrecy on his operator and clerk, ordered his fast mare harnessed, and gone to his private office.

"Read that!" said he to his secretary. "It was about time for some trouble of this kind, and now I'm going to let Uncle Sam take care of his mails. If I don't get to the reservation before the General's turned in, I shall have to wake him up. Wait for me, please."

The gray mare made the six miles to the military reservation in just half an hour. The General was smoking his last cigar, and was alert in an instant; and before the superintendent had finished the jorum of "hot Scotch" hospitably tendered, the orders had gone by wire to the commanding officer at Fort ——, some distance east of Barker's, and been duly acknowledged.

Returning to the station, the superintendent remarked to the waiting secretary:

"The General's all right. Of course we can't tell that this is not a sell; but if those Perry hounds mean business they'll get all the fight they want—and if they've got any souls—which I doubt—may the Lord have mercy on them!"

He prepared several despatches, two of which were as follows:

"Mr. Henry Sinclair:

"On No. 17, Pawnee Junction:

This telegram your authority to take charge of train on which you are, and demand obedience of all officials and trainmen on road. Please do so, and act in accordance with information wired station agent at Pawnee Junction."

To the Station Agent:

"Reported Perry gang will try wreck and rob No. 17 near —xth mile-post, Denver Division, about nine Thursday night. Troops will await train at Fort ——. Car ordered ready for them. Keep everything secret, and act in accordance with orders of Mr. Sinclair."

"It's worth about ten thousand dollars," sententiously remarked he, "that Sinclair's on that train. He's got both sand and brains. Good-night," and he went to bed and slept the sleep of the just.

III

The sun never shone more brightly and the air was never more clear and bracing than when Sinclair helped his wife off the train at Pawnee Junction. The station-master's face fell as he saw the lady, but he saluted the engineer with as easy an air as he could assume, and watched for an opportunity to speak to him alone. Sinclair read the despatches with an unmoved countenance, and after a few minutes' reflection simply said: "All right. Be sure to keep the matter perfectly quiet." At breakfast he was *distrait* —so much so that his wife asked him what was the matter. Taking her aside, he at once showed her the telegrams.

"You see my duty," he said. "My only thought is about you, my dear child. Will you stay here?"

She simply replied, looking into his face without a tremor:

"My place is with you." Then the conductor called "All aboard," and the train once more started.

Sinclair asked Foster to join him in the smoking compartment and tell him the promised story, which the latter did. His rescue at Barker's, he frankly and gratefully said, *had* been the turning point in his life. In brief, he had "sworn off" from gambling and drinking, had found honest employment, and was doing well.

"I've two things to do now, Major," he added; "first, I must show my gratitude to you; and next"—he hesitated a little—"I want to find that poor girl that I left behind at Barker's. She was engaged to marry me, and when I came to think of it, and what a life I'd have made her lead, I hadn't the heart till now to look for her; but, seeing I'm on the right track, I'm going to find her, and get her to come with me. Her father's an—old scoundrel, but that ain't her fault, and I ain't going to marry *him*."

"Foster," quietly asked Sinclair, "do you know the Perry gang?"

The man's brow darkened.

"Know them?" said he. "I know them much too well. Perry is as ungodly a cutthroat as ever killed an emigrant in cold blood, and he's got in his gang nearly all those hounds that tried to hang me. Why do you ask, Major?"

Sinclair handed him the despatches. "You are the only man on the train to whom I have shown them," said he.

Foster read them slowly, his eyes lighting up as he did so. "Looks as if it was true," said he. "Let me see! Fort ——. Yes, that's the —th infantry. Two of their boys were killed at Sidney last summer by some of the same gang, and the regiment's sworn vengeance. Major, if this story's on the square, that crowd's goose is cooked, and *don't you forget it!* I say, you must give me a hand in."

"Foster," said Sinclair, "I am going to put responsibility on your shoulders. I have no doubt that, if we be attacked, the soldiers will dispose of the gang; but I must take all possible precautions for the safety of the passengers. We must not alarm them. They can be made to think that the troops are going on a scout, and only a certain number of resolute men need be told of what we expect. Can you, late this afternoon, go through the cars, and pick them out? I will then put you in charge of the passenger cars, and you can post your men on the platforms to act in case of need. My place will be ahead."

"Major, you can depend on me," was Foster's reply. "I'll go through the train and have my eye on some boys of the right sort, and that's got their shooting-irons with them."

Through the hours of that day on rolled the train, still over the crisp buffalo grass, across the well-worn buffalo trails, past the prairie-dog villages. The passengers chatted, dozed, played cards, read, all unconscious, with the exception of three, of the coming conflict between the good and the evil forces bearing on their fate; of the fell preparations making for their disaster; of the grim preparations making to avert such disaster; of all of which the little wires alongside of them had been talking back and forth. Watkins had telegraphed that he still saw no reason to doubt the good faith of his warning, and Sinclair had reported his receipt of authority and his acceptance thereof. Meanwhile, also, there had been set in motion a measure of that power to which appeal is so reluctantly made in time of peace. At Fort ——, a lonely post on the plains, the orders had that morning been issued for twenty men under Lieutenant Halsey to parade at 4 P. M., with overcoats, two days' rations, and ball cartridges; also for Assistant Surgeon Kesler to report for duty with the party. Orders as to destination were communicated direct to the lieutenant from the post commander, and on the minute the little column moved, taking the road to the station. The regiment from which it came had been in active service among the Indians on the frontier for a long time, and the officers and men were tried and seasoned fighters. Lieutenant Halsey had been well known at the West Point balls as the "leader of the german." From the last of these balls he had gone straight to the field, and three years had given him an enviable reputation for *sang-froid* and determined bravery. He looked every inch the soldier as he walked along the trail, his cloak thrown back and his sword tucked under his arm. The doctor, who carried a Modoc bullet in some inaccessible part of his scarred body, growled good-naturedly at the need of walking, and the men, enveloped in their army-blue overcoats, marched easily by fours. Reaching the station, the lieutenant called the agent aside, and with him inspected, on a siding, a long platform car on which benches had been placed and secured. Then he took his seat in the station and quietly waited, occasionally twisting his long blond mustache. The doctor took a cigar with the agent, and the men walked about or sat on the edge of the platform. One of them, who obtained a surreptitious glance at his silent commander, told his companions that there was trouble ahead for somebody.

"That's just the way the leftenant looked, boys," said he, "when we was laying for them Apaches that raided Jones's Ranch and killed the women and little children."

In a short time the officer looked at his watch, formed his men, and directed them to take their places on the seats of the car. They had hardly done so when the whistle of the approaching train was heard. When it came up, the conductor, who had his instructions from Sinclair, had the engine detached and backed on the siding for the soldiers' car, which thus came between it and the foremost baggage car when the train was again made up. As arranged, it was announced that the troops were to be taken a certain distance to join a scouting party, and the curiosity of the passengers was but slightly excited. The soldiers sat quietly in their seats, their repeating rifles held between their knees, and the officer in front. Sinclair joined the latter, and had a few words with him as the train moved on. A little later, when the stars were shining brightly overhead, they passed into the express car, and sent for the conductor and other trainmen, and for Foster. In a few words Sinclair explained the position of affairs. His statement was received with perfect coolness, and the men only asked what they were to do.

"I hope, boys," said Sinclair, "that we are going to put this gang to-night where they will make no more trouble. Lieutenant Halsey will bear the brunt of the fight, and it only remains for you to stand by the interests committed to your care. Mr. Express Agent, what help do you want?" The person addressed, a good-natured giant, girded with a cartridge belt, smiled as he replied:

"Well, sir, I'm wearing a watch which the company gave me for standing off the James gang in Missouri for half an hour, when we hadn't the ghost of a soldier about. I'll take the contract, and welcome, to hold *this* fort alone."

"Very well," said Sinclair. "Foster, what progress have you made?"

"Major, I've got ten or fifteen as good men as ever drew a bead, and just red-hot for a fight."

"That will do very well. Conductor, give the trainmen the rifles from the baggage car and let them act under Mr. Foster. Now, boys, I am sure you will do your duty. That is all."

From the next station Sinclair telegraphed "All ready" to the superintendent, who was pacing his office in much suspense. Then he said a few words to his brave but anxious wife, and walked to the rear platform. On it were several armed men, who bade him good-evening, and asked "when the fun was going to begin." Walking through the train, he found each platform similarly occupied, and Foster going from one to the other. The latter whispered as he passed him:

"Major, I found Arizona Joe, the scout, in the smokin' car, and he's on the front platform. That lets me out, and although I know as well as you that there ain't any danger about that rear sleeper where the madam is, I ain't a-going to be far off from her." Sinclair shook him by the hand; then he looked at his watch. It was half-past eight. He passed through the baggage and express cars, finding in the latter the agent sitting behind his safe, on which lay two large revolvers. On the platform car he found the soldiers and their commander sitting silent and unconcerned as before. When Sinclair reached the latter and nodded, he rose and faced the men, and his fine voice was clearly heard above the rattle of the train.

"Company, 'ten*tion!*" The soldiers straightened themselves in a second.

"With ball cartridge, *load!*" It was done with the precision of a machine. Then the lieutenant spoke, in the same clear, crisp, tones that the troops had heard in more than one fierce battle.

"Men," said he, "in a few minutes the Perry gang, which you will remember, are going to try to run this train off the track, wound and kill the passengers, and rob the cars and the United States mail. It is our business to prevent them. Sergeant Wilson" (a gray-bearded non-commissioned officer stood up and saluted), "I am going on the engine. See that my orders are repeated. Now, men, aim low, and don't waste any shots." He and Sinclair climbed over the tender and spoke to the engine-driver.

"How are the air-brakes working?" asked Sinclair.

"First-rate."

"Then, if you slowed down now, you could stop the train in a third of her length, couldn't you?"

"Easy, if you don't mind being shaken up a bit."

"That is good. How is the country about the —xth mile-post?"

"Dead level, and smooth."

"Good again. Now, Lieutenant Halsey, this is a splendid head-light, and we can see a long way with my night glass. I will have a—"

"—2d mile-pole just past," interrupted the engine-driver.

"Only one more to pass, then, before we ought to strike them. Now, lieutenant, I undertake to stop the train within a very short distance of the gang. They will be on both sides of the track, no doubt; and the ground, as you hear, is quite level. You will best know what to do."

The officer stepped back. "Sergeant," called he, "do you hear me plainly?"

"Yes, sir."

"Have the men fix bayonets. When the train stops, and I wave my sword, let half jump off each side, run up quickly, and form line *abreast of the engine*—not ahead."

"Jack," said Sinclair to the engine-driver, "is your hand steady?" The man held it up with a smile. "Good. Now stand by your throttle and your airbrake. Lieutenant, better warn the men to hold on tight, and tell the sergeant to pass the word to the boys on the platforms, or they will be knocked off by the sudden stop. Now for a look ahead!" and he brought the binocular to his eyes.

The great parabolic head-light illuminated the track a long way in advance, all behind it being of course in darkness. Suddenly Sinclair cried out:

"The fools have a light there, as I am a living man; and there is a little red one near us. What can that be? All ready, Jack! By heaven! they have taken up two rails. Now *hold on, all!* STOP HER!!"

The engine-driver shut his throttle-valve with a jerk. Then, holding hard by it, he sharply turned a brass handle. There was a fearful jolt—a grating —and the train's way was checked. The lieutenant, standing sidewise, had drawn his sword. He waved it, and almost before he could get off the engine the soldiers were up and forming, still in shadow, while the bright light was thrown on a body of men ahead.

"Surrender, or you are dead men!" roared the officer. Curses and several shots were the reply. Then came the orders, quick and sharp:

"Forward! Close up! Double-quick! Halt! FIRE!" . . . It was speedily over. Left on the car with the men, the old sergeant had said:

"Boys, you hear. It's that —— Perry gang. Now, don't forget Larry and Charley that they murdered last year," and there had come from the soldiers a sort of fierce, subdued *growl*. The volley was followed by a bayonet charge, and it required all the officer's authority to save the lives even of those who "threw up their hands." Large as the gang was (outnumbering the troops), well armed and desperate as they were, every one was dead, wounded, or a prisoner when the men who guarded the train platforms ran up. The surgeon, with professional coolness, walked up to the robbers, his instrument case under his arm.

"Not much for me to do here, Lieutenant," said he. "That practice for Creedmoor is telling on the shooting. Good thing for the gang, too. Bullets are better than rope, and a Colorado jury will give them plenty of that."

Sinclair had sent a man to tell his wife that all was over. Then he ordered a fire lighted, and the rails relaid. The flames lit a strange scene as the passengers flocked up. The lieutenant posted men to keep them back.

"Is there a telegraph station not far ahead, Sinclair?" asked he. "Yes? All right." He drew a small pad from his pocket, and wrote a despatch to the post commander.

"Be good enough to send that for me," said he, "and leave orders at Barker's for the night express eastward to stop for us, and bring a posse to take care of the wounded and prisoners. And now, my dear Sinclair, I suggest that you get the passengers into the cars, and go on as soon as those rails are spiked. When they realize the situation, some of them will feel precious ugly, and you know we can't have any lynching."

Sinclair glanced at the rails and gave the word at once to the conductor and brakemen, who began vociferating, "All aboard!" Just then Foster appeared, an expression of intense satisfaction showing clearly on his face, in the firelight.

"Major," said he, "I didn't use to take much stock in special Providence, or things being ordered; but I'm darned if I don't believe in them from this day. I was bound to stay where you put me, but I was uneasy, and wild to be in the scrimmage; and, if I had been there, I wouldn't have taken notice of a little red light that wasn't much behind the rear platform when we stopped. When I saw there was no danger there I ran back, and what do you think I found? There was a woman in a dead faint, and just clutching a lantern that she had tied up in a red scarf, poor little thing! And, Major, it was Sally! It was the little girl that loved me out at Barker's, and has loved me and waited for me ever since! And when she came to, and knew me, she was so glad she 'most fainted away again; and she let on as it was her that gave away the job. And I took her into the sleeper, and the madam, God bless her!—she knew Sally before and was good to her—she took care of her and is cheering her up. And now, Major, I'm going to take her straight to Denver, and send for a parson and get her married to me, and she'll brace up, sure pop."

The whistle sounded, and the train started. From the window of the "sleeper" Sinclair and his wife took their last look at the weird scene. The lieutenant, standing at the side of the track, wrapped in his cloak, caught a glimpse of Mrs. Sinclair's pretty face, and returned her bow. Then, as the car passed out of sight, he tugged at his mustache and hummed:

"Why, boys, why,
Should we be melancholy, boys,
Whose business 'tis to die?"

In less than an hour, telegrams having in the meantime been sent in both directions, the train ran alongside the platform at Barker's; and Watkins, imperturbable as usual, met Sinclair, and gave him his letters.

"Perry gang wiped out, I hear, Major," said he. "Good thing for the country. That's a lesson the 'toughs' in these parts won't forget for a long time. Plucky girl that give 'em away, wasn't she? Hope she's all right."

"She is all right," said Sinclair with a smile.

"Glad of that. By the way, that father of her'n passed in his checks to-night. He'd got one warning from the Vigilantes, and yesterday they found out he was in with this gang, and they was a-going for him; but when the telegram come, he put a pistol to his head and saved them all trouble. Good riddance to everybody, I say. The sheriff's here now, and is going east on the next train to get them fellows. He's got a big posse together, and I wouldn't wonder if they was hard to hold in, after the 'boys in blue' is gone."

In a few minutes the train was off, and its living freight—the just and the unjust, the reformed and the rescued, the happy and the anxious. With many of the passengers the episode of the night was already a thing of the past. Sinclair sat by the side of his wife, to whose cheeks the color had all come back; and Sally Johnson lay in her berth, faint still, but able to give an occasional smile to Foster. In the station on the Missouri the reporters were gathered about the happy superintendent, smoking his cigars, and filling their note-books with items. In Denver, their brethren would gladly have done the same, but Watkins failed to gratify them. He was a man of few words. When the train had gone, and a friend remarked: "Hope they'll get through all right, now," he simply said: "Yes, likely. Two shots don't 'most always go in the same hole." Then he went to the telegraph instrument. In a few minutes he could have told a story as wild as a Norse *saga,* but what he said, when Denver had responded, was only—

"No. 17, fifty-five minutes late."

JAUNE D'ANTIMOINE

BY THOMAS ALLIBONE JANVIER

Thomas Allibone Janvier (born in Philadelphia in 1849) began work as a journalist in his native city in 1870. In 1881 he went to spend several years in Colorado, and New and Old Mexico—sojourns which left their impression upon his literary work. A well-known writer of short stories, Janvier is especially skilled in the delineation of the picturesque foreign life of New York.

JAUNE D'ANTIMOINE

BY THOMAS ALLIBONE JANVIER

DOWN Greenwich way—that is to say, about in the heart of the city of New York—in a room with a glaring south light that made even the thought of painting in it send shivers all over you, Jaune d'Antimoine lived and labored in the service of Art.

By all odds, it was the very worst room in the whole building; and that was precisely the reason why Jaune d'Antimoine had chosen it, for the rent was next to nothing: he would have preferred a room that rented for even less. It certainly was a forlorn-looking place. There was no furniture in it worth speaking of; it was cheerless, desolate. A lot of studies of animals were stuck against the walls, and a couple of finished pictures—a lioness with her cubs, and a span of stunning draught-horses—stood in one corner, frameless. There was good work in the studies, and the pictures really were capital—a fact that Jaune himself recognized, and that made him feel all the more dismal because they so persistently remained unsold. Indeed, this animal painter was having a pretty hard time of it, and as he sat there day after day in the shocking light, doing honest work and getting no return for it, he could not help growing desperately blue.

But to-day Jaune d'Antimoine was not blue, for of a sudden he had come to be stayed by a lofty purpose and upheld by a high resolve: and his purpose and resolve were that within one month's time he would gain for himself a new suit of clothes! There were several excellent reasons which together served to fortify him in his exalted resolution. The most careless observer could not fail to perceive that the clothes which he wore—and which were incomparably superior to certain others which he possessed, but did not wear—were sadly shabby; and Vandyke Brown had asked him to be best man at his wedding; and further—and this was the strongest reason of all—Jaune d'Antimoine longed, from the very depths of his soul, to make himself pleasing in the eyes of Rose Carthame.

How she managed it none but herself knew; but this charming young person, although the daughter of a widowly exile of France who made an uncertain living by letting lodgings in the region between south and west of Washington Square, always managed to dress herself delightfully. It is true that feminine analysis might reveal the fact that the materials of which her gowns were made were of the cheapest product of the loom; yet was feminine envy aroused—yea, even in the dignified portion of Fifth Avenue that lies not south but north of Washington Square—by the undeniable style of these same gowns, and by their charming accord with the stylish gait and air of the trig little body who wore them. Therefore it was that when Monsieur Jaune graciously was permitted to accompany Mademoiselle Rose in her jaunts into the grand quarter of the town, the propriety of her garments and the impropriety of his own brought a sense of desolation upon his spirit and a great heaviness upon his loyal heart.

For Jaune loved Rose absolutely to distraction. To say that he would have laid his coat in the mud for her to walk over does not—the condition of the coat being remembered—imply a very superior sort of devotion. He would have done more than this; he would have laid himself in the mud, and most gladly, that he might have preserved from contamination her single pair of nice shoes. Even a cool and unprejudiced person, being permitted to see these shoes—and he certainly would have been, for Rose made anything but a mystery of them—would have declared that such gallant sacrifice was well bestowed.

The ardor of Jaune's passion was increased—as has been common in love matters ever since the world began—by the knowledge that he had a rival; and this rival was a most dangerous rival, being none other than Madame Carthame's second-story-front lodger, the Count Siccatif de Courtray. Simply to be the second-story-front lodger carries with it a most notable distinction in a lodging-house; but to be that and a count too was a combination of splendors that placed Jaune's rival on a social pinnacle and kept him there. Not that counts are rare in the region between west and south of Washington Square; on the contrary, they are rather astonishingly plentiful. But the sort of count who is very rare indeed there is the count who pays his way as he goes along. Now, in the matter of payments, at least so far as Madame Carthame was concerned, the Count Siccatif de Courtray was exemplary.

That there was something of a mystery about this nobleman was undeniable. Among other things, he had stated that he was a relative of the Siccatifs of Harlem—the old family established here in New Amsterdam in the early days of the Dutch Colony. Persons disposed to comment invidiously upon this asserted relationship, and such there were, did not fail to draw attention to the fact that the Harlem Siccatifs, without exception, were fair, while the Count Siccatif de Courtray was strikingly dark; and to the further fact that, if the distinguished American family really was akin to the Count, its several members were most harmoniously agreed to give him the cold shoulder. With these malicious whisperings, however, Madame Carthame did not concern herself. She was content, more than content, to take the Count as he was, and at his own valuation. That he was a proscribed Bonapartist, as he declared himself to be, seemed to her a reasonable and entirely credible statement; and it certainly had the effect of creating about him a halo of romance. Though not proscribed, Madame Carthame herself was a Bonapartist, and a most ardent one; a fact, it may be observed, concerning which the Count assured himself prior to the avowal of his own political convictions. When, on the 20th of April, he came home wearing a cluster of violets in his buttonhole, and bearing also a bunch of these imperial flowers for Madame Carthame, and with the presentation confessed his own imperialistic faith and touched gloomily upon the sorry reward that it had brought him—when this event occurred, Madame Carthame's kindly feelings toward her second-floor lodger were resolved into an abiding faith and high esteem. It was upon this auspicious day that the conviction took firm root in her mind that the Count Siccatif de Courtray was the heaven-sent husband for her daughter Rose.

That Rose approved this ambitious matrimonial project of her mother's was a matter open to doubt; at least her conduct was such that two diametrically opposite views were entertained in regard to her intentions. On the one hand, Madame Carthame and the Count Siccatif de Courtray believed that she had made up her mind to live in her mother's own second-story front and be a countess. On the other hand, Jaune d'Antimoine, whose wish, perhaps, was father to his thought, believed that she would not do anything of the sort. Jaune gladly would have believed, also, that she cherished matrimonial intentions in quite a different, namely, an artistic, direction; but he was a modest young fellow, and suffered his hopes to be greatly diluted by his fears. And, in truth, the conduct of Rose was so perplexing, at times so atrociously exasperating, that a person much more deeply versed in women's ways than this young painter was, very well might have been puzzled hopelessly; for if ever a born flirt came out of France, that flirt was Rose Carthame.

Of one thing, however, Jaune was convinced: that unless something of a positive nature was done, and done speedily, for the improvement of his outward man, his chance of success was gone forever. Already, Madame Carthame eyed his seedy garments askance; already, for Rose had admitted the truth of his suspicions in this dismal direction, Madame Carthame had instituted most unfavorable comparisons between his own chronic shabbiness and the no less chronic splendor of the Count Siccatif de Courtray. Therefore, it came to pass—out of his abstract need for presentable habiliments, out of his desire to appear in creditable form at Vandyke Brown's wedding, and, more than all else, out of his love for Rose—that Jaune d'Antimoine registered a mighty oath before high heaven that within a month's time a new suit of clothes should be his!

Yet the chances are that he would have gone down Christopher Street to the North River, and still further down, even into a watery grave—as he very frequently thought of doing during this melancholy period of his existence—had not his fortunes suddenly been irradiated by the birth in his mind of a happy thought. It came to him in this wise: He was standing drearily in front of a ready-made clothing store on Broadway, sadly contemplating a wooden figure clad in precisely the morning suit for which his soul panted, when suddenly something gave him a whack in the back. Turning sharply, and making use of an exclamation not to be found in the French dictionaries compiled for the use of young ladies' boarding-schools, he perceived a wooden framework, from the lower end of which protruded the legs of a man. From a cleft in the upper portion of the framework came the apologetic utterance, "Didn't mean ter hit yer, boss," and then the structure moved slowly away through the throng. Over its four sides, he observed, were blazoned announcements of the excellences of the garments manufactured by the very clothing establishment in front of which he stood.

The thought came idly into his mind that this method of advertising was clumsy, and not especially effective; followed by the further thought that a much better plan would be to set agoing upon the streets a really gentlemanly-looking man, clad in the best garments that the tailoring people manufactured—while a handsome sign upon the man's back, or a silken banner proudly borne aloft, should tell where the clothes were made, and how, for two weeks only, clothes equally excellent could be bought there at a tremendous sacrifice. And then came into his mind the great thought of his life: he would disguise himself by changing his blond hair and beard to gray, and by wearing dark eye-glasses, and thus disguised he would be that man! Detection he believed to be impossible, for merely dressing himself in respectable clothes almost would suffice to prevent his recognition by even the nearest of his friends. With that prompt decision which is the sure sign of genius backed by force of character, he paused no longer to consider. He acted. With a firm step he entered the clothing establishment; with dignity demanded a personal interview with its proprietor; with eloquence presented to that personage his scheme.

"You will understand, sare," he said, in conclusion, "that these clothes such as yours see themselves in the best way when they are carried by a man very well made, and who 'as the air *comme il faut*. I 'ave not the custom to say that I am justly that man. But now we talk of *affaires*. Look at me and see!" And so speaking, he drew himself up his full six feet, and turned slowly around. There could not be any question about it: a handsomer, a more distinguished-looking man was not to be found in all New York. With the added dignity of age, his look of distinction would be but increased.

The great head of the great tailoring establishment was visibly affected. Original devices in advertising had been the making of him. He perceived that the device now suggested to him was superior to anything that his own genius had struck out. "It's a pretty good plan," he said, meditatively. "What do you want for carrying it out?"

"For you to serve two weeks, I ask but the clothes I go to wear."

For a moment the tailor paused. In that moment the destinies of Jaune d'Antimoine, of Rose Carthame, of the Count Siccatif de Courtray, hung in the balance. It was life or death. Jaune felt his heart beating like a trip-hammer. There was upon him a feeling of suffocation. The silence seemed interminable; and the longer it lasted, the more did he feel that his chances of success were oozing away, that the crisis of his life was going against him. Darkness, the darkness of desolate despair, settled down upon his soul. Mechanically he felt in his waistcoat pocket for a five-cent piece that he believed to be there—for the stillness, the restful oblivion of the North River were in his mind. His fingers clutched the coin convulsively, thankfully. At least he would not be compelled to walk down Christopher Street to his death: he could pay his way to eternity in the one-horse car. Yet even while the blackness of shattered hope seemed to be closing him in irrevocably, the glad light came again. As the voice of an angel sounded the voice of the tailor; and the words which the tailor spake were these:

"Young man, it's a bargain!"

But the tailor, upon whom Heaven had bestowed shrewdness to an extraordinary degree, perceived in the plan proposed to him higher, more artistic possibilities than had been perceived in it by its inventor. There was a dramatic instinct, an appreciation of surprise, of climax, in this man's mind that he proceeded to apply to the existing situation. With a wave of his hand he banished the suggested sign on the walking advertiser's back, and the suggested silken banner. His plan at once was simpler and more profound. Dressed in the highest style of art, Jaune was to walk Broadway daily between the hours of 11 A. M. and 2 P. M. He was to walk slowly; he was to look searchingly in the faces of all young women of about the age of twenty years; he was to wear, over and above his garments of price, an air of confirmed melancholy. That was all.

"But of the advertisement? 'Ow ——"

"Now, never you mind about the advertisement, young man. Where that is going to come in is my business. But you can just bet your bottom dollar that I don't intend to lose any money on you. All that you have to do is just what I've told you; and to be well dressed, and walk up and down Broadway for three hours every day, and look in all the girls' faces, don't strike me as being the hardest work that you might be set at. Now come along and be measured, and day after to-morrow you shall begin."

As Jaune walked slowly homeward to his dismal studio, he meditated deeply upon the adventure before him. He did not fancy it at all; but it was the means to an end, and he was braced morally to go through with it without flinching. For the chance of winning Rose he would have stormed a battery single-handed; and not a bit more of moral courage would have been needed for such desperate work than was needed for the execution of the bloodless but soul-trying project that he had in hand. For the life and spirit of him, though, he could not see how the tailor was to get any good out of this magnificent masquerading.

In one of the evening papers, about a week later, there appeared a half-column romance that quite took Jaune d'Antimoine's breath away. It began with a reference to the distinguished elderly gentleman who, during the past week, had been seen daily upon Broadway about the hour of noon; who gazed with such intense though respectful curiosity into every young woman's face; who, in the gay crowd, was conspicuous not less by the elegance of his dress than by his air of profound melancholy. Then briefly, but precisely, the sorrowful story of the Marquis de —— ("out of consideration for the nobleman's feelings" the name was withheld) was told: how, the son of a peer of France, he had married, while yet a minor, against the wishes of his stern father; how his young wife and infant daughter had been spirited away by the stern father's orders; how on his death-bed the father had confessed his evil deed to his son, and had told that mother and child had been banished to America, where the mother speedily had died of grief, and where the child, though in ignorance of her noble origin, had been adopted by an enormously rich American, about whom nothing more was known than the fact that he lived in New York. The Marquis, the article stated, now was engaged in searching for his long-lost daughter, and among other means to the desired end had hit upon this—of walking New York's chief thoroughfare in the faith that should he see his child his paternal instinct would reveal to him her identity.

"I calculate that this will rather whoop up public interest in our performance," said the tailor, cheerfully, the next day, as he handed the newspaper containing the pleasing fiction to Jaune. "That's my idea, for a starter. I've got the whole story ready to come out in sections—paid a literary feller twenty dollars to get it up for me. And you be careful to-day when you are interviewed" (Jaune shuddered) "to keep the story up—or" (for Jaune was beginning a remonstrance) "you can keep out of it altogether, if you'd rather. Say you must refuse to talk upon so delicate a subject, or something of that sort. Yes, that's your card. It'll make the mystery greater, you know—and I'll see that the public gets the facts, all the same."

The tailor chuckled, and Jaune was unutterably wretched. He was on the point of throwing up his contract. He opened his mouth to speak the decisive words—and shut it again as the thought came into his mind that his misery must be borne, and borne gallantly, because it was all for the love of Rose.

That day there was no affectation in his air of melancholy. He was profoundly miserable. Faithful to his contract, he looked searchingly upon the many young women of twenty years whom he met; and such of them as were possessors of tender hearts grew very sorrowful at sight of the obvious woe by which he was oppressed. His woe, indeed, was keen, for the newspaper article had had its destined effect, and he was a marked man. People turned to look at him as people had not turned before; it was evident that he was a subject of conversation. Several times he caught broken sentences which he recognized as portions of his supposititious biography. His crowning torture was the assault of the newspaper reporters. They were suave, they were surly, they were insinuatingly sympathetic, they were aggressively peremptory—but all alike were determined to wring from him to the uttermost the details of the sorrow that he never had suffered, of the life that he never had lived. It was a confusing sort of an experience. He began to wonder, at last, whether or not it were possible that he could be somebody else without knowing it; and if it were, in whom, precisely, his identity was vested. Being but a simple-minded young fellow, with no taste whatever for metaphysics, this line of thought was upsetting.

While involved in these perplexing doubts and the crowd at the Fifth Avenue crossing, he was so careless as to step upon the heel of a lady in front of him. And when the lady turned, half angrily, half to receive his profuse apologies, he beheld Mademoiselle Carthame. The face of this young person wore an expression made up of not less than three conflicting emotions: of resentment of the assault upon the heel of her one pair of good shoes, of friendly recognition of the familiar voice, of blank surprise upon perceiving that this voice came from the lips of a total stranger. She looked searchingly upon the smoked glasses, obviously trying to pry into the secret of the hidden eyes. Jaune's blood rushed up into his face, and he realized that detection was imminent. Mercifully, at that moment the crowd opened, and with a bow that hid his face behind his hat he made good his retreat. During the remaining half hour of his walk, he thought no more of metaphysics. The horrid danger of physical discovery from which he had escaped so narrowly filled him with a shuddering alarm. Nor could he banish from his mind the harrowing thought that perhaps, for all his gray hair and painted wrinkles and fine clothes, Rose in truth had recognized him.

That night an irresistible attraction drew him to the Carthame abode. In the little parlor he found the severe Madame Carthame, her adorable daughter, and the offensive Count Siccatif de Courtray. Greatly to his relief, his reception was in the usual form: Madame Carthame conducted herself after the fashion of a well-bred iceberg; Rose endeavored to mitigate the severity of her parent's demeanor by her own affability; the Count, as much as possible, ignored his presence. Jaune could not repress a sigh of relief. She had not recognized him.

But his evening was one of trial. With much vivacity, Rose entertained the little company with an account of her romantic adventure with the French nobleman who had come to America in quest of his lost daughter; for she had read the newspaper story, and had identified its hero with the assailant of her heel. She dwelt with enthusiasm upon the distinguished appearance of the unhappy foreigner; she ventured the suggestion, promptly and sternly checked by her mamma, that she herself might be the lost child; she grew plaintive, and expressed a burning desire to comfort this stricken parent with a daughter's love, and, worst of all, she sat silent, with a far-away look in her charming eyes, and obviously suffered her thoughts to go astray after this handsome Marquis in a fashion that made even the Count Siccatif de Courtray fidget, and that filled the soul of Jaune d'Antimoine with a consuming jealousy—not the less consuming because of the absurd fact that it was jealousy of himself! As he walked home that night through the devious ways of Greenwich to his dismal studio, he seriously entertained the wish that he never had been born.

The next day all the morning papers contained elaborate "interviews" with the Marquis: for each of the several reporters who had been put on the case, believing that he alone had failed to get the facts, and being upheld by a lofty determination that no other reporter should "get a beat on him," had evolved from his own inner consciousness the story that Jaune, for the best of reasons, had refused to tell. The stories thus told, being based upon the original fiction, bore a family resemblance to each other; and as all of them were interesting, they stimulated popular curiosity in regard to their hero to a very high pitch. As the result of them, Jaune found himself the most conspicuous man in New York. During the three hours of his walk he was the centre of an interested crowd. Several benevolent persons stopped to tell him of fatherless young women with whom they were acquainted, and to urge upon him the probability that each of these young women was his long-lost child. The representatives of a dozen detective bureaus introduced themselves to him, and made offer of their professional services; a messenger from the chief of police handed him a polite note tendering the services of the department and inviting him to a conference. It was maddening.

But worst of all were his meetings with Rose. As these multiplied, the conviction became irresistible that they were not the result of chance; indeed, her manner made doubt upon this head impossible. At first she gave him only a passing glance, then a glance somewhat longer, then a look of kindly interest, then a long look of sympathy; and at last she bestowed upon him a gentle, almost affectionate, smile that expressed, as plainly as a smile could express, her sorrow for his misery and her readiness to comfort him. In a word, Rose Carthame's conduct simply was outrageous!

The jealous anger which had inflamed Jaune's breast the night before swelled and expanded into a raging passion. He longed to engage in mortal combat this stranger who was alienating the affection that should be his. The element of absurdity in the situation no longer was apparent to him. In truth, as he reasoned, the situation was not absurd. To all intents and purposes he was two people and it was the other one of him, not himself at all, who was winning Rose's interest, perhaps her love. For a moment the thought crossed his mind that he would adjust the difficulty in his own favor by remaining this other person always. But the hard truth confronted him that every time he washed his face he would cease to be the elderly Marquis, with the harder truth that the fabulous wealth with which, as the Marquis, the newspapers had endowed him was too entirely fabulous to serve as a basis for substantial life. And being thus cut off from hope, he fell back upon jealous hatred of himself.

That night the evening paper in which the first mention of the mysterious French nobleman had been made contained an article cleverly contrived to give point to the mystery in its commercial aspect. The fact had been observed, the article declared, that the nobleman's promenade began and ended at a prominent clothing establishment on Broadway; and then followed, in the guise of a contribution toward the clearing up of the mystery, an interview with the proprietor of the establishment in question. However, the interview left the mystery just where it found it, for all that the tailor told was that the Marquis had bought several suits of clothes from him; that he had shown himself to be an exceptionally critical person in the matter of his wearing apparel; that he had expressed repeatedly his entire satisfaction with his purchases. In another portion of the paper was a glaring advertisement, in which the clothing man set forth, in an animated fashion, the cheapness and desirability of "The Marquis Suit"—a suit that "might be seen to advantage on the person of the afflicted French nobleman now in our midst who had honored it with his approval, and in whose honor it had been named." Upon reading the newspaper narrative and its advertisement pendant, Jaune groaned aloud. He was oppressed by a horror of discovery, and here, as it seemed to him in his morbidly nervous condition, was a clew to his duplex identity sufficiently obvious to be apparent even to a detective.

The Count Siccatif de Courtray, as has been intimated, went so far as to fidget while listening to Mademoiselle Carthame's vivacious description of her encounter with the handsome Marquis. Being regaled during the ensuing evening with a very similar narrative—a materially modified version of the events which had aroused in so lively a manner the passion of jealousy in the breast of Jaune d'Antimoine—the Count ceased merely to fidget and became the prey to a serious anxiety. He determined that the next day, quite unobtrusively, he would observe Mademoiselle Carthame in her relations with this unknown but dangerously fascinating nobleman; and also that he would give some attention to the nobleman himself. This secondary purpose was strengthened the next morning, while the Count was engaged with his coffee and newspaper, by his finding in the "Courrier des Etats-Unis" a translation of the paragraph stating the curious fact that the daily walk of the Marquis began and ended at the Broadway tailor shop.

Having finished his breakfast, the Count leisurely betook himself to Broadway. As he slowly strolled eastward, he observed on the other side of the street Jaune d'Antimoine, in his desperately shabby raiment, hurriedly walking eastward also. The Count murmured a brief panegyric upon M. d'Antimoine, in which the words "cet animal" alone were distinguishable. They were near Broadway at this moment, and to the Count's surprise M. d'Antimoine entered the clothing establishment from which the Marquis departed upon his daily walk. Could it be possible, he thought, that fortune had smiled upon the young artist, and that he was about to purchase a new suit of clothes? The Count entertained the charitable hope that such could not be the case.

It was the Count's purpose, in order that he might follow also the movements of Mademoiselle Carthame, to follow the Marquis from the beginning to the end of his promenade. He set himself, therefore, to watching closely for the appearance of the grief-stricken foreigner, moving carelessly the while from one shop-window to another that commanded a view of the field. At the end of half an hour, when the Count was beginning to think that the object of his solicitude was a myth, out from the broad portal of the clothing establishment came the Marquis in all his glory—more glorious, in truth, than Solomon, and more melancholy than the melancholy Jaques. And yet for an instant the Count Siccatif de Courtray was possessed by the absurd fancy that this stately personage was Jaune d'Antimoine! Truly, here was the same tall, handsome figure, the same easy, elegant carriage, the same cut of hair and beard. But the resemblance went no further, for beard and hair were gray almost to whiteness, the face was pale and old, and the clothes, so far from being desperately seedy, were more resplendent even than the Count's own. No, the thought was incredible, preposterous, and yet the Count could not discharge it from his mind. He stamped his foot savagely; this mystery was becoming more interesting than pleasing.

In the crowd that the Marquis drew in his wake, as

he slowly, sadly sauntered up Broadway, the Count had no difficulty in following him unobserved. The situation was that of the previous day, only it was intensified, and therefore, to its hero, the more horrible. The benevolent people with stray fatherless young women to dispose of were out in greater force; the detectives were more aggressive; the newspaper people were more persistent; the general public was more keenly interested in the whole performance. And Rose —most dreadful of all—was more outrageous than ever! The Count grew almost green with rage during the three hours that he was a witness of this young woman's scandalous conduct. A dozen times she met the Marquis in the course of his walk, and each time that she met him she greeted him with a yet more tender smile. A curious fact that at first surprised, then puzzled, then comforted the Count was the very obvious annoyance which these flattering attentions caused their recipient. Evidently, he persistently endeavored to evade the meetings which Rose as persistently and more successfully endeavored to force upon him. Within the scope of M. de Courtary's comprehension only one reason seemed to be sufficient to explain the determination on the part of the Marquis to resist the advances of a singularly attractive young woman, whose good disposition toward him was so conspicuously, though so irregularly, manifested: a fear of recognition. And this reason adjusted itself in a striking manner to the queer notion that had come into his mind that the Marquis was an ideal creation whose reality was Jeaune d'Antimoine. The thought was absurd, irrational, but it grew stronger and stronger within him—and became an assured conviction when, shortly after the promenade of the Marquis had ended, Jaune came forth from the clothing store in his normal condition of shabbiness and youth. The Count was not in all respects a praiseworthy person, but among his vices was not that of stupidity. Without any very tremendous mental effort he grasped the fact that his rival had sold himself into bondage as a walking advertisement, and, knowing this, a righteous exultation filled his soul. Jaune's destiny, so far as Mademoiselle Carthame was concerned, he felt was in his power: and he was perplexed by no nice doubts as to the purpose to which the power that he had gained should be applied.

Untroubled by the knowledge that his secret was discovered, Jaune entered upon the last day of his martyrdom. It was the most agonizing day of all. The benevolent persons, the reporters, the detectives, the crowd surging about him, drove him almost to madness. He walked as one dazed. And above and over all he was possessed by a frenzy of jealousy that came of the offensively friendly smiles which Rose bestowed upon him as she forced meetings upon him again and again. It was with difficulty that he restrained himself from laying violent hands upon this bogus Marquis who falsely and infamously had beguiled away from him the love for which he gladly would have given his life. Only the blood of his despicable rival, he felt, would satisfy him. He longed to find himself with a sword in his hand on a bit of smooth turf, and the villanous Marquis over against him, ready to be run through. The thought was so delightful, so animating, that involuntarily he made a lunge—and had to apologize confusedly to an elderly gentleman whom he had poked in the back with his umbrella.

At last the three hours of torture, the last of his two weeks of hateful servitude, came to an end. Pale beneath his false paleness, haggard beyond his false haggardness of age, he entered the clothing store and once more was himself. With a gladness unspeakable he washed off his wrinkles and washed out the gray from his hair and beard; with a sense of infinite satisfaction that, a fortnight earlier, he would not have believed possible, he resumed his shabby old clothes. Had he chosen to do so, he might have walked away in the new and magnificent apparel which he now fairly had earned; but just at present his loathing for these fine garments was beyond all words.

The tailor fain would have had the masquerade continue longer, for, as he frankly stated, "The Marquis Suit" was having a tremendous sale. But Jaune was deaf not only to the tailor's blandishments, but to his offers of substantial cash. "Not for the millions would I be in this part of the Marquis for one day yet more," he said firmly. And he added, "I trust to you in honor, sare, that not never shall my name be spoken in this affair."

"Couldn't speak it if I wanted to, my dear boy. It's a mystery to me how you're able to say it yourself! Well, I'd like you to run the 'Marquis' for another week; but if you won't, you won't, I suppose, so there's an end of it. I'm sorry you haven't enjoyed it. I have. It's been as good a thing as I ever got hold of. Now give me your address and I'll have your clothes sent to you. Don't you want some more? I don't mind letting you have a regular outfit if you want it. One good turn, you know—and you've done me a good turn, and that's a fact."

But Jaune declined this liberal offer, and declined also to leave his address, which would have involved a revelation of his name. It was a comfort to him to know that his name was safe—a great comfort. So the garments of the forever departed Marquis were put up in a big bundle, and Jaune journeyed homeward to his studio in Greenwich—bearing his sheaves with him—in a Bleecker Street car.

"Well, you are a cheeky beggar, d'Antimoine," said Vandyke Brown, cheerfully, the next morning, as he came into Jaune's studio with a newspaper in his hand. "So you are the Marquis who has been setting the town wild for the last week, eh? And whom did you bet with? And what started you in such a crazy performance, anyway? Tell me all about it. It's as funny—Good heavens! d'Antimoine, what's the matter? Are you ill?" For Jaune had grown deathly pale and was gasping.

"I do not know of what it is that you talk," he answered, with a great effort.

"Oh, come now, that's too thin, you know. Why, here's a whole column about it, telling how you made a bet with somebody that you could set all the town to talking about you, and yet do it all in such a clever disguise that nobody would know who you really were, not even your most intimate friends. And I should say that you had won handsomely. Why, I've seen you on Broadway a dozen times myself this last week, and I never had the remotest suspicion that the Marquis was you. I must say, though," continued Brown, reflectively, and looking closely at Jaune, "that it was stupid of me. I did think that you had a familiar sort of look; and once, I remember, it did occur to me that you looked astonishingly like yourself. It—it was the clothes, you see, that threw me out. Where ever did you get such a stunning rig? I don't believe that I'd have known you dressed like that, even if you hadn't been gray and wrinkled. But tell me all about it, old man. It must have been jolly fun!"

"Fun!" groaned Jaune; "it was the despair!" And then, his heart being very full and his longing for sympathy overpowering, Jaune told Brown the whole story. "But what is this of one bet, my dear Van," he concluded, "I do not of the least know."

"Well, here it all is in the paper, anyway. Calls you 'a distinguished animal-painter,' and alludes to your 'strikingly vigorous "Lioness and Cubs" and powerful "Dray Horses" at the last spring exhibition of the Society of American Artists.' Must be somebody who knows you, you see, and somebody who means well by you, too. There's nothing at all about your being an advertisement; indeed, there's nothing in the story but a good joke, of which you are the hero. It's an eccentric sort of heroism, to be sure; but then, for some unknown reason, people never seem to believe that artists are rational human beings, so your eccentricity will do you no harm. And it's no end of an advertisement for you. Whoever wrote it meant well by you. And, by Jove! I know who it is! It's little Conté Crayon. He's a good-hearted little beggar, and he likes you ever so much, for I've heard him say so; but how he ever got hold of the story, and especially of such a jolly version of it, I don't see."

At this moment, by a pleasing coincidence, Conté Crayon himself appeared with the desired explanation. "You see," he said, "that beast of a Siccatif de Courtray hunted me up yesterday and told me the yarn about you and the slop-shop man. He wanted me to write it up and publish it, 'as a joke,' he said; but it was clear enough that he was in ugly earnest about it. And so, you see, I had to rush it into print in the way I chose to tell it—which won't do you a bit of harm, d'Antimoine—in order to head him off. The blackguard meant to get you into a mess, and if I'd hung fire he'd have told somebody else about it, and had the real story published. Of course, you know, there's nothing in the real story that you need be ashamed of; but if it had been told, you certainly would have been laughed at, and nasty people would have said nasty things about it. And as there wasn't any time to lose, I had to print it first and then come here and explain matters afterward. And what I've got to say is this: Just you cheek it out and say that it *was* a bet, and that you won it! Brown and I will back you up in it, and so will the slop-shop man. I've been to see him this morning, and he is so pleased with the way that 'The Marquis Suit' is selling, and with the extra free advertisement that he has got out of my article, that he's promised to adopt the bet version in his advertisement in all the papers. He is going to advertise that The Marquis Suit is so called because everybody who wears it looks like a marquis—just as you did. This cuts the ground right from under the Count's feet, you see; for nobody'd believe him on his oath if they could help it.

"And now I must clear out. I've got a race at Jerome Park at two o'clock. It's all right, d'Antimoine; I assure you it's all right—but I should advise you to punch the Count's head, all the same."

Vandyke Brown thought it was all right, too, as he talked the matter over with Jaune after little Conté Crayon had gone. But Jaune refused to be comforted. So far as the public was concerned he admitted that Conté Crayon's story had saved him, but he was oppressed by a great dread of what might be the effect of the truth upon Rose. For Juane d'Antimoine was too honest a gentleman even to think of deceiving his mistress. He must tell her the whole story, without reserve, and as she approved or disapproved of what he had done must his hopes of happiness live or die.

"Better have it out with her to-day, and be done with it," counseled Brown.

"Ah! it is well for you to speak of a 'urry, my good

Van; but it is not you who go to execute your life. No, I 'ave not the force to go to-day. To-day I go to make a long walk. Then this night I sleep well. Tomorrow, in the morning, do I go to affront my destiny." And from this resolution Jaune was not to be moved.

Yet it was an unfortunate resolution, for it gave the Count Siccatif de Courtray time and opportunity for a flank movement. In the Count's breast rage and astonishment contended for the mastery as he contemplated the curious miscarriage of his newspaper assault. He had chosen this line of attack partly because his modesty counseled him to keep his own personality in the background, partly because the wider the publicity of his rival's disgrace the more complete would that disgrace be. But as his newspaper ally failed him, he took the campaign into his own hands; that is to say, he hurried to tell the true story, and a good deal more than the true story, to Rose and Madame Carthame.

Concerning its effect upon Rose, he was in doubt; but its effect upon Madame Carthame was all that he could desire. This severe person instantly took the cue that the Count dexterously gave her by affecting to palliate Jaune's erratic conduct. He urged that, inasmuch as M. d'Antimoine was a conspicuous failure as an artist, for him to engage himself to a tailor as a walking advertisement, so far from being a disgrace to him, was greatly to his credit. And Madame Carthame promptly and vehemently asserted that it wasn't. She refused to regard what he had done in any other light than that of a crime. She declared that never again should his offensive form darken her door. Solemnly she forbade Rose from recognizing him when in the future they should chance to meet. And then she abated her severity to the extent of thanking the Count with tears in her eyes for the service that he had done her in tearing off this viper's disguise. Naturally, the Count was charmed by Madame Carthame's energetic indignation. He perceived that his unselfish investigations of the actions of Monsieur Jaune were bearing excellent fruit. Already, as he believed, the way toward his own happiness was smooth and clear. As the Count retired from this successful conference, he laughed softly to himself: nor did he pause in his unobtrusive mirth to reflect that those laugh best who laugh last.

And thus it came to pass that when Jaune, refreshed by sound slumber and a little cheered by hope, presented himself the next morning at Madame Carthame's gates, fate decreed that Rose herself should open the gates to him—in response to his ring—and in her own proper person should tell him that she was not at home. In explanation of this obviously inexact statement she announced to him her mother's stern decree. Being but a giddy young person, however, and one somewhat lacking in fit reverence of maternal authority, she added, on her own account, that in half an hour or so she was going up Fourth Street to the Gansevoort market, and that Fourth Street was a public thoroughfare, upon which M. d'Antimoine also had a perfect right to walk.

In the course of this walk, while Jaune gallantly carried the market-basket, the story that Rose already had heard from the Count Siccatif de Courtray was told again—but told with a very different coloring. For Mademoiselle Carthame clearly perceived how great the sacrifice had been that Jaune had made for her sake, and how bravely, because it was for her sake, it had been made. There was real pathos in his voice; once or twice he nearly broke down. Possibly it was because she did not wish him to see her eyes that she manifested so marked an interest in the shop windows as they walked along.

"And so that adorable Marquis was unreal?" queried Mademoiselle Carthame sadly, and somewhat irrelevantly, when Jaune had told her all.

"He was not adorable. He was a disgusting beast!" replied M. d'Antimoine savagely.

"I—I loved him!" answered Rose, turning upon Jaune, at last, her black eyes. They did not sparkle, as was their wont, but they were wonderfully lustrous and soft.

Jaune looked down into the market-basket and groaned.

"And—and I love him still. I think, I—I hope, that he will live always in my heart."

The voice of Mademoiselle Carthame trembled, and her hand grasped very tightly the bag of carrots that they had been unable to make a place for in the basket: they were coming back from the market now.

Jaune did not look up. For the life of him he could not keep back a sob. It was bitter hard, he felt, that out of his love for Rose should come love's wreck; and harder yet that the rival who had stolen her from him should be himself! Through the mist of his misery he seemed to hear Rose laughing softly. Could this be so? Then, indeed, was the capstone set upon his grief!

"Jaune!"

He started, and so violently that a cabbage, with half a dozen potatoes after it, sprang out of the basket and rolled along the pavement at her feet. His bowed head rose with a jerk, and their eyes met full. In hers there was a look half mocking, that as he gazed changed into tenderness; into his, as he saw the change and perceived its meaning, there came a look of glad delight.

"As though you could deceive *me!* Why, of course, I knew you from the very first!"

Then they collected the potatoes and the cabbage and walked slowly on, and great happiness was in their hearts.

The world was a brighter world for Jaune d'Antimoine when he gave into Rose's hand the market-basket on her own doorstep, and turned reluctantly away. But there still were clouds in it. Rose had admitted that two things were necessary before getting married could be thought of at all seriously: something must be done by which the nose of the Count Siccatif de Courtray would be disjointed; something must be done to assure Madame Carthame that M. d'Antimoine, in some fashion at least a little removed from semi-starvation, could maintain a wife.

It was certain that until these things were accomplished Madame Carthame's lofty resolution to transform her daughter into a countess, and her stern disapprobation of Jaune as a social outcast, never would be overcome.

As events turned out, it was the second of these requirements that was fulfilled first.

Mr. Badger Brush was a very rich sporting man, whose tastes were horsey, but whose heart was in the right place. It was his delight to make or to back extraordinary wagers. Few New Yorkers have forgotten that very queer bet of his that resulted in putting high hats on all the Broadway telegraph poles. When Mr. Brush read the story of Jaune d'Antimoine's wager, therefore, he was greatly pleased with its originality; and when, later in the day, he fell in with little Conté Crayon at Jerome Park, he pressed that ingenious young newspaper man for additional particulars. And knowing the whereabouts of Mr. Badger Brush's heart, Conté Crayon did not hesitate to tell the whole story—winding up with the pointed suggestion that inasmuch as the hero of the story was an animal-painter of decided, though as yet unrecognized, ability, Mr. Brush could not do better than manifest his interest in a practical way by giving him an order. The sporting man rose to the suggestion with a commendable promptness and warmth.

"I don't care a blank if it wasn't a bet," he said, heartily. "That young man has pluck, and he deserves to be encouraged. I'll go down and see him to-morrow, and I'll order a portrait of Celeripes; a life-size, thousand-dollar portrait, by Jove! Celeripes deserves it, after the pot of money he brought me at Long Branch, and your friend deserves it too. And I have some other horses that I want painted, and some dogs—he paints dogs, I suppose? And I know a lot of other fellows who ought to have their horses painted, and I'll start them along at him. I'll give him all the painting he can handle in the next ten years. For it *was* a bet, you see, after all. Didn't he back his cleverness in disguise against the wits of the whole town? And didn't the slop-shop man put up the stakes? And didn't he just win in a canter? I should rather think he did! Of course it was a bet, and a mighty good one at that. Gad! Crayon, it's the best thing that's been done in New York for years. It's what I call first-class cheek. I couldn't have done it better, sir, myself!"

Thus it fell out that half an hour after Jaune got back to his studio from that memorable walk to the Gansevoort market, he had the breath-taking-away felicity of booking a thousand-dollar order, and of receiving such obviously trustworthy assurances of many more orders that his wildest hopes of success in a moment were resolved into substantial realities. When he was alone again he certainly would have believed that he had been dreaming but for the fact that Mr. Badger Brush had insisted upon paying half the price of the picture down in advance; for whatever this good-hearted, horsey gentleman did, he did thoroughly well. The crisp notes, more than Jaune ever had seen together in all his life before—save once, when he took a dealer's check for ten dollars to a bank and looked through the wire screen while the bank man haughtily cashed it—lay on the table where Mr. Badger Brush had left them; and their blissful presence proved that his happiness was not a dream, but real.

From the corner into which, loathingly, he had kicked it, he drew forth the bundle containing "The Marquis Suit." With a certain solemnity he resumed these garments of price in which he had suffered so much torture, and, being clad, boldly presented himself to Madame Carthame with a formal demand for her daughter's hand. And in view of the sudden and prodigious change that had come over M. d'Antimoine's fortunes, almost was Madame Carthame persuaded that the matrimonial plans which she had laid out for her daughter might be changed. Yet did she hesitate before announcing that their Median and Persian quality might be questioned: for the hope that Rose might be a countess lay very close to Madame Carthame's heart. However, her determination was shaken, which was a great point gained.

And presently—for Jaune's star was triumphantly in the ascendant—it was completely destroyed. The instrument of its destruction was Mr. Badger Brush's groom, Stumps.

Stumps was a talkative creature, and whenever he came down to Jaune's studio, as he very often did while the portrait of Celeripes was in progress, he had a good deal to say over and above the message that he brought, as to when the horse would be free for the next "sitting" in the paddock at Mr. Brush's country place, where Jaune was painting him. And Jaune, who was one of the best-natured of mortals, usually suffered Stumps to talk away until he was tired.

"You might knock me down with a wisp of hay, you might, indeed, sir," said the groom one morning a fortnight after the picture had been begun—the day but one, in fact, before that set for Vandyke Brown's wedding. "Yes, sir," he continued, "with a wisp of hay, or even with a single straw! Here I've been face to face with my own father's brother's son, and I've put out my hand to him, and he's turned away short and pretended as he didn't know me and went off! And they tells me at his lodgin', for I follered him a-purpose to find him out, that he calls hisself a Frenchman, and says as how his name—which it is Stumps, and always has been—is Count Sikativ de Cortray!"

Jaune's palette and brushes fell to the floor with a crash. "Is it posseeble that you do tell me of the Comte Siccatif de Courtray? Are you then sure that you do not make one grand meestake? Is it 'im truly that you 'ave seen?"

"Him, sir? Why, in course it's him. Haven't I knowed him ever since he wasn't higher'n a hoss's fetlock? Don't I tell you as me and him's fust cousins? Him? In course it's him—the gump!"

"Then, my good Stump, you will now tell me of this wonder all."

It's not much there is to tell, sir, and wat there is

isn't to his credit. His father was my father's brother. My father was in the hoss line out Saint John's Wood way—in Lunnon, you know, sir—and his father lived in our street and was a swell barber. Uncle'd married a French young 'ooman as was dressmakin' and had been a lady's maid; it's along of his mother that he gets his Frenchness, you see. He was an only son, he was, and they made a lot of him—dressin' him fine, and coddlin' him, and sendin' him to school like anythink. Uncle was doin' a big trade, you see, and makin' money fast. Then, when he was a young fellow of twenty or so, and after he'd served at barberin' with his father for a couple of years, he took service with young Lord Cadmium—as had his 'cousin' livin' in a willa down our way and came to uncle's to be barbered frequent. And wen Lord Cadmium went sudden-like over to the Continent, wishin' to give his 'cousin' the slip, havin' got sick of her, Stumps he went along. That's a matter of ten years ago, sir, and blessed if I've laid eyes on him since until I seed him here in New York to-day. Uncle died better'n two year back, aunt havin' died fust, and he left a tidy pot of money to Stumps; and I did hear that Stumps, who'd been barberin' in Paris, had giv' up work when he got the cash and had set up to be a gentleman, but I didn't know as he'd set up to be a count too. The like of this I never did see!"

"And you are then sure, you will swear, my good Stump, that this are the same man?"

"Swear, sir! I'll swear to it 'igh and low and all day long! But I must be goin', sir. You will please to remember that the hoss will be ready for you at ten o'clock to-morrow mornin', sharp."

Jaune rushed down to Vandyke Brown's studio for counsel as to whether he should go at once to the Count's lodgings and charge him with fraud to his face, or should make the charge first to Madame Carthame. But Brown was out. Nor was he in old Madder's studio, though about this time he was much more likely to be there than in his own. Old Madder said that Brown had taken Rose over to Brooklyn, to the Philharmonic, and he believed that they were going to dinner at Mr. Mangan Brown's afterward, and would not be in till late; and he seemed to be pretty grumpy about it.

Jaune fumed and fretted away what was left of the afternoon and a good part of the evening. At last Brown and Rose came home, and Brown, with a very bad grace, suffered himself to be led away from old Madder's threshold. To do him justice, though, when he had heard the story that Jaune had to tell, he was all eagerness. His advice was to make the attack instantly; and without more words they set off together, walking briskly through the chill air of the late October night.

As they were passing along Macdougal Street—midway between Bleecker and Houston, in front of the row of pretty houses with verandas all over their fronts—Jaune suddenly gripped Brown's arm and drew him quickly within one of the little front yards and into the shadow of the high iron steps.

"Look!" he said.

On the other side of the street, in the light of the gas-lamp that stands in the centre of the block, was the Count himself. For the moment that he was beneath the gas-lamp they saw him clearly. His face was set in an expression of gloomy sternness; his rapid, resolute walk indicated a definite purpose; he carried a little bundle in his hand.

"What a villain he looks!" whispered Brown. "Upon my soul, I do believe that he is going to murder somebody!"

"Ah, the vile animal! We will pursue," answered Jaune, also in a whisper.

Giving the Count a start of a dozen house fronts, they stepped out from their retreat and followed him cautiously. He walked quickly up Macdougal Street until he came out on Washington Square. For a moment he paused—by Sam Wah's laundry—and then turned sharply to the left along Fourth Street. At a good pace he crossed Sixth Avenue, swung around the curve that Fourth Street makes before beginning its preposterous journey northward, went on past the three little balconied houses whose fronts are on Washington Place, and so came out upon the open space where Washington Place and Barrow Street and Fourth Street all run into each other. It was hereabout that Wouter Van Twiller had his tobacco farm a trifle less than two centuries ago.

The Count stopped, as though to get his bearings. and while they waited for him to go on Brown nudged Jaune to look at the delightfully picturesque frame house, set in a deep niche between two high brick houses, with the wooden stair elbowing up its outside to its third story. It came out wonderfully well in the moonlight, but Jaune was too much excited even to glance at it.

At the next group of corners—where Fourth Street crosses Grove and Christopher Streets at the point where they go sidling into each other along the slanting lines of the little park—the Count halted again. Evidently, the exceeding crookedness of Greenwich Village puzzled him—as well it might. Presently a Christopher Street car came along and set him straight; and thus guided, he started resolutely westward, as though heading for the river.

"Is it posseeble that he goes 'imself to drown?" suggested d'Antimoine.

"No such good luck," Brown answered shortly.

Coming out on what used to be called "the Strand" —West Street they call it now—the Count bore away from the lights of the Hoboken Ferry and from the guarded docks of the White Star and Anchor lines of steamers, skirted the fleet of oyster boats, and so came to the quiet pier at the foot of Perry Street, where the hay barges unload. This pier runs a long way out into the river, for it is a part of what was called Sapokamikke Point in Indian times. The Count stopped and looked cautiously around him, but his pursuers promptly crouched behind a dray and became invisible.

As he went out upon the pier, though, they were close upon his heels—walking noiselessly over the loose hay and keeping themselves hidden in the shadow of the barges and behind the piles of bales. At the very end of the pier he stopped. Jaune and Brown, hidden by a bale of hay, were within five feet of him. Their hearts were beating tremendously. There had been no tragical purpose in their minds when they started, but it certainly did look now as though they were in the thick of a tragedy. In the crisp October moonlight the Count's face shone deathly pale; they could see the fingers of his right hand working convulsively; they could hear his labored breathing. Below him was the deep, black water, lapping and rippling as the swirl of the tide sucked it into the dark, slimy recesses among the piles. In its bosom was horrible death. The Count stepped out upon the very edge of the pier and gazed wofully down upon the swelling waters. His dismal purpose no longer admitted of doubt. Involuntarily the two followed him until they were close at his back. Little as they loved him, they could not suffer him thus despairingly to leave the world.

But instead of casting himself over the edge of the pier, the Count slowly raised the hand that held the bundle, with the obvious intention of throwing the bundle and whatever was the evil secret that it contained into the river's depths. Quick as thought, Brown had seized the upraised arm, and Jaune had settled upon the other arm with a grip like a vise.

"No, you don't, my boy! Let's see what it is before it goes overboard. Hold fast, d'Antimoine!"

The Count struggled furiously, but hopelessly.

"It's no use. You may as well give in, Stumps!"

As Brown uttered this name the Count suddenly

became limp. The little bundle that he had clutched tightly through the struggle dropped from his nerveless hand, and fell open as it struck the ground. And there, gleaming in the moonlight, a brace of razors, a stubby brush, a stout pair of shears, lay loosely in the folds of a barber's jacket!

And this was the sorry climax to the brilliant romance of the proscribed Bonapartist, the Count Siccatif de Courtray!

Jaune, who was a generous-hearted young fellow, was for setting free his crestfallen rival at once, and so having done with him. Brown took a more statesmanlike view of the situation. "We will let him go after he has owned up to Madame Carthame what a fraud he is," he said. The Count winced when this sentence was pronounced, but he uttered no remonstrance. The shock of the discovery had completely demoralized him.

It was after midnight when they reached Madame Carthame's dwelling, and Rose herself, with her hair done up in curl papers, opened the door for them. When she recognized the three visitors and perceived that the Count was in custody, and at the same moment remembered her curl papers, on her face the gaze of astonishment and the blush of maidenly modesty contended for the right of way.

Madame Carthame fairly was in bed—as was evident from the spirited conversation between herself and her vivacious daughter that was perfectly audible through the folding doors which separated the little parlor from her bedroom. It was evident, also, that she was indisposed to rise. However, her indisposition was overcome and in the course of twenty minutes or so she appeared arrayed in a frigid dignity and a loose wrapper. Rose, meanwhile, had taken off her curl papers, and Jaune regarded her tumbled hair with ecstasy.

The tribunal being assembled, the prisoner was placed at the bar and the trial began. It was an eminently irregular trial, looking at it from a legal point of view, for the verbal evidence all was hearsay. But it also was extra-legal in that it was brief and decisive. Brown gave his testimony in the shape of a repetition of the story that Jaune had told him had been told by Mr. Badger Brush's groom; and when this was concluded, Jaune produced the jacket, razors, shears, and shaving brush, and stated the circumstances under which they had been found. Then the prosecution rested.

Being questioned by the court—that is to say, by Madame Carthame—in his own defence, the Count replied gloomily that he hadn't any. "When I saw that horse fellow," he said, "I knew that I was likely to get into trouble, and that was the reason why I wanted to get rid of these things. And now the game is up. It is all true. I was a barber. I am not a count. My real name is Stumps."

Then it was that Madame Carthame, blissfully ignorant of the fact that she had neglected to remove her nightcap, stood up in her place, with her wrapper gathered about her in a statuesque fashion, and in a tragic tone uttered the single word:

"Sortez!"

And the Count went!

Out, out into the chill and gloom of night went the false Count, never to return; and with him went Madame Carthame's fond hope that her daughter would be a countess, which also was the last barrier in the way of Jaune d'Antimoine's love. Perceiving that the force of fate inexorably was pressing upon her, Madame Carthame—still in her night-cap—bestowed upon Rose and Jaune the maternal blessing in a manner that, even allowing for the nightcap, was both stately and severe.

As at Vandyke Brown's wedding Jaune d'Antimoine was radiantly magnificent in "The Marquis Suit," adding splendor to the ceremony and rendering himself most pleasing in the eyes of Rose Carthame; so, a month later, he was yet more radiant when he wore the famous suit again, in the church of Saint Vincent de Paul, and was himself married.

Conté Crayon brought Mr. Badger Brush down to the wedding, and the groom came too, and the tailor got wind of it and came without being asked—and had to be implored not to work it up into an advertisement, as he very much wanted to do. Mrs. Vandyke Brown, just home from her wedding journey, was the first—after the kiss of Madame Carthame had been sternly bestowed—to kiss the bride; and Mr. Badger Brush irreverently whispered to Conté Crayon that he wished, by gad! he had her chance!

OLE 'STRACTED

BY THOMAS NELSON PAGE

Thomas Nelson Page (born in Oakland, Virginia, April 23, 1853) represents the generation of Southerners who were too young to fight but not to feel during the Civil War. In the middle eighties he published a number of stories in the "Century Magazine" which presented with loving sympathy charming views of the old aristocratic régime that it had become a literary fashion sweepingly to condemn. These tales of courtly ideals on the part of the masters, and affecting loyalty on the side of the slaves, were gathered together and published in 1887 in a volume entitled "In Ole Virginia." "Marse Chan," "Meh Lady," and "Ole 'Stracted," the present selection, are the favorites of the collection.

OLE 'STRACTED

BY THOMAS NELSON PAGE

"AWE, little Ephum! *awe,* little E-phum! ef you don' come 'long heah, boy, an' rock dis chile, I'll buss you haid open!" screamed the high-pitched voice of a woman, breaking the stillness of the summer evening. She had just come to the door of the little cabin, where she was now standing, anxiously scanning the space before her, while a baby's plaintive wail rose and fell within with wearying monotony. The log cabin, set in a gall in the middle of an old field all grown up in sassafras, was not a very inviting-looking place; a few hens loitering about the new hen-house, a brood of half-grown chickens picking in the grass and watching the door, and a runty pig tied to a "stob," were the only signs of thrift; yet the face of the woman cleared up as she gazed about her and afar off, where the gleam of green made a pleasant spot, where the corn grew in the river bottom; for it was her home, and the best of all was she thought it belonged to them.

A rumble of distant thunder caught her ear, and she stepped down and took a well-worn garment from the clothes-line, stretched between two dogwood forks, and having, after a keen glance down the path through the bushes, satisfied herself that no one was in sight,

This story is reprinted, by permission, from the book entitled "In Ole Virginia." Copyright, 1887, by Charles Scribner's Sons.

"Mammy, Ole 'Stracted say you must bring he shut; he say he marster comin' to-night."

"How he say he is?" inquired the woman, with some interest.

"He ain' say—jes say he want he shut. He sutny is comical—he layin' down in de baid." Then, having relieved his mind, Eph went to sleep in the cradle.

" 'Layin' down in de baid?' " quoted the woman to herself as she moved about the room. "I 'ain' nuver hern 'bout dat befo'. Dat sutny is a comical ole man anyways. He say he used to live on dis plantation, an' yit he al'ays talkin' 'bout de gret house an' de fine kerridges dee used to have, an' 'bout he marster comin' to buy him back. De 'ain' nuver been no gret house on dis place, not sence I know nuttin 'bout it, 'sep de overseer house whar dat man live. I heah Ephum say Aunt Dinah tell him de ole house whar used to be on de hill whar dat gret oak-tree is in de pines bu'nt down de year he wuz born, an' he ole marster had to live in de overseer house, an' hit break he heart, an' dee teck all he niggers, an' dat's de way *he* come to blongst to we all; but dat ole man ain' know nuttin 'bout dat house, 'cause hit bu'nt down. I wonder whar he did come from?" she pursued, "an' what he sho' 'nough name? He sholy couldn' been named 'Ole 'Stracted,' jes so; dat ain' no name 'tall. Yit ef he ain' 'stracted, 'tain' nobody is. He ain' even know he own name," she continued, presently. "Say he marster'll know him when he come—ain' know de folks is free; say he marster gwi buy him back in de summer an' kyar him home, an' 'bout de money he gwine gi' him. Ef he got any money, I wonder he live down dyah in dat evil-sperit hole." And the woman glanced around with great complacency on the picture-pasted walls of her own by no means sumptuously furnished house. "Money!" she repeated aloud, as she began to rake in the ashes, "He ain' got nuttin. I got to kyar him piece o' dis bread now," and she went off into a dream of what they would do when the big crop on their land should be all in, and the last payment made on the house; of what she would wear, and how she would dress the children, and the appearance she would make at meeting, not reflecting that the sum they had paid for the property had never, even with all their stinting, amounted in any one year to more than a few dollars over the rent charged for the place, and that the eight hundred dollars yet due on it was more than they could make at the present rate in a lifetime.

"Ef Ephum jes had a mule, or even somebody to help him," she thought, "but he ain' got nuttin. De chil'n ain big 'nough to do nuttin but eat; he 'ain' not no brurrs, an' he deddy took 'way an' sold down Souf de same time my ole marster whar dead buy him; dat's what I al'ays heah 'em say, an' I know he's dead long befo' dis, 'cause I heah 'em say dese Virginia niggers carn stan' hit long deah, hit so hot, hit frizzle 'em up, an' I reckon he die befo' he ole marster, whar I heah say die of a broked heart torectly after dee teck he niggers an' sell 'em befo' he face. I heah Aunt Dinah say dat, an' dat he might'ly sot on he ole servants, spressaly on Ephum deddy, whar named Little Ephum, an' whar used to wait on him.

Dis mus' 'a' been a gret place dem days, 'cordin' to what dee say." She went on: "Dee say he sutny live strong, wuz jes rich as cream, an' weahed he blue coat an' brass buttons, an' lived in dat ole house whar was up whar de pines is now, an' whar bu'nt down, like he owned de wull. An' now look at it; dat man own it all, an' cuttin' all de woods off it. He don't know nuttin 'bout black folks, ain' nuver been fotch up wid 'em. Who ever heah he name 'fo' he come heah an' buy de place, an' move in de overseer house, an' charge we all eight hundred dollars for dis land, jes 'cause it got little piece o' bottom on it, an' forty-eight dollars rent besides, wid he ole stingy wife whar oon' even gi' 'way buttermilk!" An expression of mingled disgust and contempt concluded the reflection.

She took the ash-cake out of the ashes, slapped it first on one side, then on the other, with her hand, dusted it with her apron, and walked to the door and poured a gourd of water from the piggin over it. Then she divided it in half; one half she set up against the side of the chimney, the other she broke up into smaller pieces and distributed among the children, dragging the sleeping Eph, limp and soaked with sleep, from the cradle to receive his share. Her manner was not rough—was perhaps even tender—but she used no caresses, as a white woman would have done under the circumstances. It was only toward the baby at the breast that she exhibited any endearments. Her nearest approach to it with the others was when she told them, as she portioned out the ash-

Thos. Nelson Page

cake, "Mammy ain't got nuttin else; but nuver min', she gwine have plenty o' good meat next year, when deddy done pay for he land."

"Hi! who dat out dyah?" she said, suddenly. "Run to de do', son, an' see who dat comin'," and the whole tribe rushed to inspect the new-comer.

It was, as she suspected, her husband, and as soon as he entered she saw that something was wrong. He dropped into a chair, and sat in moody silence, the picture of fatigue, physical and mental. After waiting for some time, she asked, indifferently. "What de matter?"

"Dat man."

"What he done do now?" The query was sharp with suspicion.

"He say he ain' gwine let me have my land."

"He's a half-strainer," said the woman, with sudden anger. "How he gwine help it? Ain' you got crap on it?" She felt that there must be a defence against such an outrage.

"He say he ain' gwine wait no longer; dat I wuz to have tell Christmas to finish payin' for it, an' I ain' do it, an' now he done change he min'."

"Tell dis Christmas comin'," said his wife, with the positiveness of one accustomed to expound contracts.

"Yes; but I tell you he say he done change he min'." The man had evidently given up all hope; he was dead beat.

"De crap's yourn," said she, affected by his surrender, but prepared only to compromise.

"He say he gwine teck all dat for de rent, and dat he gwine drive Ole 'Stracted 'way too."

"He ain' nuttin but po' white trash!" It expressed her supreme contempt.

"He say he'll gi' me jes one week mo' to pay him all he ax for it," continued he, forced to a correction by her intense feeling, and the instinct of a man to defend the absent from a woman's attack, and perhaps in the hope that she might suggest some escape.

"He ain' nuttin sep po' white trash!" she repeated. "How you gwine raise eight hundred dollars at once? Dee kyarn nobody do dat. Gord mout! He ain' got good sense."

"You ain' see dat corn lately, is you?" he asked. "Hit jes as rank! You can almos' see it growin' ef you look at it good. Dat's strong land. I know dat when I buy it."

He knew it was gone now, but he had been in the habit of calling it his in the past three years, and it did him good to claim the ownership a little longer.

"I wonder whar Marse Johnny is?" said the woman. He was the son of her former owner; and now, finding her proper support failing her, she instinctively turned to him. "He wouldn' let him turn we all out."

"He ain' got nuttin, an' ef he is, he kyarn get it in a week," said Ephraim.

"Kyarn you teck it in de co't?"

"Dat's whar he say he gwine have it ef I don' git out," said her husband, despairingly.

Her last defence was gone.

"Ain' you hongry?" she inquired.

"What you got?"

"I jes gwine kill a chicken for you."

It was her nearest approach to tenderness, and he knew it was a mark of special attention, for all the chickens and eggs had for the past three years gone to swell the fund which was to buy the home, and it was only on special occasions that one was spared for food.

The news that he was to be turned out of his home had fallen on him like a blow, and had stunned him; he could make no resistance, he could form no plans. He went into a rough estimate as he waited.

"Le' me see: I done wuck for it three years dis Christmas done gone; how much does dat meck?"

"An' fo' dollars, an' five dollars, an' two dollars an' a half last Christmas from de chickens, an' all dem ducks I done sell he wife, an' de washin' I been doin' for 'em; how much is dat?" supplemented his wife.

"Dat's what I say!"

His wife endeavored vainly to remember the amount she had been told it was; but the unaccounted-for washing changed the sum and destroyed her reliance on the result. And as the chicken was now approaching perfection, and required her undivided attention, she gave up the arithmetic and applied herself to her culinary duties.

Ephraim also abandoned the attempt, and waited in a reverie, in which he saw corn stand so high and rank over his land that he could scarcely distinguish the bulk, and a stable and barn and a mule, or maybe two—it was a possibility—and two cows which his wife would milk, and a green wagon driven by his boys, while he took it easy and gave orders like a master, and a clover patch, and wheat, and he saw the yellow grain waving, and heard his sons sing the old harvest song of "Cool Water" while they swung their cradles, and—

"You say he gwine turn Ole 'Stracted out, too?" inquired his wife, breaking the spell. The chicken was done now, and her mind reverted to the all-engrossing subject.

"Yes; say he tired o' ole 'stracted nigger livin' on he place an' payin' no rent."

"Good Gord A'mighty! Pay rent for dat ole pile o' logs! Ain't he been mendin' he shoes an' harness for rent all dese years?"

" 'Twill kill dat ole man to tu'n him out dat house," said Ephraim; "he ain 'nuver stay away from dyah a hour since he come heah."

"Sutny 'twill," assented his wife; then she added, in reply to the rest of the remark, "Nuver min'; den we'll see what he got in dyah." To a woman, that was at least some compensation. Ephraim's thoughts had taken a new direction.

"He al'ays feared he marster'd come for him while he 'way," he said, in mere continuance of his last remark.

"He sen' me wud he marster comin' to-night, an' he want he shut," said his wife, as she handed him his supper. Ephraim's face expressed more than interest; it was tenderness which softened the rugged lines as he sat looking into the fire. Perhaps he thought of the old man's loneliness, and of his own father torn away and sold so long ago, before he could even remember, and perhaps very dimly of the beauty of the sublime devotion of this poor old creature to his love and his trust, holding steadfast beyond memory, beyond reason, after the knowledge even of his own identity and of his very name was lost.

The woman caught the contagion of his sympathy.

"De chil'n say he mighty comical, an' he layin' down in de baid," she said.

Ephraim rose from his seat.

"Whar you gwine?"

"I mus' go to see 'bout him," he said, simply.

"Ain' you gwine finish eatin'?"

"I gwine kyar dis to him."

"Well, I kin cook you anurr when we come back," said his wife, with ready acquiescence.

In a few minutes they were on the way, going single file down the path through the sassafras, along which little Eph and his followers had come an hour before, the man in the lead and his wife following, and, according to the custom of their race, carrying the bundles, one the surrendered supper and the other the neatly folded and well-patched shirt in which Ole 'Stracted hoped to meet his long-expected loved ones.

As they came in sight of the ruinous little hut which had been the old man's abode since his sudden appearance in the neighborhood a few years after the war, they observed that the bench beside the door was deserted, and that the door stood ajar—two circumstances which neither of them remembered ever to have seen before; for in all the years in which he had been their neighbor Ole 'Stracted had never admitted any one within his door, and had never been known to leave it open. In mild weather he occupied a bench outside, where he either cobbled shoes for his neighbors, accepting without question anything they paid him, or else sat perfectly quiet, with the air of a person waiting for some one. He held only the briefest communication with anybody, and was believed by some to have intimate relations with the Evil One, and his tumble-down hut, which he was particular to keep closely daubed, was thought by such as took this view of the matter to be the temple where he practiced his unholy rites. For this reason, and because the little cabin, surrounded by dense pines and covered with vines which the popular belief held "pizenous," was the most desolate abode a human being could have selected, most of the dwellers in that section gave the place a wide berth, especially toward nightfall, and Ole 'Stracted would probably have suffered but for the charity of Ephraim and his wife, who, although often wanting the necessaries of life themselves, had long divided it with their strange neighbor. Yet even they had never been admitted inside his door, and knew no more of him than the other people about the settlement knew.

His advent in the neighborhood had been mysterious. The first that was known of him was one summer morning, when he was found sitting on the bench beside the door of this cabin, which had long been unoccupied and left to decay. He was unable to give any account of himself, except that he always declared that he had been sold by some one other than his master from that plantation, that his wife and boy had been sold to some other person at the same time for twelve hundred dollars (he was particular as to the amount), and that his master was coming in the summer to buy him back and take him home, and would bring him his wife and child when he came. Everything since that day was a blank to him, and as he could not tell the name of his master or wife, or even his own name, and as no one was left old enough to remember him, the neighborhood having been entirely deserted after the war, he simply passed as a harmless old lunatic laboring under a delusion. He was devoted to children, and Ephraim's small brood were his chief delight. They were not at all afraid of him, and whenever they got a chance they would slip off and steal down to his house, where they might be found any time squatting about his feet, listening to his accounts of his expected visit from his master, and what he was going to do afterward. It was all of a great plantation, and fine carriages and horses, and a house with his wife and the boy.

This was all that was known of him, except that once a stranger, passing through the country, and hearing the name Ole 'Stracted, said that he heard a similar one once, long before the war, in one of the Louisiana parishes, where the man roamed at will, having been bought of the trader by the gentleman who owned him, for a small price, on account of his infirmity.

"Is you gwine in dyah?" asked the woman, as they approached the hut.

"Hi! yes; 'tain' nuttin' gwine hu't you; an' you say Ephum say he be layin' in de baid?" he replied, his mind having evidently been busy on the subject.

"An' mighty comical," she corrected him, with exactness born of apprehension.

"Well? I 'feared he sick."

"I ain' nuver been in dyah," she persisted.

"Ain' de chil'n been in dyah?"

"Dee say 'stracted folks oon hu't chil'n."

"Dat ole man oon hu't nobody; he jes tame as a ole tomcat."

"I wonder he ain' feared to live in dat lonesome ole house by hisself. I jes lieve stay in a graveyard at once. I ain' wonder folks say he sees sperrits in dat hanty-lookin' place." She came up by her husband's side at the suggestion. "I wonder he don' go home."

"Whar he got any home to go to sep heaven?" said Ephraim.

"What was you mammy name, Ephum?"

"Mymy," said he, simply.

They were at the cabin now, and a brief pause of doubt ensued. It was perfectly dark inside the door, and there was not a sound. The bench where they had heretofore held their only communication with their strange neighbor was lying on its side in the weeds which grew up to the very walls of the ruinous cabin, and a lizard suddenly ran over it, and with a little rustle disappeared under the rotting ground-sill. To the woman it was an ill omen. She glanced furtively behind her, and moved nearer her husband's side. She noticed that the cloud above the pines was getting a faint yellow tinge on its lower border, while it was very black above them. It filled her with dread, and she was about to call her husband's notice to it, when a voice within arrested their attention. It was very low, and they both listened in awed silence, watching the door meanwhile as if they expected to see something supernatural spring from it.

"Nem min'—jes wait—'tain so long now—he'll be heah torectly," said the voice. "Dat's what he say—gwine come an' buy me back—den we gwine home."

In their endeavor to catch the words they moved nearer, and made a slight noise. Suddenly the low, earnest tone changed to one full of eagerness.

"Who dat?" was called in sharp inquiry.

" 'Tain' nobody but me an' Polly, Ole 'Stracted," said Ephraim, pushing the door slightly wider open and stepping in. They had an indistinct idea that the poor deluded creature had fancied them his longed-for loved ones, yet it was a relief to see him bodily.

"Who you say you is?" inquired the old man, feebly.

"Me an' Polly."

"I done bring you shut home," said the woman, as if supplementing her husband's reply. "Hit all bran' clean, an' I done patch it."

"Oh, I thought—" said the voice, sadly.

They knew what he thought. Their eyes were now accustomed to the darkness, and they saw that the only article of furniture which the room contained was the wretched bed or bench on which the old man was stretched. The light sifting through the chinks in the roof enabled them to see his face, and that it had changed much in the last twenty-four hours, and an instinct told them that he was near the end of his long waiting.

"How is you, Ole 'Stracted?" asked the woman.

"Dat ain' my name," answered the old man, promptly. It was the first time he had ever disowned the name.

"Well, how is you, Ole— What I gwine to call you?" asked she, with feeble finesse.

"I don' know—he kin tell you."

"Who?"

"Who? Marster. He know it. Ole 'Stracted ain' know it; but dat ain' nuttin. *He* know it—got it set down in de book. I jes waitin' for 'em now."

A hush fell on the little audience—they were in full sympathy with him, and, knowing no way of expressing it, kept silence. Only the breathing of the old man was audible in the room. He was evidently nearing the end. "I mighty tired of waitin'," he said, pathetically. "Look out dyah and see ef you see anybody," he added suddenly.

Both of them obeyed, and then returned and stood silent; they could not tell him no.

Presently the woman said, "Don' you warn put you' shut on?"

"What did you say my name was?" he said.

"Ole 'Str—" She paused at the look of pain on his face, shifted uneasily from one foot to the other, and relapsed into embarrassed silence.

"Nem min'! dee'll know it—dee'll know me 'dout any name, oon dee?" He appealed wistfully to them both. The woman for answer unfolded the shirt. He moved feebly, as if in assent.

"I so tired waitin'," he whispered; "done 'mos gin out, an' he oon come; but I thought I heah little Eph to-day?" There was a faint inquiry in his voice.

"Yes, he wuz heah."

"Wuz he?" The languid form became instantly alert, the tired face took on a look of eager expectancy. "Heah, gi' m'y shut quick. I knowed it. Wait; go over dyah, son, and git me dat money. He'll be heah torectly." They thought his mind wandered, and merely followed the direction of his eyes with theirs. "Go over dyah quick—don't you heah me?"

And to humor him Ephraim went over to the corner indicated.

"Retch up dyah, an' run you' hand in onder de second jice. It's all in dyah," he said to the woman —"twelve hunderd dollars—dat's what dee went for. I wucked night an' day forty year to save dat money for marster; you know dee teck all he land an' all he niggers an' tu'n him out in de old fiel'? I put 'tin dyah 'ginst he come. You ain' know he comin' dis evenin', is you? Heah, help me on wid dat shut, gal

—I stan'in' heah talkin' an' maybe ole marster waitin'. Push de do' open so you kin see. Forty year ago," he murmured, as Polly jammed the door back and returned to his side—"forty year ago dee come an' leveled on me: marster sutny did cry. 'Nem min',' he said, 'I comin' right down in de summer to buy you back an' bring you home.' He's comin', too—nuver tol' me a lie in he life—comin' dis evenin.' Make 'aste." This in tremulous eagerness to the woman, who had involuntarily caught the feeling, and was now with eager and ineffectual haste trying to button his shirt.

An exclamation from her husband caused her to turn around, as he stepped into the light and held up an old sock filled with something.

"Heah, hol you' apron," said the old man to Polly, who gathered up the lower corners of her apron and stood nearer the bed.

"Po' it in dyah." This to Ephraim, who mechanically obeyed. He pulled off the string, and poured into his wife's lap the heap of glittering coin—gold and silver more than their eyes had ever seen before.

"Hit's all dyah," said the old man, confidentially, as if he were rendering an account. "I been savin' it ever sence dee took me 'way. I so busy savin' it I ain' had time to eat, but I ain' hongry now; have plenty when I git home." He sank back exhausted. "Oon marster be glad to see me?" he asked presently in pathetic simplicity. "You know we grewed up togerr? I been waitin' so long I 'feared dee 'mos' done forgit me. You reckon dee is?" he asked the woman, appealingly.

"No, suh, dee ain' forgit you," she said, comfortingly.

"I know dee ain'," he said, reassured. "Dat's what he tell me—he ain' nuver gwine forgit me." The reaction had set in, and his voice was so feeble now it was scarcely audible. He was talking rather to himself than to them, and finally he sank into a doze. A painful silence reigned in the little hut, in which the only sign was the breathing of the dying man. A single shaft of light stole down under the edge of the slowly passing cloud and slipped up to the door. Suddenly the sleeper waked with a start, and gazed around.

"Hit gittin' mighty dark," he whispered, faintly. "You reckon dee'll git heah 'fo' dark?"

The light was dying from his eyes.

"Ephum," said the woman, softly, to her husband.

The effect was electrical.

"Heish! you heah dat!" exclaimed the dying man, eagerly.

"Ephum"—she repeated. The rest was drowned by Ole 'Stracted's joyous exclamation.

"Gord! I knowed it!" he cried, suddenly rising upright, and, with beaming face, stretching both arms toward the door. "Dyah dee come! Now watch 'em smile. All y'all jes stand back. Heah de one you lookin' for. Marster—Mymy—heah's Little Ephum!" And with a smile on his face he sank back into his son's arms.

The evening sun, dropping on the instant to his setting, flooded the room with light; but as Ephraim gently eased him down and drew his arm from around him, it was the light of the unending morning that was on his face. His Master had at last come for him, and after his long waiting, Ole 'Stracted had indeed gone home.

OUR CONSUL AT CARLSRUHE

BY F. J. STIMSON

Frederic Jesup Stimson is a prominent lawyer of Boston. He is a member of the New York and Boston bars and is a special lecturer at Harvard. He has been more or less identified with State politics in Massachusetts for a great many years, was Assistant Attorney-General of the State in 1884-85, general counsel to the United States Industrial Commission, and Democratic candidate for Congress in 1902. In addition to being the author of several novels, essays, etc., Mr. Stimson has written a number of law books. His earlier novels were published under the pen-name of "J. S. of Dale." Mr. Stimson's latest novel is entitled "In Cure of Her Soul." The hero of the story, Austin Pinckney, is a son of the "Consul at Carlsruhe."

OUR CONSUL AT CARLSRUHE

BY F. J. STIMSON ("J. S. OF DALE")

DIED.—*In Baden, Germany, the 22d instant, Charles Austin Pinckney, late U. S. Consul at Carlsruhe, aged sixty years.*

There: most stories of men's lives end with the epitaph, but this of Pinckney's shall begin there. If we, as haply God or Devil can, could unroof the houses of men's souls, if their visible works were of their hearts rather than their brains, we should know strange things. And this alone, of all the possible, is certain. For bethink you, how men appear to their Creator, as He looks down into the soul, that matrix of their visible lives we find so hard to localize and yet so sure to be. For all of us believe in self, and few of us but are forced, one way or another, to grant existence to some selves outside of us. Can you not fancy that men's souls, like their farms, would show here a patch of grain, and there the tares; there the weeds and here the sowing; over this place the rain has been, and that other, to one looking down upon it from afar, seems brown and desolate, wasted by fire or made arid by the drought? In this man's life is a poor beginning, but a better end; in this other's we see the foundations, the staging, and the schemes of mighty structures, now stopped, given over, or abandoned; of vessels, fashioned for the world's seas, now rotting on the stocks. Of this one all seems ready but the launching, of that the large keelson only has been laid; but both alike have died unborn, and the rain falls upon them, and the mosses grow: the sound of labor is far off, and the scene of work is silent. Small laws make great changes; slight differences of adjustment end quick in death. Small, now, they would seem to us; but to the infinite mind all things small and great are alike; the spore of rust in the ear is very slight, but a famine in the corn will shake the world.

Pinckney's life the world called lazy; his leisure was not fruitful, and his sixty years of life were but a gentleman's. Some slight lesion may have caused paralysis of energy, some clot of heart's blood pressed upon the soul: I make no doubt our doctors could diagnose it, if they knew a little more. Tall and slender, he had a strange face, a face with a young man's beauty; his white hair gave a charm to the rare smile, like new snow to the spring, and the slight stoop with which he walked was but a grace the more. In short, Pinckney was interesting. Women raved about him; young men fell in love with him; and if he was selfish, the fault lay between him and his Maker, not visible to other men. There are three things that make a man interesting in his old age: the first, being heroism, we may put aside; but the other two are regret and remorse. Now, Mr. Pinckney's fragrance was not of remorse—women and young men would have called it heroism: it may have been.

As much heroism as could be practiced in thirty-six years of Carlsruhe.

Why Carlsruhe? That was the keynote of inquiry; and no one knew. Old men spoke unctuously of youthful scandals; women dreamed. I suspect even Mrs. Pinckney wondered, about as much as the plowed field may wonder at the silence of the autumn. But Pinckney limped gracefully about the sleepy avenues which converge at the Grand Duke's palace, like a wakeful page in the castle of the Sleeping Beauty. Pinckney was a friend of the Grand Duke's, and perhaps it was a certain American flavor persisting in his manners which made him seem the only man at the Baden court who met his arch-serene altitude on equal terms. For one who had done nothing and possessed little, Pinckney certainly preserved a marvelous personal dignity. His four daughters were all married to scions of Teutonic nobility; and each one in turn had asked him for the Pinckney arms, and quartered them into the appropriate check-square with as much grave satisfaction as he felt for the far-off patch of Hohenzollern, or of Hapsburg in sinister chief. Pinckney had laughed at it and referred them to the Declaration of Independence, clause the first; but his wife had copied them from some spoon or sugar bowl. She was very fond of Pinckney, and no more questioned him why they always lived in Carlsruhe than a Persian would the sun for rising east. Now and then they went to Baden, and her cup was full.

Pinckney died of a cold, unostentatiously, and was buried like a gentleman; though the Grand Duke actually wanted to put the court in mourning for three days, and consulted with his chamberlain whether it would do. Mrs. Pinckney had preceded him by some six years; but she was an appendage, and her husband's deference had always seemed in Carlsruhe a trifle strained. It was only in these last six years that any one had gossiped of remorse, in answer to the sphinx-like question of his marble brow. Such questions vex the curious. Furrows trouble nobody—money matters are enough for them; but white smoothness in old age is a bait, and tickles curiosity. Some said at home he was a devil and beat his wife.

But Pinckney never beat his wife. Late in the last twilight of her life she had called him to her, and excluded even the four daughters, with their stout and splendid barons; then, alone with him, she looked to him and smiled. And suddenly his gentleman's heart took a jump, and the tears fell on her still soft hands. I suppose some old road was opened again in the gray matter of his brain. Mrs. Pinckney smiled the more strongly and said—not quite so terribly as Mrs. Amos Barton: "Have I made you happy, dearest Charles?" And Charles, the perfect-mannered, said she had; but said it stammering. "Then," said she, "I die very happily, dear." And she did; and Pinckney continued to live at Carlsruhe.

The only activities of Pinckney's mind were critical. He was a wonderful orator, but he rarely spoke. People said he could have been a great writer, but he never wrote, at least nothing original. He was the art and continental-drama critic of several English and

American reviews; in music, he was a Wagnerian, which debarred him from writing of it except in German; but the little Court Theatre at Carlsruhe has Wagner's portrait over the drop-curtain, and the consul's box was never empty when the mighty heathen legends were declaimed or the holy music of the Grail was sung. In fiction of the earnest sort, and poetry, Pinckney's critical pen showed a marvelous magic, striking the scant springs of the author's inspiration through the most rocky ground of incident or style. He had a curious sympathy with youthful tenderness. But, after all, as every young compatriot who went to Baden said, what the deuce and all did he live in Baden for? Miles Breeze had said it in 'Fifty, when he made the grand tour with his young wife, and dined with him in Baden-Baden; that is, when Breeze dined with him, for his young wife was indisposed and could not go. Miles Breeze, junior, had said it, as late as 'Seventy-six, when he went abroad, ostensibly for instruction, after leaving college. He had letters to Mr. Pinckney, who was very kind to the young Baltimorean, and greatly troubled the Grand Duke his Serenity by presenting him as a relative of the Bonapartes. Many another American had said it, and even some leading politicians: he might have held office at home: but Pinckney continued to live in Carlsruhe.

His critical faculties seemed sharpened after his wife's death, as his hair grew whiter; and if you remember how he looked before you must have noticed that the greatest change was in the expression of his face. There was one faint downward line at either side of his mouth, and the counterpart at the eyes; a doubtful line which, faint as it was graven, gave a strange amount of shading to the face. And in speaking of him still earlier, you must remember to take your india-rubber and rub out this line from his face. This done, the face is still serious; but it has a certain light, a certain air of confidence, of determination, regretful though it be, which makes it loved by women. Women can love a desperate, but never begin to love a beaten, cause. Women fell in love with Pinckney, for the lightning does strike twice in the same place; but his race was rather that of Lohengrin than of the Asra, and he saw it, or seemed to see it, not. Still, in these times those downward lines had not come, and there was a certain sober light in his face as of a sorrowful triumph. This was in the epoch of his greatest interestingness to women.

When he first came to Carlsruhe, he was simply the new consul, nothing more; a handsome young man, almost in his honeymoon, with a young and pretty wife. He had less presence in those days, and seemed absorbed in his new home, or deeply sunk in something; people at first fancied he was a poet, meditating a great work, which finished, he would soon leave Carlsruhe. He never was seen to look at a woman, not overmuch at his wife, and was not yet popular in society.

But it was true that he was newly married. He was married in Boston, in 'Forty-three or four, to Emily Austin, a far-off cousin of his, whom he had known (he himself was a Carolinian) during his four years at Cambridge. For his four years in Cambridge were succeeded by two more at the Law School; then he won a great case against Mr. Choate, and was narrowly beaten in an election for Congress; after that it surprised no one to hear the announcement of his engagement to Miss Austin, for his family was unexceptionable and he had a brilliant future. The marriage came in the fall, rather sooner than people expected, at King's Chapel. They went abroad, as was natural; and then he surprised his friends and hers by accepting his consulship and staying there. And they were imperceptibly, gradually, slowly, and utterly forgotten.

The engagement came out in the spring of 'Forty-three. And in June of that year young Pinckney had gone to visit his *fiancée* at Newport. Had you seen him there, you would have seen him in perhaps the brightest rôle that fate has yet permitted on this world's stage. A young man, a lover, rich, gifted, and ambitious, of social position unquestioned in South Carolina and the old Bay State—all the world loved him, as a lover; the many envied him, the upper few desired him. Handsome he has always remained.

And the world did look to him as bright as he to the world. He was in love, as he told himself, and Miss Austin was a lovable girl; and the other things he was dimly conscious of; and he had a long vacation ahead of him, and was to be married late in the autumn, and he walked up from the wharf in Newport swinging his cane and thinking on these pleasant things.

Newport, in those days, was not the paradise of cottages and curricles, of lawns and laces, of new New Yorkers and Nevada miners; it was the time of big hotels and balls, of Southern planters, of Jullien's orchestras, and of hotel hops; such a barbarous time as the wandering New Yorker still may find, lingering on the simple shores of Maine, sunning in the verdant valleys of the Green Mountains; in short, it was Arcadia, not Belgravia. And you must remember that Pinckney, who was dressed in the latest style, wore a blue broadcloth frock coat, cut very low and tight in the waist, with a coat-collar rolling back to reveal a vast expanse of shirt-bosom, surmounted by a cravat of awful splendor, bow-knotted and blue-fringed. His trousers were of white duck, his boots lacquered, and he carried a gold-tipped cane in his hand. So he walked up the narrow old streets from the wharf, making a sunshine in those shady places. It was the hottest hour of a midsummer afternoon; not a soul was stirring, and Pinckney was left to his own pleasant meditations.

He got up the hill and turned into the park by the old mill; over opposite was the great hotel, its piazzas deserted, silent even to the hotel band. But one flutter of a white dress he saw beneath the trees, and then it disappeared behind them, causing Pinckney to quicken his steps. He thought he knew the shape and motion, and he followed it until he came upon it suddenly, behind the trees, and it turned.

A young girl of wonderful beauty, rare, erect carriage, and eyes of a strange, violet-gray, full of much meaning. This was all Pinckney had time to note; it was no one he had ever seen before. He had gone up like a hunter, sure of his game, and too far in it to retract. The embarrassment of the situation was such that Pinckney forgot all his cleverness of manner, and blurted out the truth like any schoolboy.

"I beg pardon—I was looking for Miss Austin," said he; and he raised his hat.

A delightful smile of merriment curled the beauty's lips. "My acquaintance with Miss Austin is too slight to justify my finding her for you; but I wish you all success in your efforts," she said, and vanished, leaving the promising young lawyer to blush at his own awkwardness and wonder who she was. As she disappeared, he only saw that her hair was a lustrous coil of pale gold-brown, borne proudly.

He soon found Emily Austin, and forgot the beauty, as he gave his betrothed a kiss and saw her color heighten; and in the afternoon they took a long drive. It was only at tea, as he was sitting at table with the Austins in the long dining-room, that some one walked in like a goddess; and it was she. He asked her name; and they told him it was a Miss Warfield, of Baltimore, and she was engaged to a Mr. Breeze.

In the evening there was a ball; and as they were dancing (for every one danced in those days) he saw her again, sitting alone this time and unattended. She was looking eagerly across the room, through the dancers and beyond; and in her eyes was the deepest look of sadness Pinckney had ever seen in a girl's face; a look such as he had thought no girl could feel. A moment after, and it was gone, as some one spoke to her; and Pinckney wondered if he had not been mistaken, so fleeting was it, and so strange. An acquaintance—one of those men who delight to act as brokers of acquaintances—who had noticed his gaze came up. "That is the famous Miss Mary Warfield," said he. "Shall I not introduce you?"

"No," said Pinckney; and he turned away rudely. To be rude when you like is perhaps one of the choicest prerogatives of a good social position. The acquaintance stared after him, as he went back to Miss Austin, and then went up and spoke to Miss Warfield himself. A moment after, Pinckney saw her look over at him with some interest; and he wondered if the man had been ass enough to tell her. Pinckney was sitting with Emily Austin; and, after another moment, he saw Miss Warfield look at her. Then her glance seemed to lose its interest; her eyelids drooped, and Pinckney could see, from her interlocutor's manner, that he was put to his trumps to keep her attention. At last he got away, awkwardly; and for many minutes the strange girl sat like a statue, her long lashes just veiling her eyes, so that Pinckney, from a distance, could not see what was in them. Suddenly the veil was drawn and her eyes shone full upon him, her look meeting his. Pinckney's glance fell, and his cheeks grew redder. Miss Warfield's face did not change, but she rose and walked unattended through the centre of the ballroom to the door. Pinckney's seat was nearer it than hers; she passed him as if without seeing him, moving with unconscious grace, though it would not have been the custom at that time for a girl to cross so large a room alone. Just then some one asked Miss Austin for a dance; and Pinckney, who was growing weary of it, went out on the piazza for a cigar, and then, attracted by the beauty of the night, strayed further than he knew, alone, along the cliffs above the sea.

The next day he was walking with Miss Austin, and they passed her, in her riding habit, waiting by the mounting stone; she bowed to Miss Austin alone, leaving him out, as it seemed to Pinckney, with exaggerated care.

"Is she not beautiful?" said Emily, ardently.

"Humph!" said Pinckney. A short time after, as they were driving on the road to the Fort, he saw her again; she was riding alone, across country, through the rocky knolls and marshy pools that form the southern part of Rhode Island. She had no groom lagging behind, but it was not so necessary then as now; and, indeed, a groom would have had a hard time to keep up with her, as she rattled up the granite slopes and down over logs and bushes with her bright bay horse. The last Pinckney saw of her she disappeared over a rocky hill against the sky; her beautiful horse flecked with foam, quivering with happy animal life, and the girl calm as a figure carved in stone, with but the faintest touch of rose upon her face, as the pure profile was outlined one moment against the sunlit blue.

"How recklessly she rides!" whispered Miss Austin to him, and Pinckney said *yes,* absently, and, whipping up his horse, drove on, pretending to listen to his fiancée's talk. It seemed to be about dresses, and rings, and a coming visit to the B——s, at Nahant. He had never seen a girl like her before; she was a puzzle to him.

"It is a great pity she is engaged to Mr. Breeze," said Miss Austin; and Pinckney woke up with a start, for he was thinking of Miss Warfield too.

"Why?" said he.

"I don't like him," said Emily. "He isn't good enough for her."

As this is a thing that women say of all wooers after they have won, and which the winner is usually at that period the first to admit, Pinckney paid little attention to this remark. But that evening he met Miles Breeze, saw him, talked with him, and heard others talk of him. A handsome man, physically; well made, well dressed, well fed; well bred, as breeding goes in dogs or horses; a good shot, a good sportsman, yachtsman, story-teller; a good fellow, with a weak mouth; a man of good old Maryland blood, yet red and healthy, who had come there in his yacht and had his horses sent by sea. A well-appointed man, in short; provided amply with the conveniences of fashionable life. A man of good family, good fortune, good health, good sense, good nature, whom it were hypercritical to charge with lack of soul. "The first duty of a gentleman is to be a good animal," and Miles Breeze performed it thoroughly. Pinckney liked him, and he could have been his companion for years and still have liked him, except as a husband for Miss Warfield.

He could not but recognize his excellence as a *parti*. But the race of Joan of Arc does not mate with Bonhomme Richard, even when he owns the next farm. Pinckney used to watch the crease of Breeze's neck, above the collar, and curse.

Coming upon Miss Austin one morning, she had said, "Come—I want to introduce you to Miss Warfield." Pinckney had demurred, and offered as an excuse that he was smoking. "Nonsense, Charles," said the girl; "I have told her you are coming." Pinckney threw away his cigar and followed, and the presentation was made. Miss Warfield drew herself almost unusually erect after courtesying, as if in protest at having to bow at all. She was so tall that, as Emily stood between them, he could meet Miss Warfield's iron-gray eyes above her head. It was the first time in Pinckney's life that he had consciously not known what to say.

"I was so anxious to have you meet Charles before he left," said Emily. Evidently, his fiancée had been expatiating upon him to this new friend, and if there is anything that puts a man in a foolish position it is to have this sort of preamble precede an acquaintance.

"An anxiety I duly shared, Miss Warfield, I assure you," said he; which was a truth spoiled in the uttering—what the conversational Frenchman terms *banale*.

"Thank you," said Miss Warfield, very simply and tremendously effectively. Pinckney, for the second time with this young lady, felt himself a schoolboy. Emily interposed some feeble commonplaces, and then, after a moment, Miss Warfield said, "I must go for my ride"; and she left, with a smile for Emily and the faintest possible glance for him. She went off with Breeze; and it gave Pinckney some relief to see that she seemed equally to ignore the presence of the man who was her acknowledged lover, as he trotted on a smart cob beside her. That evening, when he went on the piazza after tea, he found her sitting alone, in one corner, with her hands folded: it was one peculiarity about this woman that she was never seen with work. She made no sign of recognition as he approached; but, none the less, he took the chair that was beside her and waited a moment for her to speak. "Have you found Miss Austin?" said the beauty, with the faintest trace of malice in her coldly modulated tones, not looking at him. "I am not looking for Miss Austin," said he; and she continued not looking at him, and so this strange pair sat there in the twilight, silent.

What was said between them I do not know. But in some way or other their minds met; for long after Miss Austin and her mother had returned from some call, long after they had all left him, Pinckney continued to pace up and down restlessly in the dark. Pinckney had never seen a woman like this. After all, he was very young; and he had, in his heart, supposed that the doubts and delights of his soul were peculiar to men alone. He thought all women—at all events, all young and worthy women—regarded life and its accepted forms as an accomplished fact, not to be questioned, and, indeed, too delightful to need it. The young South Carolinian, in his ambitions, in his heart-longings and heart-sickenings, in his poetry, even in his emotions, had always been lonely; so that his loneliness had grown to seem to him as merely part of the day's work. The best women, he knew, where the best housewives; they were a rest and a benefit for the war-weary man, much as might be a pretty child, a bed of flowers, a strain of music. With Emily Austin he should find all this; and he loved her as good, pretty, amiable, perfect in her way. But now, with Miss Warfield—it had seemed that he was not even lonely.

Pinckney did not see her again for a week. When he met her, he avoided her; she certainly avoided him. Breeze, meantime, gave a dinner. He gave it on his yacht, and gave it to men alone. Pinckney was of the number.

The next day there was a driving party; it was to drive out of town to Purgatory, a pretty place, where there is a brook in a deep ravine with a verdant meadow-floor; and there they were to take food and drink, as is the way of humanity in pretty places. Now it so happened that the Austins, Miss Warfield, Breeze, and Pinckney were going to drive in a party, the Austins and Miss Warfield having carriages of their own; but at the last moment Breeze did not appear, and Emily Austin was incapacitated by a headache. She insisted, as is the way of loving women, that "Charles should not lose it"; for to her it was one of life's pleasures, and such pleasures satisfied her soul. (It may be that she gave more of her soul to life's duties than did Charles, and life's pleasures were thus adequate to the remainder; I do not know.) Probably Miles Breeze also had a headache; at all events, he did not, at the last moment, appear. It was supposable that he would turn up at the picnic; Mrs. Austin joined her daughter's entreaty; Miss Warfield was left unattended; in fine, Pinckney went with her.

Miss Warfield had a solid little phaeton with two stout ponies: she drove herself. For some time they were silent; then, insensibly, Pinckney began to talk and she to answer. What they said I need not say —indeed I could not, for Pinckney was a poet, a man of rare intellect and imagination, and Miss Warfield was a woman of this world and the next; a woman who used conventions as another might use a fan, to screen her from fools; whose views were based on the ultimate. But they talked of the world, and of life in it; and when it came to an end, Pinckney noted to himself this strange thing, that they had both talked as of an intellectual problem, no longer concerning their emotions—in short, as if this life were at an end, and they were two dead people discussing it.

So they arrived at the picnic, silent; and the people assembled looked to one another and smiled, and said to one another how glum those two engaged people looked, being together, and each wanting another. Mr. Breeze had not yet come; and as the people scattered while the luncheon was being prepared, Pinckney and she wandered off like the others. They went some distance—perhaps a mile or more—aimlessly; and then, as they seemed to have come about to the end of the valley, Pinckney sat down upon a rock, but she did not do so, but remained standing. Hardly a word had so far been said between them; and then Pinckney looked at her and said:

"Why are you going to marry Mr. Breeze?"

"Why not?"—listlessly.

"You might as well throw yourself into the sea," said Pinckney; and he looked at the sea which lay beyond them shimmering.

"That I had not thought of," said she; and she looked at the sea herself with more interest. Pinckney drew a long breath.

"But why this man?" he said at length.

"Why that man?" said the woman; and her beautiful lip curled, with the humor of the mind, while her eyes kept still the sadness of the heart, the look that he had seen in the ballroom. "We are all poor," she added; then scornfully, "it is my duty to marry."

"But Miles Breeze?" persisted Pinckney.

The lip curled almost to a laugh. "I never met a better fellow than Miles," said she; and the thought was so like his own of the night before that Pinckney gasped for breath. They went back, and had chicken croquettes and champagne, and a band that was hidden in the wood made some wild Spanish music.

Going home, a curious thing happened. They had started first and far preceded all the others. Miss Warfield was driving; and when they were again in the main road, not more than a mile from the hotel, Pinckney saw ahead of them, coming in a light trotting buggy of the sort that one associates with the gentry who call themselves "sports," two of the gentlemen whom he had met at Breeze's dinner the night before. Whether Miss Warfield also knew them he did not know; but they evidently had more wine than was good for them, and were driving along in a reckless manner on the wrong side of the road. The buggy was much too narrow for the two; and the one that was driving leaned out toward them with a tipsy leer. Pinckney shouted at him, but Miss Warfield drove calmly on. He was on the point of grasping the reins, but a look of hers withheld him, and he sat still, wondering; and in a moment their small front wheel had crashed through both the axles and spiderweb wheels of the trotting buggy. The shock of the second axle whirled them round, and Pinckney fell violently against the dasher, while Miss Warfield was thrown clear of the phaeton on the outer side. But she had kept the reins, and before Pinckney could get to her she was standing at her horses' heads, patting their necks calmly, with a slight cut in her forehead where she had fallen, and only her nostril quivering like theirs, as the horses stood there trembling. The buggy was a wreck, and the horse had disappeared; and the two men, sobered by the fall, came up humbly to her to apologize. She heard them silently, with a pale face like some injured queen's; and then, bowing to them their dismissal, motioned Pinckney into the phaeton, which, though much broken, was still standing, and, getting in herself, drove slowly home.

"She might have killed herself," thought Pinckney, but he held his peace, as if it were the most natural course of action in the world. To tell the truth, under the circumstances he might have done the same alone.

Then it began. Pinckney could not keep this woman out of his head. He would think of her at all times, alone and in company. Her face would come to him in the loneliness of the sea, in the loneliness of crowds; the strong spirit of the morning was hers, and the sadness of the sunset and the wakeful watches of the night. Her face was in the clouds of evening, in the sea-coal fire by night; her spirit in the dreams of summer morns, in the hopeless breakers on the stormy shores, in the useless, endless effort of the sea. Her eyes made some strange shining through his dreams; and he would wake with a cry that she was going from him, in the deepest hours of the night, as if in the dreams he had lost her, vanishing forever in the daily crowd. Then he would lie awake until morning, and all the laws of God and men would seem like cobwebs to his sorrow, and the power of it freezing in his heart. This was the ultimate nature of his being, to follow her, as drop of water blends in drop of water, as frost rends rock. Let him then follow out his law, as other beings do theirs; gravitation has no conscience; should he be weaker than a drop of water, because he was conscious, and a man?

So these early morning battles would go on, and character, training, conscience, would go down before the simpler force, like bands of man's upon essential nature. Then, with the first ray of the dawn, he would think of Emily Austin, sleeping near him, perhaps dreaming of him, and his mad visions seemed to fade; and he would rise exhausted, and wander out among the fresh fields and green dewy lanes, and calm, contentful trees, and be glad that these things were so; yet could these not be moved, nor their destiny be changed. And as for him, what did it matter?

So the days went by. And Emily Austin looked upon him with eyes of limitless love and trust, and Pinckney did not dare to look upon himself; but his mind judged by day-time and his heart strove by night. Hardly at all had he spoken to Miss Warfield since; and no reference had ever been made between them to the accident, or to the talk between them in the valley. Only Pinckney knew that she was to be married very shortly; and he had urged Miss Austin to hasten their own wedding.

Emily went off with her mother to pay her last visit among the family, and to make her preparations; and it was deemed proper that at this time Pinckney should not be with her. So he stayed in Newport five long days alone; and during this time he never spoke to Miss Warfield. I believe he tried not to look at her: she did not look at him. And on the fifth night

Pinckney swore that he must speak to her once more, whatever happened.

In the morning there was talk of a sailing party; and Pinckney noted Breeze busying himself about the arrangements. He waited; and at noon Breeze came to him and said that there was a scarcity of men: would he go? Yes. They had two sail-boats, and meant to land upon Conanicut, which was then a barren island without a house, upon the southern end, where it stretches out to sea.

Pinckney did not go in the same boat with Breeze and Miss Warfield; and, landing, he spent the afternoon with others and saw nothing of her. But after dinner was over, he spoke to her, inviting her to walk; and she came, silently. A strange evening promenade that was: they took a path close on the sheer brink of the cliffs, so narrow that one must go behind the other. Pinckney had thought at first she might be frightened, with the rough path, and the steepness of the rocks, and the breakers churning at their base; but he saw that she was walking erect and fearlessly. Finally she motioned him to let her go ahead; and she led the way, choosing indiscriminately the straightest path, whether on the verge of the sea or leading through green meadows. A few colorless remarks were made by him, and then he saw the folly of it, and they walked in silence. After nearly an hour, she stopped.

"We must be getting back," she said.

"Yes," said he, in the same tone; and they turned; she still leading the way, while he followed silently.

They were walking toward the sunset; the sun was going down in a bank of dense gray cloud, but its long, level rays came over to them, across a silent sea. She walked on over the rugged cliff, like some siren, some genius of the place, with a sure, proud grace of step; she never looked around, and his eyes were fixed upon the black line of her figure, as it went before him, toward the gray and blood-red sunset. It seemed to him this was the last hour of his life; and even as he thought his ankle turned, and he stumbled and fell, walking unwittingly into one of the chasms, where the line of the cliff turned in. He grasped a knuckle of rock, and held his fall, just on the brink of a ledge above the sea. Miss Warfield had turned quickly and seen it all; and she leaned down over the brink, with one hand around the rock and the other extended to help him, the ledge on which he lay being some six feet below. Pinckney grasped her hand and kissed it.

Her color did not change at this; but, with a strange strength in her beautiful lithe figure, she drew him up steadily, he helping partly with the other hand, until his knees rested on the path again. He stood up with some difficulty, as his ankle was badly wrenched.

"I am afraid you can not walk," said she.

"Oh, yes," he answered; and took a few steps to show her. The pain was great; but she walked on, and he followed, as best he could, limping. She looked behind now, as if to encourage him; and he set his teeth and smiled.

"We must not be late," she said. "It is growing dark, and they will miss us."

But they did not miss them; for when they got to the landing-place, both the sail-boats had left the shore without them. There was nothing but the purple cloud-light left by this time; but Pinckney fancied he could see her face grow pale for the first time that day.

"We must get home," she said, hurriedly. "Is there no boat?"

Pinckney pointed to a small dory on the beach, and then to the sea. In the east was a black bank of cloud, rifted now and then by lightning; and from it the wind came down and the white caps curled angrily toward them.

"No matter," said she; "we must go."

Pinckney found a pair of oars under the boat, and dragged it, with much labor, over the pebbles, she helping him. The beach was steep and gravelly, with short breakers rather than surf; and he got the bow well into the water and held it there.

"Get in," said he.

Miss Warfield got into the stern, and Pinckney waded out, dragging the flat-bottomed boat until it was well afloat. Then he sprang in himself, and, grasping the oars, headed the boat for the Fort point across the channel, three miles away. She sat silently in the stern, and it was too dark for him to see her face. He rowed savagely.

But the wind was straight ahead, and the sea increasing every moment. They were not, of course, exposed to the full swell of the ocean; but the wide sea-channel was full of short, fierce waves that struck the little skiff repeated rapid blows, and dashed the spray over both of them.

"Are you not afraid?" said he, calmly. "It is growing rougher every minute."

"Oh, no, Mr. Pinckney," said she. "Pray keep on."

Pinckney noticed a tremor of excitement in her voice; but by a flash of lightning that came just then he saw her deep eyes fixed on his, and the pure white outline of her face undisturbed. So he rowed the harder, and she took a board there was and tried to steer; and now and then, as the clouds were lit, he saw her, like a fleeting vision in the night.

But the storm grew stronger; and Pinckney knew the boat that they were in was not really moving at all, though, of course, the swash of the waves went by and the drifted spray. He tried to row harder, but with the pain in his ankle and the labor he was nearly exhausted, and his heart jumped in his chest at each recover. "Can you not make it?" said she, in the dark; and Pinckney vowed that he could, and set his teeth for a mighty pull. The oar broke, and the boat's head fell rapidly off in the trough of the sea. He quickly changed about his remaining oar, and with it kept the head to the wind.

"We must go back," he said, panting.

"I know," said she. The windstorm was fairly upon them; and, in spite of all his efforts, an occasional wave would get upon the beam and spill its frothing crest into the boat. Pinckney almost doubted whether it would float until it reached the shore; but Miss Warfield did not seem in the least disturbed, and spoke without a tremor in her voice. The lightning had stopped now, and he could not see her.

He had miscalculated the force of the wind and waves, however; for in a very minutes they were driven broadside back upon the beach, almost at the same place from which they had started. Miss Warfield sprang out quickly, and he after, just as a wave turned the dory bottom upward on the stones.

"They will soon send for us," he said; and stepping painfully up the shore, he occupied himself with spreading her shawl in a sheltered spot for them to wait in. She sat down, and he beside her. He was very wet, and she made him put some of the shawl over himself. The quick summer storm had passed now, with only a few big drops of rain; and the moon was breaking out fitfully through veils of driving clouds and their storm-scud. By its light he looked at her, and their eyes met. Pinckney groaned aloud, and stood up. "Would that they would never come; would God that we could—"

"We can not," said she, softly, in a voice that he had never heard from her before—a voice with tears in it; and the man threw himself down at her feet, inarticulate, maddened. Then, with a great effort at control, not touching her, but looking straight into her eyes, he said, in blunt, low speech: "Miss Warfield, I love you—do you know it?"

Her head sank slowly down; but she answered,

very low, but clearly, *yes*. Then their eyes met again; and, by some common impulse, they rose and walked apart. After a few steps, he stopped, being lame, and leaned against the cliff; but she went on until her dark figure was blended with the shadows of the crags.

So, when the boat came back, its sail silvered by the moonlight, they saw it, and, coming down, they met again; but only as the party were landing on the beach. Several of the party had come back; and Mr. Breeze, who was among them, was full of explanation how he had missed the first boat and barely caught the second, supposing that his fiancée was in the first. An awkward accident, but easily explained by Pinckney, with the sprain in his ankle; and, indeed, the others were too full of excuses for having forgotten them to inquire into the causes of their absence together.

Pinckney went to his room, and had a night of delirium. Toward morning, his troubled wakefulness ended, and he fell into a dream. He dreamed that in the centre of the world was one green bower, beneath a blossoming tree, and he and Miss Warfield were there. And the outer world was being destroyed, one sphere by fire and the other by flood, and there was only this bower left. But they could not stay there, or the tree would die. So they went away, he to the one side and she to the other, and the ruins of the world fell upon them, and they saw each other no more.

In the morning his delirium left him, and his will resumed its sway. He went down, and out into the green roads, and listened to the singing of the birds; and then out to the cliff-path, and there he found Miss Warfield sitting as if she knew that he would come. He watched her pure face while she spoke, and her gray eyes: the clear light of the morning was in them, and on the gleaming sea beyond.

"You must go," said she.

"Yes," he said, and that was all. He took her hand for one moment, and lifted it lightly to his lips; then he turned and took the path across the fields. When he got to the first stile, he looked around. She was still sitting there, turned toward him. He lifted his hat, and held it for a second or two; then he turned the corner of the hedge and went down to the town.

Thus it happened that this story, which began sadly, with an epitaph, may end with wedding bells:

MARRIED. *At King's Chapel, by the Rev. Dr. A——, the 21st of September, Charles Austin Pinckney to Emily, daughter of the late James Austin.*

END OF VOLUME TWO